BREATH

GHOST MOUNTAIN WOLF SHIFTERS BOOK 5

AUDREY FAYE

SHELLEY

I don't think I made enough cookies.

I glance over at the sturdy pantry shelves that are one of the very best parts of our new cook shack. They aren't bending under the weight of what's piled on them, but it's not for lack of trying. Five kinds of jerky, more hard-boiled eggs than I used to make in a year, an entire shelf of Mikayla's honey berry bars, enough muffins and cookies that the last batches in the oven are likely ridiculous, and so many bowls of nuts and neatly stacked fruits that the nice folks at the grocery store in town think we're about to hibernate for the winter.

Strange fizzy bubbles rise inside my ribs and try their best to kick my foolish worries to the curb. They don't win that fight—but it matters that they try.

Mikayla looks up from the floor, where she's teaching

Mellie the fine art of punching bread dough so that it can rise again, and grins. "Are we ready?"

Not a chance, but we won't starve. "Maybe. Has Ebony heard from Rio yet?" He left at the crack of dawn to meet the truck convoy that's bringing up the two school-and-greenhouse buildings. One for us, one for the cats.

Mikayla shrugs, but I know she's got one ear tuned to the owl hoots outside. She knows what every last one of them means. Just one of the many small reasons that my wolf feels safer when she's around. Which I will never tell her, because young hearts deserve to be as free as we can make them, but I suspect she knows anyhow.

Mellie, who has somehow stolen Reilly's special purple shirt for the third day this week, makes an impressively correct fist and starts punching the next bowl in the long line of rising dough. Grandpa Cleve watches from the end, his furry nose practically touching the last bowl. We're all pretending to ignore him. Rio got the temporary lines that deliver power and water and heated floors hooked up to the cook shack about two minutes after Eliza and Danielle and Brown finished building it. Myrna showed up with an old gray wolf ten minutes after that, waved Cleve over to the corner, and told him to make some noise if the floor got too warm to be comfortable.

He left an hour later, but he's come back every day since.

This is the first day he's allowed himself to stay close

to a pup, however. Mikayla might need some onions to chop soon so that she can have herself a little sniffle.

We all look up at the sound of steps in the doorway. Ebony rubs her bare arms briskly. "Brrr. It's getting cold out there. Can a hungry wolf get a snack, or do I have to wait until lunchtime?"

Mellie cheerfully punches another bowl of bubbly dough.

I shake my head. So much for her pantry-guarding instincts.

Ebony grins and helps herself to a honey berry bar. "Need any more help in here?"

I snort. There's been a constant stream of people and wolves underfoot ever since the cook shack opened for business. Not that I can blame them. I've been baking barefoot for a week. The heated floors are wondrous, for toes and for bread dough and for elderly wolf bones, too, and Rio says that we don't have to worry about wasting heat, even though there aren't any walls. "Not unless people keep eating the snacks we made for the work crews."

My wolf shudders a little as I finish speaking. I spent my last six years in the kitchen saying as little as possible, but Cleve needs to be reminded of more than just the sweetness of a frisky pup with bread dough in her hair. This is a good pack for submissives. A safe one. One where our weaknesses aren't allowed to harm the pack and our strengths are allowed to feed it.

Ebony watches me with proud eyes—and tries to tuck her guilt away where I can't see it.

Silly dominant. Today isn't for regrets, mine or hers. "Is Rio close?"

She chuckles. "Yes. About thirty minutes out, based on Fallon's last report. Ben won't let her do another run until she drinks her tea and lets him rub her feet, just in case pregnancy got hard in the last hour."

Mikayla giggles. "That's just going to get tea poured on his head."

Her baby pack moved to the new den even faster than my kitchen, but the bonds they forged in their few short weeks together haven't diminished a bit. And poor Ben does tend to hover. "So long as she doesn't throw it at his head. We've already broken three mugs this month."

Mellie, who was responsible for two of them, shifts into wolf form and yips.

Ebony swoops her up before pup paws meet with bread dough, and nuzzles her nose against Mellie's furry one. "I need a partner to come out to the road with me and keep an eye out for Rio and his big truck."

"Too late," says Hayden, sticking his head through what would be a window if this cook shack wasn't as open to the elements as a naked toddler's bottom. "They've been spotted. They made good time down the logging road."

I eye him. The trucks were supposed to be coming one at a time. "They?"

He makes a wry face. "One delivery truck, followed by a motley crew of cats and ravens who insist that we need help carrying things in from the road. Kel thinks we might have a few hawks lurking, too."

Ebony sighs. "They know that we're perfectly capable of doing this ourselves, right?"

Hayden snorts. "Reese said they're coming to learn from our mistakes."

Friends are precious, even if they're sometimes annoying. "We can always send a crew over to help with their setup." We already built the ravens a pool shack. I somehow got convinced to paint a small mural on the inside, where it was dim and cozy and hard to see my mistakes.

Mikayla grins at me. "I bet they're just coming for the cookies."

They might try to make it seem like that, because Reese and Tressie and Kendra are tricky alphas, every last one of them. I eye the pantry shelves. I know how much food Reilly and Brown and Rio ate after they relocated my kitchen appliances.

I've got just enough time to whip up one more batch of cookies.

HAYDEN

There are generals with less determination in their eyes than Shelley Martins has right now. Which is absolutely gorgeous, but it needs a slight course adjustment. I make my way into the expansive interior of the nicest cook shack on the continent and send Cleve muted pleased-alpha vibes as I walk by. He doesn't cower, which pleases my wolf immensely.

I wrap an arm around the shoulders of the woman who runs our kitchen and somehow thinks I'm going to let her stay there while joy arrives as several hundred carefully boxed-and-labeled parts. "Cleve can supervise the snacks. I need your strong arms to carry pipes and panels and bags of concrete mix."

The wolf on the floor startles. So does the one who thought I was just giving her a quick hug on my way to stealing a muffin. She shakes her head adamantly. "I'll stay here and make sure everyone gets fed."

Ebony snorts and tosses me a muffin from the cooling rack. "Everyone's going to be at the truck trying to grab a load twice as big as they can carry. We need all the level heads out there so that we don't end up with bent pipes and wall panels that got accidentally walked into trees."

I love it when my betas do all my work and leave me to eat really good muffins. This one tastes like nuts and Lissa's favorite apple tea. I try not to drool too much. The heated floors in this place are currently our pack's most prized possession. Rio swears the hot water pipes are held together with duct tape and chewing gum, but that hasn't dimmed their magic in the slightest.

Mikayla, down on the floor surrounded by big metal bowls, winks at Cleve. "If level heads are needed, I guess that means Hayden can stay here and guard the berry bars, and you and me had better get ourselves to the road."

She's not quite a teenager anymore, but she does the job of one like a pro. I grin at her. "I like this plan."

Ebony rolls her eyes. "Shelley, get our alpha out of here before he finds the extra-spicy jerky and sets his tongue on fire. Mik, you can take this rugrat with you." She deposits a furry Mellie on the ground and gives her the kind of look that keeps even dominant pups from jumping on their elders.

I grab a couple of water canteens and sling them over my shoulders. There's one more thing to lock down, but I'm pretty sure Ebony's got it handled.

She winks at the wolf who's edging his way into the shadows. "Cleve can guard the bread dough. Howl if it starts to take over the kitchen, okay? We'll be back in a jiffy."

Hesitation.

She squats down. "Molly is with Kennedy and Hoot. She's doing great, and one of them will come find you right away if she needs you."

Shelley's shoulders soften under my arm. She has a soft spot for the gangly, gulping teenager who walked into Dorie's camp a couple of weeks ago, clinging to Cleve's fur, and announced in a voice rusty with disuse that she wanted to go to school.

Dorie didn't let a tiny detail like having no idea who Molly was get in her way at all. By the time I got up there and discovered that Molly can't let an adult male who isn't Cleve anywhere near her, the pack's teenagers had closed ranks around the new stray in their midst and Reilly had enrolled her in ninth grade.

The grandfather wolf lying on the floor doesn't answer, but the lines of his body change into ones that look a whole lot less like retreat.

I nudge Shelley toward the door. She'll understand the power of leaving Grandpa Cleve to guard something of importance to his pack.

She smiles faintly and takes one last look around her domain. Then she steps out of what would be a door if any of the walls had been filled in. I'm not sure whether Brown intended to leave the cook shack this open to the elements, but Shelley's quiet, delighted sigh the first time he let her stand inside the half-built walls decided the matter. Our new kitchen is a place of fall breezes and delicious smells, happily chatting helpers, and brilliant light.

Especially once the extra skylights that accidentally fell onto the delivery truck get here. Brown might have intended for this shack to be strictly temporary, but Rio took one look at the small hands holding up boards as Eliza and Danielle nailed them, and the careful consultations over Brandy's drawings, and Lissa and Shelley as they planned shelf layouts deep into the night, and decided something entirely different.

Which will probably make Brown growl, but that isn't today's fight. I glance back at Ebony, who's gathering more canteens and delaying just long enough to make sure we haven't pushed Cleve more than his wolf can handle. Then I head off down the path toward our old den and the road and a sentinel who is bringing in a truck full of pieces of our future.

SHELLEY

I'm being ridiculous. I know it, and my wolf knows it, but I can't get either of us to calm down. She wants to run and hunt in the woods for a truck and howl to the daylight moon of her discoveries. Wolves don't know what schools are, or greenhouses, but they know all about dens. A piece of our pack's heart is arriving today.

I didn't expect to be here to see it—someone always needs to tend to hearth and home, and that's felt like my purpose ever since I was Kelsey's size. But the yellow-gold wolf running at my side knew better, and so does the one still in her human skin who is running after us with a bunch of clothes in her arms, giggling.

Even my wolf knows that's a really good sound.

There's a small brown wolf running somewhere in the trees, too, but Ebony won't let Mellie get lost, and for a toddler, this is a decent run. It's pure foolishness for a woman with a rapidly growing collection of wrinkles and gray hairs, but my wolf can hardly remember why those human things matter. She's too happy to be out here running through her woods.

Breathing in freedom.

It's easier to do when I'm a wolf. My human form fought Samuel's dominance in as many small ways as I could, and I've got the scars, inside and out, to prove it.

My wolf shakes her head. Today isn't about fighting or about the state of my scars. It's about pack, one that

Samuel doesn't control anymore. The alpha running beside me, his tongue lolling, radiates good with every cheerful paw he puts on the ground, and he'll keep doing it all day long, even if one of the pups bangs his thumb with a hammer or a clumsy submissive spills his drink.

I inhale the crisp fall morning and run around a boulder just big enough to make my hips complain if I try to leap over it. These moments in my fur are precious, and I don't want to spoil them with sad memories. Not on this day. I want to collect new ones and tuck them away for safekeeping, just like Fallon does with her shiny things.

A yellow-gold wolf bumps against me companionably.

My wolf bumps him right back. Muffin thief.

Amusement glints in the one eye she can see.

I shake my head and slow to a trot. Mikayla isn't far behind with our clothes, and I don't want to greet our new greenhouse school naked as a jaybird.

Hayden shifts beside me. He doesn't give two hoots about being naked and neither does Mellie when he catches her, but they both pull on the pants and hoodies and sneakers Mikayla hands out when she arrives, her eyes dancing and her cheeks rosy in the fall air.

Ebony looks at her sneakers and hands one to me. "Since I don't have two left feet, I think this one's yours."

Hayden chuckles. "That will teach you to buy matching shoes."

Lissa found a really good deal, which means half the adult pack is sporting brand new green-and-purple sneakers. I slip mine on and tie neat bows in my laces. Slowly, because I've got a watcher. She hasn't quite worked out the very last part, but she'll have it soon enough.

I look up when I'm done and smile at Kelsey. "Has everyone made it, sweet pea?" It's not a fair question for a four-year-old, even one who's got a birthday coming and can almost tie her shoes, but Kelsey does pack math better than anyone except for maybe Rio, and he would disagree with me.

She nods solemnly. Then she reaches for Mikayla's hand and leads her off to parts unknown.

Hayden smiles at their departing backs. "Apparently we're not important enough to rate an escort."

If Samuel had said those words, there would have been bloodshed looming. He always needed to be the most important person in a room or a seedy bar or a forest. Hayden Scott hunts the woods for stray socks or washes every last dish in my kitchen without a whiff of arrogance—and every time he does it, my ribs find a little more space to breathe.

I'm not brave like Lissa, who unbound her ribs all at once, or Myrna, who never gave them an inch of what lived in her heart. But slowly, one slightly bigger breath at a time, I'm salvaging whatever is left of Shelley Martins.

Today, it feels like it just might be enough.

I look over at the man who's steadily, silently, patiently waiting for me to fight my demons and take the hand he's offering me. He leads us through the last stand of brushy trees into the clearing that passes for our parking lot and normally doesn't have much more in it than Rio's pickup truck or a half-pile of pea gravel.

It doesn't have either of those things this morning. Instead, there's chaos. Milling ravens and cats and hawks and teenagers, and more wolves from the baby packs than I expected, and enough different conversations happening all at once that it sounds like a party exploded in our quiet woods.

I look around quickly, because we have a lot of pack members who don't do parties all that well, yet. I'm not the only one scanning. We've learned a lot about what they need in the past few weeks. Things that should have been obvious but weren't—not until Fallon made us see.

But we have learned, and apparently our visitors somehow have, too. Tressie and Reese and Kendra and Hayden have alpha eyes everywhere. I can't see our betas, which just means they're doing their jobs silently, and the teenagers of all four packs are moving in ways that look cheerful and innocent and are rapidly finding buddies for everyone who wants one and a few who don't.

I hide a grin at Kenny's scowl. He flatly refuses to let his pack save him, but so far, we're doing a terrible job of listening. Stinky is already chattering away as he tugs Kenny out of the trees, and Brown offers a companionable growl as they join him on the periphery of the milling crowd.

I'm not worried about Kenny. Today will be about carrying heavy loads, and he's never let a packmate do that while his own shoulders were unburdened. It's the light days that are hard for him, not the ones full of work.

We are much alike, he and I.

I look at the two minders who have flanked me. "I'm fine. Truly."

Moon Girl doesn't say anything. She just rests her furry head against the side of my leg. Ghost leans into my shoulder. "I'm glad you're here. I wasn't sure you would come."

The two of us have had ourselves some long and interesting conversations as we gathered up the last lettuce and cucumbers of the season from our old garden. Not about my scars—those aren't stories for fifteen-year-old ears. But we've spoken of tricky and tender things, all the same. Hope, and composting, and how to cultivate courage. "Grandpa Cleve is watching the bread dough."

Which I didn't make. Myrna is better with yeast than I am. I stick to good, old-fashioned baking soda.

Ghost smiles, her fingers scratching behind Moon Girl's ears. "That's really good."

It is. Tiny, baby steps, but huge ones, all the same.

I take a deep breath and let it out—and let those strange fizzy bubbles in my ribs rise again.

2

RIO

I've driven a hundred trucks or more, delivering the assembly blocks of new den buildings to eager, waiting shifter packs all over the continent. It's not precisely my job, but Jules makes sure we all get a turn to see and feel our work come to life.

Today is reaching for me so hard that it's a wonder my ass is still in its damn seat. Ryder, sitting in the truck beside me, grins. "Don't drive into a tree, mister. That's precious cargo we're hauling."

She has no idea.

Well, she has some. I remember the scraggly kid she once was, staring in wonder at the tree-house den we hauled up the side of a mountain to where her small pack still lives. She drags me back there once a year or so. It's never boring. Neither is the woman who gets Home-

Wild's goods from Whistler to anywhere they need to go. "Just remember the rules, okay?"

She grunts. She's not happy about them. She lives to see the pieces come together, but I've given her the same instructions as I gave the motley crew in the vans and trucks behind us, and Kel is supposed to be disseminating them to the birds who have been circling overhead for the last half hour. A message straight from my sentinel gut.

They can schlep and carry all they want. We build.

I navigate a sharp bend in this road to the middle of nowhere, which is a tight squeeze courtesy of a pothole that has delusions of grandeur. Ryder chuckles. "I'll make some cats help me fill that up when we leave."

I don't ask if she's got the supplies for pothole filling. I've seen her pull a small crane out of her back pocket. "Will the other two trucks get through?"

She snorts. "If they can't, they're fired."

Ryder fires everyone at least twice a week. Not the most traditional management technique ever, but her crew would jump through fire for her, my wolf included. I take a deep breath. She's helped to settle him nicely. "Thanks."

She reaches over and squeezes my shoulder. "I miss you like fuck, dude, but I'm glad you found your place."

I lay my big hand over hers. She knows what it is to leave a family—and to make your place in a new one.

She grins. "I'll be nice, I promise."

I roll my eyes. She defines that term in the same general vicinity as Brown and Ames do. "Do you even know what that word means?"

She snickers. "Sure. I'll be totally sweet. Until the first wolf runs something into a rock. Then it will be time for my outside manners."

Her outside manners normally get a well-deserved workout at a delivery, but she has absolutely no idea how carefully the pieces of this building are about to be carried through the woods. My pack has been practicing for days with tree trunks and spare boards and an inventively assembled wall that was far more awkward than anything Ryder would ever permit onto one of her trucks. Kel made them stop two hours after dark last night. I think we're better prepared than some of his missions.

I squint ahead of me. We're not all going to fit into the parking lot, and I expected there to be shifters milling all over the road by now.

Then I see them.

Not milling. Standing at attention, two lines of them, holding hands or resting them on furry heads, and flanking a place of honor that is so very clearly meant to hold a really big truck.

My eyes blur.

Ryder's fist lands in my ribs. "Don't you dare hit a tree, Rio Marczak. Or any of those adorable pups." She starts bouncing on the seat beside me. "That's Kelsey, right? And Reilly. He's so stinking small. Does he know how big he's going to get? And there's Myrna. She's just like Adrianna described her, and that's Lissa beside her, and I bet that's Fallon, and Kennedy, and I have to talk to Danielle because Jules wants to steal her. You should probably make sure that doesn't actually work. It's a really good offer. Oh, and there's Ebony. I talked to her last week, and that's Ghost beside her, right?"

I rub my new tender spot, make a note to save Danielle from Hayden's baby sister, and grin. Apparently I'm not going to have to make introductions.

SHELLEY

It's so big.

I stare at the enormous truck as it inches forward into the space we've made for it. I've walked the ground with the stakes and string that show where our new school is going to be, and looked out at the view that we'll be able to see from the greenhouse, and tracked the sunlight that will land on our indoor garden so we could work out how to use the precious, warm space to grow the most goodness.

I still somehow expected the delivery to be so much smaller.

I stare as Rio hops out of the truck on one side and a woman who is almost as wide as she is tall climbs down from the other. She flashes me a grin, like she knows exactly who I am, and then she cups her hands to her mouth. "Yo, Ghost Mountain Pack. Your delivery is here."

She's got a voice like a foghorn, but her last words still get drowned in a lot of noise as hawks land and cats and ravens come out of the woodwork and a really excited bear cub roars loudly enough to shake the sides of the truck.

I step out of the way as Ghost moves forward, collecting up Reilly as she goes. The other team leaders move forward, too, and assemble in a line in front of the short woman with the foghorn voice.

She grins. "I'm Ryder. You must be the folks in charge of getting all of this through the woods to your den."

My wolf wants to lick her. The team leaders are mostly teenagers and some of them are sprouting fur at being this close to a stranger, and she's acting like it's all business as usual.

Reilly gulps and nods. "Yes."

She nods cheerfully. "Good. You're Reilly, right? Rio tells me you're smart and careful and you know to take a rest when you need one instead of being a big dope who thinks his muscles are his best feature."

Kennedy snickers and flexes her arms. Hoot elbows her in the ribs.

Ryder fist-bumps Hoot. Then her eyes swing unerringly to a teenager who hasn't said a word. "So, how do we work this? I unload to you, and you'll supervise everyone else?"

Kennedy and Hoot and Reilly all beam at the friendly stranger who got it exactly right.

Ghost clears her throat. "Yes, but give us a minute to get all the new people into teams, okay?" She turns around and eyes the crowd behind her. "We weren't expecting quite so many of you."

The raven alpha chuckles. "Ever tried to tell cats or birds that they can't do something fun?"

Ghost's lips quirk. "Some."

Tressie winks. "Anyone who doesn't behave will be sent away without any cookies. Tell us how to be useful."

My wolf watches, worried. Ghost is getting really good at being bossy, but we really weren't expecting this many people. She doesn't look too nervous, though. Her baby pack and the other team leaders they recruited are already pulling out their special bandanas.

Ghost holds one up in the air. "Anyone wearing one of these is in charge of a team. That means you follow their instructions unless they're really dumb or might get somebody hurt. All the Ghost Mountain shifters already have a team leader. New people, find someone from our pack to pair up with, because we did a lot of practicing, and we learned a lot of ways not to walk things into trees."

I shuffle myself over Moon Girl's way. I didn't expect to be here this morning, but I practiced just like everyone else. She was the best leader for my wolf. She's calm and gets the job done, and she's got an uncanny sense for how to guide ungainly objects through the forest.

Stinky slides past in front of me on his way over to Kennedy's team, towing Sienna and Sierra behind him. There are some discreet hand signals happening, but they're not really necessary. Everyone is cheerfully finding a buddy, and nobody seems to care that the teenagers are in charge.

Reese touches a hand to Hoot's bright-yellow bandana. "These are really smart."

Ghost dips her chin. "Thanks. They were Shelley's idea."

My cheeks warm. I don't know how I got pulled into this. All I did was find some stretchy fabric in town.

Ryder grins at Hayden. "When can I steal her?"

He snorts. "Ghost or Shelley?"

She winks at me. "Both."

Rio wraps his arm around her shoulders. "No stealing my packmates, remember?"

She scowls. "Spoilsport."

Myrna cackles. "I like her. Can we keep her?"

Rio rolls his eyes. "Can we start unloading these trucks? Pretty please? Or my boss is going to get cranky, because she needs them back for a new delivery next week."

Ryder smirks. "Your boss can be bribed with really good cookies and you know it."

Reese snickers. "So can the rest of us. Why do you think we're here?"

Every head in the clearing nods, like that's an entirely reasonable reason to spend a day tromping through the forest carrying heavy things.

My wolf sits on me so I don't run straight back to camp to throw a new batch of cookies into the oven. She stays there as I breathe, as I remember that we have wall panels to carry and this isn't Samuel's domain anymore. I don't have to instantly jump anytime there's something that needs to be done.

Hayden smiles at me, like maybe he saw what my bossy wolf did and he's proud of her.

I dip my head.

Moon Girl's fingers slide into mine. She knows what it is to see approval in an alpha's eyes and still shake.

"The cookies are all back at camp because Ghost is smart like that." Kennedy grins and leans against her quieter friend. She also casts me a quick, searching look that sees almost as much as Hayden's did. "So let's get this stuff off the truck before I starve."

Ryder nods, and just like that, we all come to attention.

My wolf quivers. I might not be ready for what this day brings—but she is.

KEL

Shelley Martins is one of my favorite people, and her human heart is attached to a wolf who quietly, insistently walked her through six years of hell and is damn determined to bring her all the way out the other side.

I'm close enough to give that wolf support if she needs it, and so is Ebony, but neither of us is going to be necessary. Shelley's wolf is solid, and if she wobbles, Kenny is about half a step away, pretending like he's just some random guy who happens to be standing on a patch of dirt near the lady who bakes cookies.

Which is bullshit, but I don't get in the way of bullshit that works on the side of healing and goodness and reluctant redemption.

I glance at Hayden, because he got Shelley here and somehow made it look like an innocent stroll in the woods, and at Ghost, who planted the seeds for what's coming next several weeks ago. We've been trying to put off making her an official pack beta because human fifteen-year-olds deserve time and space to be young and irresponsible, but her wolf isn't going to let us do that for much longer.

She meets my eyes and smiles faintly. Then she follows Ryder around to the back of the truck, the pack flowing and re-forming around the two of them like we do this every day. Which is a testament to a whole lot of things, and so far, none of them have required more than a hint of Ryder's prodigious talents with unruly, disorganized strangers.

I'll have to send Brown her way. She'll be sad if she doesn't get to use her outside voice at least once.

Ryder raises the door on the back of the truck, which is impressive and noisy and cuts off all chatter as Ghost Mountain Pack gets its first look at the bones of our new school. It's mostly a sea of the specialty pressed packing cardboard that HomeWild recycles and remakes onsite. Countless rows of neatly stacked and labeled boxes that hint at very little besides the magnitude of the task ahead of us.

Reilly exhales into the hush. "Wow."

I hide a grin. The kid doesn't look daunted at all. I

wonder if he has any idea how many trips he's about to take through the woods.

Ryder winks at him and then finds Hayden in the crowd. "I've got the two special items you requested, and then I'll have Ghost here figure out who should be taking everything else."

Ghost has the brains to look a little daunted. Reilly just beams at the new friend who is delivering his wildest dreams. Hayden makes his way forward, pulling on the cloak of alpha authority he uses so rarely. Ghost might have planted these particular seeds, but Hayden grew them into monster zucchini.

When he decides to throw his alpha weight around, he does it right.

Ryder raises a wry eyebrow, but the rest of her manages to stay appropriately solemn as she reaches for a box twice as tall as she is and neatly hefts it off the truck and nearly onto Hayden's toes. "This here is the door of your school. I figure you know where it's headed."

Hayden smiles a little. "Sounds heavy. Might need a bear to carry it."

Smart hands push an eleven-year-old bear cub forward. Brown does his best to hide behind the crowd.

Hayden lays his hand on Reilly's shoulder. "Every student in Ghost Mountain Pack is going to step through this door nearly every day in the years to come. Do you think you can get it safely to where it needs to go?"

Reilly lays his cheek on the cardboard packaging, a bear cub entirely overwhelmed.

Ryder sniffles as she turns and grabs a second large,

flat box. This one she sets down far more carefully. "This one's gonna need someone really responsible. Not you, Hayden Scott."

He grins at her. "I only ran a window into a tree once."

She snorts. "It ran into a tree after you tried to use it to slide down a hill because you thought glass might be slippery like snow."

Even Reilly grins at that, and a whole lot of wolves relax. The bar has been set. They can all manage to be more responsible than their alpha.

Hayden smiles at his pack. "Some of you will remember a day, shortly after I first got here, when I asked what you wanted in your new den."

The words are simple enough. The sense of alpha ritual he just wrapped around them isn't simple at all. Every wolf who was there inhales quietly. Remembering.

The rest wait. Quiet. Reverent.

Lissa nods, her entire being full of love for her mate. "Shelley was the first one to speak up. She asked for light. For windows."

"She did." Hayden's eyes find a wolf who absolutely didn't expect to be noticed in this moment. He lays his hand on the big, flat box. "Carry the first window for us, Shelley Martins. Walk this big, beautiful piece of light into our new den."

Shelley stares. At Lissa, at Hayden, at Reilly, at the cardboard-clad window. "I can't carry that."

Reilly grins. "Of course not. That's why we have teams, remember?"

Ghost, standing on the end of the truck with very well-hidden satisfaction in her eyes, gives him a fraction of a nod that makes him glow. Kenny, who is no slouch as a beta either, snorts and pushes Shelley forward. "Collect up your window, woman."

She stares at the boxed window like it might eat her.

Kennedy strolls over and lays her hand on Reilly's door. "I better carry this one. I'd totally walk a window into a tree." She shoots a grin at her alpha. "Even I'm not dumb enough to try sliding one down a hill, though."

I shake my head at Ebony. We had some plans on how to get this show moving. Once again, the teenagers are making us irrelevant.

Hoot slides past Kenny and pats Shelley's shoulder. "I'll help you." Moon Girl and Brandy and Katrina step up silently behind her. I'm close enough to hear Kenny's resigned sigh as he realizes that he just got surrounded by wolves he can't growl at without getting his ass chewed.

I grin. I discussed the teams with him as we practiced carries and buddied up packmates like Moon Girl and Brandy who might have to leave suddenly. I might not have shared all my reasoning, however.

He glares at me, a guy finally figuring out some of the team-building math way too late.

Too bad. We've got one window in solid hands, and one guy who can't slink off into the woods because he doesn't want to do anything that might earn him cookies.

I scowl at him another second for good measure. Then I take a quick look around, because with this many cats, something is bound to go wrong pretty much immediately. Ebony is heading for the door team, probably because Kennedy and Sienna are already trying to talk Reilly into a route that will resemble an obstacle course instead of a sedate walk in the woods. Ravi joins them, which makes my wolf smile. I don't know if anyone has told him yet, but he'll be walking through that door most days, too.

Ryder reaches into the truck for a much smaller box, jumps down, and hands it to the small girl holding Ravi's hand. "This is the most important part of the door, cutie. It's the hinges to attach it to everything else. Think you can get it to your den without losing any of the parts?"

Jade, who has no idea what a hinge might be, nods solemnly.

Ebony looks a little concerned. I'm not. There's not a chance in hell that Ryder doesn't have spare hinges on one of the trucks, and she believes in empowering girls with a fierceness that involves recruitment as soon as they can walk. A quirk aided and abetted by her alpha, her boss, and pretty much everyone else in Whistler Pack.

The door and window teams get themselves sorted using the quiet hoots we worked out over the last several days, which startles the hawks and ravens and amuses the fuck out of the cats.

Ryder shoots me a sharp look. Her team communicates that way, but she clearly wasn't expecting it from a bunch of amateurs.

I don't bother telling her what she'll figure out for herself in the next few minutes. I just watch as my pack orients around the two cardboard boxes that have been neatly anointed with our pack story and assigned to bearers who will feel every step of this journey in their bones.

We're all silent as eleven packmates, one window, one door, and a set of hinges make their way into the woods with slow, awkward majesty.

Heading home.

3

SHELLEY

"I had no idea windows were this heavy." Wrinkles grins at me and extracts a granola bar from the pouch on my hip. My hands are busy carrying my sixth and final window of the day. She holds up the bar. "Anyone need a bite?"

"Me." Kennedy somehow manages to turn around and look at us while not mangling some innocent tree with her armload of pipes. "I think we're lost. It can't possibly take this long to walk to Banner Rock."

She's made more trips than the rest of us combined. And helped Mikayla kick me out of the kitchen every time I've had what they consider to be enough of a chance to catch my breath, because apparently windows can't make it through the forest without my help. I nod down at my pouch. "There's jerky in there, too."

Wrinkles holds up a handful. "Already got it." She

eyes Kenny. "And this time you're eating some or I'm making you sit with the pups when we get back."

Good for her. I forced him onto a stool in my kitchen earlier and made him eat a bowl of chili, but I don't think he's touched anything since, and he's still far too thin to be working this hard without fuel.

He eyes Wrinkles with a death stare that bounces right off. "Not hungry."

Kennedy snorts. "You must really want some healer tea. I hear this batch is really awful, by the way. Rio thinks maybe someone dropped a sock in by accident."

Wrinkles chortles. "The socks are never accidental."

Kenny grunts. "Next trip I'm carrying pipes like all the other cranky loners."

I don't think there will be a next trip. The trucks were looking awfully barren.

Kennedy shakes her armful of pipes cheerfully. "Not cranky. Not a loner."

She collected up that armful when Brandy needed a sudden break, but our baby alpha rarely lets facts get in the way of a good story. We're all getting really good at helping our packmates slide in and out of the shadows as they need.

Including my wolf. She bites my ankles every time I try to hide away for too long, and when that doesn't work, she acquires help. I smile at Kenny. He's really done very well at not being too grumpy, and he's made almost as many trips as Kennedy. "Mikayla's making up some honey ham sandwiches. You'll eat one of those."

Reese snorts from his spot off Kenny's flank. He's

carrying some boxes of bolts that will feel like small boulders by the time we get to the den. "That sounds like bear food."

I roll my eyes his way. He's been a steady presence all day, making people laugh and encouraging them to take a rest and starting sword fights with accidentally dropped pipes and generally making sure a bunch of earnest wolves don't work ourselves into the ground. While somehow still carrying an awful lot of wall panels.

Our pack does not lack for friends.

I look up as more birds fly overhead. Rio and Kendra rigged some carry loops for the hawks and ravens, and there are currently a bunch of steel beams zooming through the sky.

Wrinkles snorts as the last hawk goes by with Mellie in his claws, instead. "How many rides has she gotten today?"

Reese grins. "She's carrying a pipe."

She is. A small, bendy one that will be part of the school's heated floor. Which I know because Ghost has made sure that every single shifter carrying a load knows its purpose, and Kelsey had two of those bendy pipes on her last trip. She came to the kitchen to show them to Grandpa Cleve.

Rio runs toward us with three pups on his heels. He ruffles Kennedy's head as he arrives. "I smell gummy bears. Who's got them?"

Silly wolf. "I think there are still some in my pouch."

He grins. "Those ones are all covered in cookie crumbs."

Reese isn't the only goofball in these parts. "Fine. Then you can wait until you get back to the cook shack and have clean ones from the bin."

Robbie shifts to human behind him and looks at me beseechingly.

My wolf sits up, worried. The pups are hungry.

Rio rolls his eyes. "He just ate three sandwiches. *Three.* And drank Myrna's big mug full of chocolate milk."

Robbie grins, shifts back to cute white wolf, and takes off after his friends.

"Save me some gummy bears. Clean ones," Rio calls back over his shoulder as he runs off after his furry charges. "And maybe try to save Brown from the cats. They're trying to convince him that the shelves in the cook shack aren't level."

I glare at Reese. His kitties need to behave. Those shelves are my prize possessions.

He just snickers.

Kennedy grins at Sierra. "Your alpha is almost as immature as ours."

Sierra, who has been shooting video most of the day, nearly trips over a tree root laughing. Which means Kennedy has to do a fancy dance to keep from bonking her on the head with a bunch of pipes. Most of which gets caught on video for posterity.

Wrinkles chuckles.

Kenny closes his eyes and shakes his head silently.

I just smile and grip my window a little tighter. My arms are sore and my fingers don't work quite right anymore and I might have to give in and sleep on the warm kitchen floor tonight if I want to be able to move in the morning. But that first slow, solemn walk through the woods and the progressively sillier ones since haven't done a thing to diminish the glow in my ribs.

I'm carrying light into our den.

HAYDEN

I look at Ryder and the three very empty trucks she's just finished checking one last time. "Miss anything?"

Ghost giggles. "Only if it's invisible."

Ryder grins. "You have no idea how many invisible boxes have come back to the workshop."

Exactly none since she took over. I put my arm around the shoulders of a fifteen-year-old who's been working logistics all day, along with the far more subtle levers of making her packmates feel important and worthy and special. "She's just trying to make sure she has enough room to kidnap you."

"Seriously." Ryder shoots me a look that says she's only half-kidding. She holds out a hand to Ghost. "I expected Rio to make my life easier than usual today. Instead, I got a real pro. If you ever want to spend a year or two down south, I need you to promise me that I can have the first chance to make you an offer."

I grab my wolf before he pounces. Ghost deserves choices.

She smiles softly. "Thanks, but these are my woods."

Ryder nods. "Yeah. Figured." She punches my shoulder. "This big doofus is lucky to have you."

Kendra strolls up, grinning. "Are we beating up on Hayden?"

I let my wolf growl. Hawk alphas don't find him at all scary. "No. You're leaving so that we can go find all the pipes you dropped before it gets dark."

She snorts. "We had ravens on our teams. Do you really think they lost shiny things?"

No. Which was an unexpected bonus when Mellie dropped a box of hex bolts while flying over a small canyon. I hold out a hand. "Thank your crew for me. They worked hard." Which is all the thanks she'll take—I've already tried half a dozen other varieties.

She chuckles. "You earned it. My hawks ate you out of house and home. Ryder here might want to kidnap Ghost. I want Shelley."

That will happen shortly after Ghost decides to be a city wolf. "Hands off my pack, you two."

"Three." Tressie, freshly landed, pulls on a hoodie that I'm pretty sure used to belong to Lissa. "Can I give you a list of who I want? I'll send them back for visits."

Ghost, tucked into my side, giggles.

About time she turned back into a teenager. I let my wolf keep cuddling her. The teenagers in this pack need every bit of affection and alpha approval I can hand out, even the ones who rarely look like they need it.

Tressie holds out her palm and offers a single, shiny

blue bead to Ghost. "I hear you've been taking really good care of Indrani. Thank you."

HomeWild's newest engineering intern has been staying with us for the last couple of weeks, putting in crazy hours with Danielle and Rio as they hook up all the uses my pack can imagine for the temporary pipes running from our underground hot spring. Ghost was the one who realized that she needed to be sprung for regular runs in the forest.

My pack's youngest beta takes the pretty bead, clearly recognizing it as the high honor it is, with a quiet smile. She doesn't have any kind of ego, but she's one of the few around here who don't underestimate their own worth. "It's been fun for Fallon to have another raven around."

Tressie chuckles. "You practically have Martha living with you, and if you need more, just say the word and I'll let them out of raven jail."

I grin. "Martha's useful to have around. She keeps Myrna out of trouble." And adds healer weight so that we don't smother our newly pregnant mamas. Cori copes with overprotective wolves reasonably well. Fallon wants to bite our tails on a regular basis. Martha understands that in a way that furry, land-bound packmates simply can't.

The raven alpha takes one last look around. "I think we're all out of your hair. We'll go bug Reese and make sure he sets up his building right."

His crew already left, mostly to get ready for an invasion. The cats are hosting an impromptu building party for their school in the morning, which will likely be preceded by some serious revelry tonight. It will also make good use of a bunch of hovering shifters who are afraid to leave this neck of the woods in case we need them.

I don't have the heart to tell them that Rio and I could erect this school ourselves. They'll figure that out in the morning. HomeWild kits are designed to be idiot-proof, and I was the lead tester on the idiot squad more times than I can count.

I squeeze Ghost's shoulders. "Let's go make sure nobody got lost in the woods, and then we'll see if we can find the building instructions before it gets dark."

It's a measure of how drunk her wolf is on alpha approval that she just nods agreeably.

Ryder pulls the door of her truck closed with a slam that rings loud in the quiet. Tressie and Kendra head toward the woods, chatting with each other and ignoring the hawks and ravens circling overhead.

I smile. Some new friends were made today.

Ghost's head settles against my shoulder. "Are you sure we can build it? There were a lot of parts."

A beta who's still young enough to show her doubts— and managed to keep them to herself all day long. I rub my cheek on the top of her head. "You did your part. Tomorrow, Reilly and Danielle and Eliza will do theirs, and I bet they'll have it totally nailed down just like you did."

She grins. "I watched the instruction video. There aren't any nails."

There aren't, which is a shame. Brown has everyone, right down to Robbie and Kelsey, well schooled in the fine art of driving a nail where it needs to go. However, bolts and screws and interlocking parts are easier for idiots—and for the careful hands that will be the corps de construction ballet tomorrow.

My official job will be backing up the choreographers, but I'm pretty sure I'll be spending the day fetching sandwiches.

I know just how many times Reilly and Danielle and Eliza have watched that video.

SHELLEY

The sun is setting and the flames of the campfire down below us are making strange shadows of the tarp-covered piles of wall panels and roof beams and floorboards and pipes.

The pipes, especially, are a mystery. Some will run hot water for warm floors, and some will irrigate our planters, and some will let us turn the whole greenhouse into a misty rainforest. I look over at Danielle, who is still squinting at the various piles, even though she can't possibly make out their details in the deepening shadows. "Got it all figured?"

She snorts. "Not even close."

"You will." Cori smiles. "Rio says that the changes

you made to the heat exchange system are so good that Ronan is probably going to cry."

Danielle squirms. "It's just temporary. They'll build the real one after Ronan gets here."

I lean into her wolf. I don't know a thing about pipes, but there isn't a chance she's going to get side-lined just because a polar bear with a fancy engineering degree shows up. Besides, I think he might end up too busy fishing with Reilly to actually get any work done. Or knitting. Or learning to fold flowers out of Ebony's shiny origami paper. "How much do you think he eats?"

Cori giggles. "Did you see how much Reilly ate today?"

Danielle groans. "It was Hayden's fault. He kept telling him that growing bears need to eat."

He's right. That poor child had to keep his appetite and his bear in check for six years, and he's sometimes still hesitant to eat as he should. "He's a pleasure to feed, and we've got plenty of groceries. I'm just not sure what a grown bear might like."

Cori shoots me a measuring look.

I ignore her. Feeding Ronan is a real concern, and if it helps keep Danielle's thoughts off her big responsibilities tomorrow morning, that's all to the good. "I asked Indrani, but she just laughed and said he eats everything."

"He likes jam, I know that much." Danielle tilts her head, thinking. "Fish, of course, and spicy food, or that's what he tells Reilly, anyhow."

I make mental notes to haggle with Martha for more spices and test out a couple of new jerky recipes.

Cori shifts her weight, adjusting the pillow behind her back.

My wolf wants to sniff and make sure she's settled safely. I tell her to chill. We're hiding out up here on this ledge because Cori needs a break from wolves who are worried that carrying a few pipes has somehow dislodged the baby in her barely rounding belly.

I do hand her the flask and cups Wrinkles gave me, though.

Cori eyes it suspiciously.

My wolf snickers. She did sniff the contents of the flask. "It's safe. Just a calming tea for us all to share." A healer who is not above using one patient to guilt the others.

Cori unscrews the lid and fills three small tin cups.

I smile as she hands me one. They're silly, dented things, garage-sale discards because the fourth cup was missing. I bought them for Kelsey, but they make their way into my hands often enough that clearly Kelsey has other ideas.

The cup nestles in my hands, radiating warmth and smelling of summer fields and something bright and fruity. I take a sip that's still hot enough to have my tongue panting. I never do wait quite long enough.

Cori reaches over and squeezes my knee. "You sound happy."

Six years ago she was a quiet young woman with haunted eyes who wouldn't have dared either the touch or the question. But even then, my soul knew hers. "It was a good day."

Danielle shakes her head. "Thirty-seven windows. What were we thinking?"

Light. So much light. "It will be good for the plants. And for the pups."

Cori smiles. "I'm going to sit in the greenhouse when I'm round and pregnant and can hardly move, and help you harvest baby tomatoes."

I have no idea if we can grow cherry tomatoes in the dead of winter, but every shifter in the gardening forum is cheering us on, and they were Cori's single, shy request. Which means Kelsey is already singing to the tomato seeds, and Reilly found us an article about growing tomato seedlings in outer space in case it might be helpful, and Mikayla is collecting tomato recipes in a folder with the date of Cori's birthday on it. "At least you know the difference between weeds and tomatoes."

Danielle chuckles. "I might need lessons. The last batch of nettles I harvested apparently wasn't nettles."

Cori grins. "That's why you're in charge of pipes and wires, and Shelley is in charge of edible things that taste good, and Wrinkles is in charge of edible things that taste bad. We all have our strengths."

I'm being credited with far too many today. "I'm in charge of baking. I'm just a helper in the garden."

Danielle snorts. "Good luck with that. Hayden has other ideas."

He's a pushy alpha. That's his job. "He has other ideas about you, too."

She shrugs a little. "I'm good at what I do. I tinker. I fix things. It's enough."

It would be if that's what her soul wanted, but it isn't. She pored over the building diagrams that Rio printed out for her, the special ones that don't usually get sent with the HomeWild kits. She spent hours studying the veins and bones and sinew of our greenhouse school and asking Indrani shy questions when she thought Rio wasn't looking.

Silly wolf. Rio is always looking, even when his eyes are elsewhere.

I take another sip of my tea. This time I don't have to dangle my tongue like an overeager pup. "I saw Hayden working on Bailey, too." He'll have plenty of help with that. A school needs teachers, after all.

Cori smiles. "They're going to get Ravi training so he can work with the smallest pups as a real teacher, not just a helper. Lissa told him while he was holding one end of a roof truss and couldn't run away."

I shake my head. "Pushy wolves, our alphas." That still isn't quite official, but up here on this ledge, no one will argue.

Danielle shoots me a saucy look. "I heard that you told Cleve to shift and put on some pants because there were wolves who needed snacks and your hands were full."

That was different. "My hands *were* full."

The two of them tip against each other, laughing quietly.

Such a different reaction than my small impertinences used to earn. I sip my tea and chase away the tears that threaten. They aren't needed.

My wolf settles her head on her tail. Happy. Proud of me.

I let her rest while she can. She'll probably need to push on me again tomorrow.

4

SHELLEY

Braden charges into the kitchen, trying to speak and catch his breath at the same time. Myrna catches him before he faceplants into the open bin of potatoes. "Is it time?"

A small, remarkably unsticky face nods and then scampers back out the door like we set fire to his tail.

Hayden makes shooing motions with his potato peeler. "Go. I promise not to burn down the kitchen."

Since the stove isn't on yet, that's probably a promise he can keep. I dry my hands and set down the towel. We haven't been in here long—just long enough to babysit the marinades Myrna has brewing for a big cookout tonight. We made pancakes over the campfire this morning so we could watch as Danielle walked her helpers through the careful layout of the pipes that go under the school floor, and Eliza used the bags that Brown lugged through the forest to mix up concrete for the footing molds, and Reilly and his team carefully laid out all the boxed windows and wall panels.

I follow Myrna out of the cook shack, our eyes blinking in the sudden sun as we eagerly scan the area where the school will be. It still looks like an ant hive, but it's changed a lot in the time it took to stir the marinades and add a few potatoes to the pot.

Danielle waves us over. "You're up. Pipe-joining duty. I need a crew who knows their left from their right."

Stinky grins and takes Robbie's hand. "That's not us. We get to go stir concrete."

Brown snorts from the big bucket he's supervising just outside the laid-out pipes. He's got what looks like a huge egg beater on the end of a drill, and the mix inside his bucket would make nice pancakes if it weren't quite so gray.

Eliza punches his arm. "Don't be a cranky bear. This is the best job and you have to share it, remember?"

He just rolls his eyes and stirs his pancake batter.

I try not to sniffle. I remember the days when Eliza never looked up, much less cheerfully punched a bear. I also remember the days when my arms didn't feel like limp spaghetti, but this isn't one of them. Hopefully I can manage pipes. We didn't get to practice this part. All of the pipes we had were old and terrible and made Rio curse. These ones are shiny and laid out in a long trail back and forth on the dirt.

Myrna and I join Ravi and Glow, who are already looking uncertainly at the work before us. My wolf thinks maybe she ought to try to fix that. I elbow Myrna. "The rest of us are quiet and follow directions. Are you sure you're supposed to be here?"

That gets a silent smile from Glow. She's one of Dorie's strays. She doesn't usually say much, but she's been reading over Ghost's shoulder in the gardening forum.

Danielle holds up two short sections of pipe. "These screw together just like a jar lid." She demonstrates and then hands the two pipes to me. "Turn left to loosen them, right to tighten them."

My hands find the motions easily. They've opened plenty of jars.

Glow scowls when she has to try twice. Ravi pulls a marker out of his pocket and calmly writes a big *L* on his left hand and hers.

Danielle shoots him a grateful look as she holds out her hand, too. "That's a really smart idea. It gets confusing after a while, especially with the bendy pipes."

Those are the ones that turn the trail of pipes around for another pass under the floor. I hold out my hand to Ravi's marker and survey the pipes. There are a lot of them. I know how kitchen assembly lines work, but this one is a bit of a mystery. "Where do we start?"

"In the middle." Glow looks really surprised that she's spoken.

Danielle's eyes widen with pleasure. "Exactly. Makes sense, right?"

Ravi puts up his hand. "Explain, please? For those of us who lack sense?"

Myrna bumps him with her shoulder. "Speak for yourself, mister. I have plenty of sense. I might have left it in the potato bin, but it's good stuff."

Glow's lips quirk.

Silly pack. I eye Danielle. "I have an alpha in my kitchen, and he's going to come across Myrna's common sense in the potato bin soon, so let's get moving, shall we?"

She chuckles. "It's pretty simple, really. We start in the middle and work out so we don't unscrew pipes that are already joined as we screw on the new ones."

Myrna blinks and tilts her head. "Nope. Not getting it."

She's been doing this lately. Owning what she doesn't understand, especially when there are teenagers and young adults around who aren't so sure that they want to go to school and put how much they don't know on display.

Danielle's face wrinkles.

I expect Ravi to help her, but it's Glow who reaches for the two short pieces of pipe we were screwing together earlier. "Do you have two more?"

Danielle's eyes clear. She reaches over to the trail of pipe and picks up a couple of short ones, quickly screwing them together.

Glow hands me two, and Ravi two. Then she positions us and nods to Myrna. "Screw them together, right here."

Myrna twists the middle two pipes, carefully at first, and then faster as the pipes cooperate. Then she stops and snorts. "I'm just undoing the other two joins, aren't I?"

I can see the one in my hands coming apart. I can also see, very clearly, why starting in the middle makes sense. And I can see that Danielle just got herself an assistant, even though Glow maybe hasn't figured that part out yet.

Myrna pats Glow's hand. "You're an excellent teacher, dear. Sometimes I learn far better from a little demonstration than a bunch of fancy words."

My wolf snorts quietly. Troublemaking elder.

Danielle clears her throat. "Are we ready?"

No, but I'm learning not to let that stop me. I carefully put the two short pipes in my hands back where they came from and step over the boundary string. My breath catches a little. This feels momentous, even if I'm a lowly helper chosen mostly because I won't make a mad dash through the carefully laid-out pipes. The old den was built before I arrived, and my cook shack rose up around me while I was sorting pots and figuring out how to get a stove and a refrigerator and a couple of very large freezers into their proper places.

Today I get to put my hands on what will be a school and a garden and a joyful, warm, sturdy monument to our pack. Today, I get to touch our new bones.

RIO

Kel snorts as he watches the activity below. "Jules is going to try to steal half the pack at this rate."

I take a swig of my chocolate milk. "She can try." We're on top of a rock with papers strewn everywhere, which is a fairly sad attempt to look busy enough that nobody will bother us. That it's working is a testament to the three people slowly feeling their way into being the leaders of this build.

Reilly and Danielle and Eliza all have doubts about their own skills, but their faith in each other is nearly infinite—and that's somehow making it work. Eliza has several entirely creditable concrete footers already hardening, and Brown, who has mixed a bag or two of concrete in his time, has steadfastly done nothing more than pour wet mix where he's told. Reilly has the wall panels, which will go up after the floor is done, already laid out in sequential order around the building area, and the helmet-clad teenagers and mamas who helped him are taking a well-deserved snack break.

Which means it's Danielle who has most of our attention at the moment. She chose this particular crew carefully, and we watch as she herds them into place in the middle of the pipe grid. My fingers tap on the rock, trying to get a read on Glow, who is the most likely to scamper. Or so I thought, right up until she started giving pipe-joining lessons.

Kel snorts. "Use your human eyes. There's plenty to see."

Glow looks up just enough that I catch her shy smile at Shelley.

My sentinel relaxes. There will be no scampering.

Shelley and Glow bend down and pick up one end of a long, straight pipe. They're not as heavy as they look, but they're awkward, all the same. Myrna and Ravi take hold of the end of the next pipe in the line, and Danielle guides them as they navigate the two ends together. There's some cursing as they figure out that left and right depend on which way you happen to be holding your pipe, but Glow solves that with quiet efficiency.

I shake my head ruefully. People with those kind of instincts for pipes and wires are hard to find, and apparently we have two of them. "Hayden needs to come up with some kind of lending arrangement where Home-Wild can borrow our packmates but has to give them back."

Kel snorts. "Right. Because Hayden paid so much attention when his sister was studying contract law."

I grin. "Maybe Lissa, then."

Kel grunts. "That might work."

It will work or a sentinel will throw his weight around. Mostly for the theatrics. Jules Scott might make a lot of dramatic noises, but she will steal her brother's wolves shortly after hell freezes over. The two of them were impacted by their father's death in very different ways, but both of them grew into adults who spend every day of their lives making home into a place of safety and refuge and belonging. She'll only make loud noises about stirring that up for the same reason Brown is stirring wet mix. To make it stronger.

Kel bumps my shoulder. "Kelsey just headed into the kitchen with her guitar."

My wolf snorts. Hayden is in there with a really big pot of potatoes. Kelsey is a step ahead of my sentinel, as usual. Even if she doesn't know exactly why today will shake her alpha.

The pipes crew have made their way to opposite ends of the first row, and are contemplating the tricky bends that will route the water flow for another pass under the floor. Glow barely pauses as she rounds her turn, but Myrna ends up cursing in at least two languages as she negotiates her first bendy pipe.

I grin. There's no way our pups are going to make it through this build without learning a few new words. Even the teenagers might pick up a few. Myrna has an impressive collection.

Danielle heads over to help the swearing part of her team. Shelley and Glow keep moving down their row with a precision that makes my wolf beam. He doesn't give a damn about pipes, but that kind of teamwork requires trust, and those two just built it really quickly.

My sentinel is amused. They aren't the pairing he predicted.

Kel shakes his head as packmates who have never built anything more complicated than a tent platform slowly, awkwardly, beautifully take the first steps to erect a greenhouse school. "This project is going to keep us really humble."

I grin. "Speak for yourself. I'm the genius who designed this thing."

He snorts. "You're next up on slinging around bags of concrete."

That's one of the very few tasks in a HomeWild build that benefits from burly muscles. "I thought that was your job."

He grins. "Nope. I'm on chili duty."

The last time I ate Kel's chili, my fur was on fire for a week. "I guess I'm eating at the pups' table again."

He chuckles. "I'll tell Hayden to make some spaghetti. I think Shelley's going to be busy for a while."

Good. The kitchen is where Shelley is painstakingly rebuilding her confidence—but my wolf is quite certain it isn't where she's going to find her joy.

SHELLEY

My arms are going to fall off. I pause long enough to push my hair out of my face and scowl at Glow, who looks as unruffled as she did when we first got started. "You carried things yesterday. I saw you. How are your arms still working?"

She smiles and screws on another pipe. At this point, she's doing all the hard work, because I lost track of my left and my right three rows ago. My job is to hold steady and not accidentally drop anything on our toes.

The next join proceeds silently, which pokes at me. I'm not usually a chatty wolf, but something in me wants a conversation today. "I've been trying to figure out if we can plant some pumpkins in under the green beans."

Glow watches her hands as she positions the next bendy pipe.

Bile slithers in my belly. "I'm sorry. I'll be quiet."

"No." A quick, hitching breath. "If you want to talk, that's fine. I like listening."

It's so hard to believe the nice words. My wolf nudges me. I need to try. "I was hoping to maybe hear your thoughts on the garden. I know you've been reading online with Ghost, and I know what it's like to have thoughts and think that nobody wants to hear them."

She glances up at me and looks back down at her hands.

Nasty, crawling shame rises up my throat. The pipe I'm holding starts to shake. "I'm sorry."

She sets her pipe against mine, catching it. Steadying it. Showing it where to go. "I was six years old when I spoke for the first time."

My wolf snaps at my shame and sends it fleeing back to its dark den. "Was it your choice, or did you not know how until then?"

She pauses. Huffs out a breath. Smiles a little. "Nobody ever asks that."

My wolf tries to figure out which way to step. They all smell funny. I lean, very gently, against Glow's shoulder.

She doesn't lean in, but she doesn't move away, either. "Choice, mostly. I got left alone a lot with some old videos to watch. So I got used to listening." A long pause. "Pumpkins sound good. I really liked the pie that Myrna made a while back."

The silly bubbles in my ribs show up out of nowhere. "Secret ingredient. She adds a little chai tea."

A quiet laugh. "I don't even really know what that is."

I grin. "I don't even really know which way we're supposed to turn this pipe."

Her laugh turns into almost a giggle.

My silly bubbles dance.

5

SHELLEY

My thighs wince as I clamber up the goat path to the ledge with the best view of the building site. Apparently my arms aren't the only part of me that got overused yesterday.

I smell the tea before I arrive. It's a new blend Wrinkles made up with fall spices and a splash of apple cider. I suspect it also hides some things to chase away sniffles and achy bones, but even the pups are drinking it cheerfully, so it can't be anything too dire.

It doesn't surprise me to see Cleve's mostly white snout lying next to a sturdy earthenware mug. I sent Hoot up here earlier with muffins and tea and one of the newly finished knitted blankets. Judging by how much of it he's got pulled up over his hips, he shifted at least long enough to pour himself some tea.

Brave old wolf. Rio says the darkness comes for Cleve when he's human.

I know a bit about that.

I sit down beside him, wincing as my muscles creak.

The dark eye surveying me looks amused.

I pour myself some tea and refill his mug. I expect he'll stay in his fur, but the hot tea gives off a stronger scent, and maybe it will warm his snout a little, too. I tug a spare corner of his blanket over my knees. "This blanket was a trial to finish, I'll have you know. Stinky helped Myrna join the knitted stripes together, and Kelsey did the pretty ruffle around the edge, and they kept starting sword fights with their crochet hooks."

He doesn't react as I tell him the story, but he doesn't wince as I say any the names of his granddaughter and his grandnephew, either.

Progress.

I take a sip of tea. It's delicious, with hints of cinnamon and brisk winds and things that make my wolf want to take a run in the forest. Which probably isn't accidental. Wrinkles has some unusual healing philosophies. So says Martha, the raven midwife, anyhow. The rest of us just drink our tea and try not to think too hard about what it might be doing to our souls.

Cleve moves a little. Stretching, maybe, but when he's done, he's lying closer to my knee.

My throat tries to close. When I first came to this pack, I was about Mikayla's age, a distant Dunn cousin looking for somewhere to matter more than I did in a pack with too many hands and not enough work. Cleve was the one who invited me into his kitchen and offered me a way to stay busy. "My muffins still aren't as good as yours."

Quiet, whiffling breaths.

I have no idea if he remembers the hundreds of batches we made together. Rio says that he might. "I made some zucchini nut ones the other day, but Mellie dropped her favorite pebble in the bowl and by the time we fished it out, I was all distracted and forgot to add baking soda. Hayden says I need to try that again when it's time for hockey season." Which didn't stop him from eating three of them.

Cleve shivers a little.

I rest my hand on his head a moment. Rio didn't say I should talk about our new alpha, but my wolf has never chosen the easy ways. "He's got a new plan to convince Bailey to be our teacher that he hatched with Reilly. They're teaching everyone about the solar system, but they're mixing up all the planets."

A sound that might be the man, deep inside his wolf, huffing out a laugh.

I take another sip of my tea. "Yesterday Bailey was carrying one of the roof beams with a bunch of the teenagers. Katrina and Hoot and Mikayla spent the whole trip from the parking lot to the den talking about how Mercury has rings and there might have been life on Jupiter and Venus isn't really a planet because it's too cold and dark."

The eye that I can see glares at me balefully.

I hide a grin. Cleve's the one who hooked Bailey on

science fiction novels back when his niece was a trouble-some teenager. "Bailey nearly bit her tongue off trying not to get involved. When she finally asked who taught them that nonsense, Hoot mumbled something about looking things up online."

His wolf whimpers a little.

Mine nudges me. We've pushed enough.

I listen. She knows plenty about keeping the darkness at bay when you're not strong enough to fight it directly. "I'll be heading back down in just a minute. We've got walls to build this afternoon."

I can't believe how fast the floor happened. As soon as we finished joining the pipes, Kenny and some of the mamas swooped in, sliding long panels underneath and over top and clicking them into long steel beams. Lissa and Cori sprayed in some special eco-insulation with a big hose, and then Danielle and Reilly activated fancy mechanical feet in the steel beams that lifted up the whole floor all at once.

Reilly says that Ronan invented those feet.

Eliza's footings will go under some of the feet in a few days, but Rio says the floor is plenty sturdy enough for us to keep building in the meantime, and he jumped on it to prove it. Which meant that a bunch of pups and teenagers and a bear cub and an elder all jumped around like hoydens, too.

Not me. I was busy holding pipes while Danielle and Glow got the temporary water flow hooked up. They promise we'll have a warm floor by sundown.

I can't even begin to sort out how I feel about that.

A snout settles on my knee.

My eyes threaten to do foolish things. "I'll be making stew tomorrow. You come by for a bowl and bring that young charge of yours." Molly has been dropping by Dorie's camp most days, but she's still skittish around the main part of the den. Too many grown men. She's got a sweet tooth, though, and I've got some fancy new cocoa powder.

Cleve's warm breath whiffs out into my lap.

I stroke the soft fur of his head. The patches behind his ears are still the charcoal and red of a much younger wolf. The one who maybe remembers what it is to feel like a useful part of pack, instead of its biggest failure.

I'm lucky, I guess. I get to feel both.

HAYDEN

I look at the bear cub with the bright orange helmet on his head and carefully don't look at the guy behind him— the one who's casting worried looks up at the ledge where Shelley is hanging out with Cleve. Kenny still spends way too much time trying to convince us that he doesn't give a damn, but his actions regularly set his pants on fire.

Reilly squints at me, trying to figure out what's caught my wolf's attention. "Do we need to take a longer break before we get started?"

Not if we want the walls up by dark. "Nope. Collect up your crews."

Kennedy snorts. "We're collected."

They are. Four teams ready to go, with everyone in helmets and work gloves, and depending on temperament, either turning a little pale or bouncing like a ping-pong ball. They've spent all morning moving wall panels around, peeling off the specialty packing cardboard and neatly piling it up to send back to HomeWild for reuse, and dutifully eating the sandwiches that Reilly insisted were part of the safety protocol.

Now it's time for the payoff.

I look around to make sure we have all the spotters, too. If this goes well, we'll be standing around and looking pretty, but if the delicate ballet of joining one panel to the next goes awry, we're the ones who need to make sure no one gets squished.

If that happens, it will also be international news. I got a text from Ryder this morning. It's absolutely killing her that we're doing this part without her. Which is part of why we're live-streaming this afternoon's events out to several hundred watching shifters, including one really overanxious polar bear.

If I drop a wall panel on my head, Jules is going to laugh for a week.

If I drop one on Reilly, I'm a dead man walking.

I look over at Fallon, who's running the video camera. She grins at me and fires off a hand signal that suggests I might be an alien.

I sigh. Our HomeWild-delivered, construction-grade helmets came equipped with googly eyes. Jules takes safety very seriously. Respecting her big brother's dignity, not so much.

Shelley slides to a halt beside me, a little breathless.

I flash her a grin. "Ready?" She's on the rescue team. Clear-headed wolves who are supposed to get pups and teenagers and pregnant mamas out of the way in the event that we have a serious screw-up.

Lissa was the first one Reilly named to the rescue team after Rio casually explained that unexpected things happen in all big builds, and smart leaders try to plan accordingly. Shelley, Ghost, Wrinkles, and Bailey are the others, which proves that he's a smart bear. The chances that I'm going to spend the next few hours standing around doing nothing, while wearing googly eyes, are really damn high.

I sigh again. This footage will probably end up in HomeWild's next ad.

Shelley shoots me an amused look and tightens her helmet strap. Her googly eyes turn to face Reilly, just like the rest of us.

He takes a deep breath—one that only shakes a little. "Are we ready?"

His crews grin at him in unison.

His eyes glow. "Okay. We're building a corner to start, just like we practiced. Team Pinecone is on the wall panel with the big letter *A*, and Team Shark has the onc with letter *B*. Does everyone remember all the steps?"

Twelve heads nod, four of them furry. Ballet rehearsals were particularly fierce for this first joining. People step into place, finding the handholds that Jules builds into the steel tongue-and-groove on the sides of each wall panel. Conveniently, they're holds that work particularly well for small hands, because HomeWild's semi-official mission is to make big dominants feel as useless as possible.

Reilly snaps two guide ropes into loops on what will be the top of the wall panels and carefully hands the other ends to the four crew members who are furry. Everyone stands calmly in place while Reilly runs through the checklist Jules sent him. Then he steps back, takes a deep breath, and looks over at Ravi and Kelsey.

Their hands land on the drum between their knees. One. Two. One. Two.

Pack sense sharpens. That's a heartbeat. A signal to our wolves to work together. Reilly lifts his hands. The first panel rises smoothly. I move in closer. The base needs to click into the steel gutter that runs around the edge of the floor. If toes are in danger, it will be now.

The wolf on the guide rope nearest to me does an excellent job of rolling her eyes.

The base slides into place with an audible *click*—and Reilly's even more audible exhale. Team Pinecone grins widely. Ravi adds a flourish to the drumbeat. Someone behind me sniffles.

Wall panel A is vertical and locked a few seconds later. The team lets go gingerly, but Jules and Ronan don't build walls that fall down after you set them up. It stands in sturdy, solitary splendor, reaching for the sky.

Reilly reaches out a hand and strokes it very gently.

Fallon, tears running down her cheeks, streams his awed touch out into the world for posterity.

My wolf hardly notices when she swings the camera over to him. He's too busy riding the whopping wave of realization that just hit his pack.

We're building our den.

SHELLEY

My wolf is beside herself, but there's no time for that. She's on the rescue team, and right now all the big, strong men in this pack are swooning and a lot of eyes are blurry and that seems exactly like when something might go disastrously wrong.

I shiver a little as I step closer to Hayden, because big emotions from my alpha are still so very hard to be near, but he deserves this moment. He made it possible, and so did a bear cub, and a video team, and a whole bunch of knitters and traders, and even a batch or two of my cookies.

I pat Hayden's arm. "Reilly, that looks very nice. I'm thinking I just might get to sleep on a warm floor tonight if you keep going."

A slightly stunned bear cub swings his gaze my way.

I smile at him, my sweet boy who has somehow managed to gather up the bruised pieces of himself and assemble them into something wondrous. "I've got cookies that just came out of the oven once this first corner is done."

He snaps to attention. So do the mamas on Team Shark. Hands find handles and snouts check their grips on ropes. Wrinkles moves in closer in case Mellie forgets how far away she needs to stand.

Hayden chuckles quietly and nuzzles my cheek. "That was very well done."

I want to protest, to tell him it was a small thing and hide it away from his notice, but my wolf won that fight months ago. We don't hide from this alpha.

Reilly signals the drummers again and the second panel starts its slow rise. This one isn't quite as easy. They have to navigate the one already in place, which means that Kennedy barely moves her head out of the way in time, and the panel clicks into the base with a screech that makes my wolf wince.

Team Shark freezes. Reilly shoots an alarmed look at Rio.

Rio grins. "Hayden, how long did it take before the wall panels you put up stopped yelling like that?"

Our alpha snorts. "About two years after I stopped dropping them on my toes."

Rio winks at the bear cub in charge. "Remember, Jules designs everything assuming that her big brother might be building it. That's an entirely normal noise. We'll probably hear it a few more times today."

Team Shark relaxes. Reilly still looks worried.

Kennedy nudges him. "It tried to eat my bandana,

but I think we still won. You have a checklist for this, right?"

Reilly nods wildly. "We need to see if the buttons on the bottom turned green."

Hoot drops to the ground and peers up at the gutter that's holding the base of the wall panel. "I see four green buttons, two of Kennedy's fingers, and a stinky fart."

Stinky and Kennedy make nearly identical faces.

Reilly giggles. Then he sobers and nods at his mom. "That means you can do the corner part."

Danielle does some kind of wizardry where the two panels meet. Glow watches over her shoulder intently. I step in a little closer, too. It looks almost like knitting, the way she's stitching them together, with loops that snug up as she pulls on the next ones until there's a nice, neat line all the way up to the top.

When she finishes, she pats the wall from the top of her short, squat ladder and grins. "Let's see if this thing starts."

Reilly rolls his eyes. "Mom. It's not an engine."

It's not. It's not even really a wall, because we've barely begun. There are dozens more wall panels to raise, and we have siding to put up on the outside and finishing boards on the inside, and that's before we even get to the parts of the greenhouse that are nothing but panels of glass.

But none of that matters to the feeling expanding inside me like it just met up with a cup of baking soda. What matters, so much more than I expected it to—is that we've begun.

6

KEL

I hold my bowl steady as Kelsey carefully spoons in more soup. She's having to scrape the dregs of the pot to fill her ladle, but that isn't diminishing her shine any. Myrna called her over to soup-dispensing duties like it was no big deal, but there wasn't a wolf in this pack who missed Kelsey's delighted murmur.

Mine is sad that we're almost out of soup, and he doesn't even like the stuff. "That's plenty for me, thanks, sweet pea."

She beams at me and sets down the ladle, reaching for one of the biscuits that look like they got made by a startled rabbit.

I shake my head. I know my limits, and I passed them about two bowls of soup and four biscuits ago. "Just this or my tummy will be making funny noises while we sleep tonight."

Her eyes light up.

I grin. There's been a lot of that going on this evening. Rio and Danielle have been having long discussions over by the heat-exchange system, and rumor has it that we're going to have warm floors by sundown. Which would be a wild waste of energy in most buildings without finished walls and a roof, but apparently a volcanic hot spring under your mountain changes the math enough that warming several dozen wolves sleeping within those half-built walls is basically a rounding error.

I glance over at the heat-exchange system. It apparently breaks a bunch of engineering rules now that Danielle has tinkered with it thoroughly. Which Ronan obviously caught a whiff of during the live-stream of the walls going up. He's been sending Reilly an increasingly desperate series of texts, begging for a close-up.

Sadly for Ronan, I have the pack phone tonight. Reilly is being filled with spicy ribs and honey baked beans and celebrated as the best wall builder in the history of dens. Which is only a slight exaggeration. Sierra and Sienna sent a video clip of the Lonely Peak Pack unloading their trucks. It involved Ryder applying duct tape to several cats and at least two wall panels accidentally walking into trees.

Kelsey pats my arm. "Eat your soup before it gets cold."

I hide a grin. She's doing a fine job of channeling Shelley. A pup could pick far worse role models. "I'll do that. Don't let Kennedy eat all the biscuits."

The baby alpha who was trying to sneak up on them,

probably just to mess with me, scowls. Then she tugs on one of the feathers in Kelsey's hair. "Dibs on you for my sleeping pile tonight. All the others snore and wiggle."

Kelsey giggles. "I like Reilly's snores."

Kennedy manages an impressive pouty face. I think Hoot's been giving her lessons. "I already asked Cori and Moon Girl and Glow, but they're all sleeping with Reilly, too."

I shake my head. There will only be one pup pile tonight, and Kennedy won't be in it because she's on patrol. But that obviously isn't deterring her from working the levers of her pack. She read one of Adrianna's blog posts on consent a couple of weeks ago, and ever since then, she's been on a mission to ask ridiculous questions of every submissive in our pack. Which means most of them have gotten to the point where they can turn her down without even a hint of unease.

Or, in Kelsey's case, with amused, sweet firmness.

I walk away with my soup bowl. Kennedy is more than capable of handling soup pots that need scrubbing, and I have another mission calling.

Lissa smiles as I walk past her. "She's in the kitchen. He's trying to sneak off to do sentry duty."

I roll my eyes. It amuses Hayden to no end when Lissa steps into alpha-wolf duties without even noticing. Someone needs to duct-tape those two to a tree until they give us the mating ceremony we deserve.

Sadly, it won't be me. I've read too many of Adrianna's blog posts.

I turn toward the trees, finishing my soup as I walk.

The guy I'm stalking isn't a submissive, which means I will get to lean on him. Consent is tricky when a guy has a bossy wolf inside him, but I'm not wrong about what I need him to do, and hopefully he'll work that out for himself.

Assuming I can find him. All my human nose can smell at the moment is squash soup, and Kenny's disappearing skills have upgraded lately. I need to chat with Ghost about equipping wolves with skills that will let them vanish until we've also equipped them with an unquenchable need to stick around and be useful.

Kenny's is still kind of wobbly.

He steps out of the trees, which my wolf notices fast enough that I don't actually brain him with my soup bowl. I do scowl, however. He's right on the edge of bad packmate manners and we both know it. "Knock it off."

He raises an eyebrow in a fairly good imitation of me. "Quit following me."

I hadn't actually gotten down to the business of doing that, yet. "I put Katrina on sentry duty. I need you at the main camp tonight." Our languaging of the various spaces of the den is still a work in progress, but he'll know what I mean.

His face says exactly what he thinks about that plan.

I don't give a fuck, but there's a dance here, and he's earned a right to it. I try to lean after I provide all the necessary information, not before. "Some wolves are going to struggle with sleeping on the school floor tonight."

He gives me a sharp look that says he knows that—and that whatever I'm up to, he doesn't like it.

Tough shit. "Shelley is probably going to be one of them."

The mask he uses when he wants to reveal exactly nothing slams into place. "Shelley had a good day. She'll be fine."

She had an amazing day. Sometimes those can be the hardest kind. "I don't know why she finds walls such a problem, but I'm guessing that you do." It's a mean swipe—he probably had to watch helplessly while it happened. Which is the kind of trauma that sometimes requires claws to even begin to release the poison.

His wolf manages not to claw back. Barely. "She used the old kitchen just fine."

She did. Which means that I didn't understand just how deep this particular trauma ran until I saw her in a kitchen without walls. "I'm not a threat, Kenny. You know that. I'm not trying to strip her naked, either. I'm asking a friend who's maybe seen her more naked than I have to have her back tonight."

He winces. "It's not like that."

The idiot guy is thinking with his wolf brain, and wolves are way too fucking literal. He and Shelley aren't mates. They're friends who walked into hell together—and who both think they weren't enough to save each other, even though they're still doing it every damn day. I growl at his shuttered eyes. "I know that, asshole."

He winces again. "Crap. Sorry."

That's progress. Ebony's, more than mine, but I'll

take it. "Tonight is the first set of walls that she's going to want to be inside in a long time." Half a wall and no roof, but trauma doesn't tend to pay a whole lot of attention to mitigating facts.

He sighs. He knows the trap I've got him in. His wolf doesn't want to be inside those walls, either.

I wait. If this trap closes, it needs to happen with his consent.

He finally gives me a reluctant nod.

That's big progress, even if he would never admit it.

SHELLEY

I somehow didn't think about this part. I look down at my sleeping bag, neatly rolled up and tucked under my arm, and wonder if I can do this. I want to do it. I desperately want to do it. Most of Dorie's crew came down from her tents, and all of Fallon's baby pack is here, and a few extras from the woods, and Cori and Eliza have pulled out all of our pillows and blankets and created an enormous, welcoming bed.

It's going to be a sleeping pile for the ages.

Reilly, surrounded by pups who are fighting sleep hard but losing to the magic of the warm floor beneath them, is right in the very center. It will be the first time in a very long time that he isn't sleeping as a bear. Kelsey brought her special pillow to share with him, and Robbie is already snoring right next to it.

Myrna and the mamas and Ravi and Dorie are trying to create some kind of order around them, which is only making partial headway against the tide of rambunctious teenagers who haven't entirely sorted themselves out yet.

I'm keeping my eye on Kennedy. She's causing half the trouble, mostly as cover for the almost-invisible herding of the most skittish wolves of Dorie's crew into sleeping places they can handle—squished in between more comfortable packmates, or over on the edges, or against a wall with a good line of sight on the woods.

"Figured out a spot, yet?"

I smile at Lissa. She's been walking on the floor in her bare feet for the last hour, humming happily. The shed she slept in with most of the mamas and pups was so very cold, and Robbie couldn't sleep in his fur to stay warm.

I swallow. I didn't sleep in mine, either—and there were endless nights that I yearned for the relative safety and anonymity of that shed. "We might not all fit. I can always go sleep in one of Dorie's tents."

Her eyes fill with sympathy and acceptance. "If you do, we've got a couple of blankets that need to head that way."

My wolf firms her hold on the nape of my neck. This is our pack. We sleep here.

I sigh. I tried negotiating with her. I reminded her that this is a pack that makes room for shadows and there's no shame in fighting this battle another day. She didn't say a word then, and she doesn't now. She's never been a chatty wolf.

Lissa steps in and rubs her cheek against mine. "If

you decide to stay, I hear that the far corner has an extra-warm spot."

It's where the water first enters from the heat-exchange system. It's also a spot that's wide open, destined to be a corner of the greenhouse once the glass walls are installed. Warmth as far away from being closed-in as possible.

My hands tremble inside my pockets.

I take a slow, deep breath. The sleeping cabins were tiny. Nothing like our big, beautiful school. The bad walls are ashes. They can't hurt me anymore. These are good walls. Walls built with pack hands that will contain learning and laughter and growing things, not fear.

An arm wraps around my waist. My wolf jerks in surprise.

Kenny grunts at Lissa. "Your man looks lonely."

Lissa glances wryly over at Hayden, who has just tucked himself in next to Robbie. Several of the sentries and both of the pregnant mamas are settling in around him—the wolves who are most soothed by proximity to their alpha.

I pat Lissa's shoulder. "There's space right next to him if you get there before Hoot falls asleep."

She studies me for a moment, and then she kisses Kenny's cheek. "If you run off into the woods tonight, somebody will hunt you down. Just so we're clear on that."

My wolf grins. She likes bossy Lissa.

Kenny stands there as she leaves, stony and silent—except for the arm around my waist. Six years ago, that was a normal thing. A pack thing. An easy bond between friends. When I began the tightrope walk of convincing Samuel that I was meant to be his mate, the few smart men who were still left kept their hands far away from me.

Kenny would find me, sometimes, in the quiet moments when Samuel had gone to town or was sleeping off a binge. But not often. The lieutenants had eyes, and we had too many others who needed us in those moments.

I let my head rest on his shoulder. "Who sent you?"

He winces. "They shouldn't have needed to."

I pat his arm. "The wolves of this pack never do leave well enough alone."

He huffs out a sound that's trying to be a laugh.

My wolf leans into him. He used to laugh so easily. Not the boisterous kind—Kenny was never loud—but his wry chuckle was one of my favorite sounds. His son chased it out of him often. Goofy, kind-hearted Jason. The boy built from all the best parts of his dad's heart.

"Dammit, don't go there, woman."

His words are low and gruff, but they aren't what surprise me most. It's his wiry frame, still leaning against mine—quietly shaking.

My wolf straightens.

He blows out a frustrated breath. "Sorry. I'll go."

Not if I can help it. I haven't felt this much of his wolf since Jason died. I pat his chest briskly. "Are we going to do this with our clothes on or off?"

He raises a reluctantly amused eyebrow.

Troublesome man. I set my sleeping bag down by the wall. "I've a mind to sleep furry. I see a spot over there by Mikayla."

He eyes the tangle of teenage and barely adult limbs and the very large black wolf they've chosen to sprawl all over. "I'll go watch the perimeter a while."

I give him the same look I give my muffins when they rise too much and make a mess of my oven.

He sighs and lets his cheek brush against the top of my head. "I don't know if I can do this, Squeaky."

The nickname cracks what little courage I have left— and somehow stiffens it right back up again. My wolf has never yearned for the most tangible bonds of pack. Mate. Sibling. Parent. Always, she's reached for the other ones. "That makes two of us, but we're going to look like fools sleeping out in the snow in a few months, so we'd best get to work."

He snorts. "I have a tent. I'll be fine."

His tent is a war zone. "Where did they move it today?"

He scowls. "Halfway up the slope to Dorie's camp. On a damn pile of scree."

I hide a grin. He keeps pitching his tent somewhere sensible and as far away from the main camp as Kel will allow it. His baby pack keeps relocating it to the most annoying spots they can find.

I might have given them an idea or two.

I lean against a friend who's trying to collect up whatever is left of himself, just like I am. "I hear that this floor is pretty level."

He growls under his breath.

I slide my fingers into his. "Come. I'm an old woman with tired arms who needs her sleep. I've got watermelon seeds to plant in the morning."

Kenny huffs out a laugh. "You might need some windows, first."

I smile. That's not how this pack does things anymore. We tend to the fragile green shoots that dare to push their heads out of the soil, no matter where and when they choose to bloom.

Even if they're still growling as we find a place to sleep.

7

SHELLEY

I look up from my early-morning tea and grimace. You know you're in trouble when all of the pack elders have come to find you. Especially at an hour when most of them aren't even usually awake yet.

Myrna snorts as she clambers up onto my rock. "You look as guilty as Stinky did when he stole the last honey berry bar."

He does that at least twice a week. Mikayla needs to start making them in much bigger batches. "Dorie's been teaching him bobcat skills. He'll be swiping them right out of people's hands, soon enough."

Wrinkles sits down and shakes her head at the bobcat in question. "Let the boy be a wolf. He's enough of a menace without you giving him extra lessons."

Dorie grins. "He needs to keep up with the big kids."

The teenagers all learned their bobcat skills for far

more serious purposes. Ones that we were united in keeping as far away from Stinky Dunn as we could. Tragedy came for him so very young. Our pack might not survive it finding him again.

Which of course means that he seeks out every other kind of trouble he can find.

Myrna bumps against my shoulder. "Pay attention. This is an official meeting of the female elders of Ghost Mountain Pack. Tara sent her vote in with Dorie."

Tara never agrees with anyone about anything. "That sounds official." And worrisome. "Am I that old already?"

Wrinkles cackles. "Nope. You're not one of the elders, you're on our agenda. We're here to boss you around."

Definitely worrisome. I take a bracing sip of tea.

Dorie smirks at my mug. "Unless there's whiskey in there, it's not going to help you."

I watched alcohol rot the sense of right and wrong of far too many good wolves to ever voluntarily add it to my tea. But they aren't here about what's in my tea, and my wolf can't imagine why else they've decided to gang up on me. Which is disconcerting. She prides herself on knowing what's going on with her pack.

Myrna chuckles and pulls a small pad of paper and a very pink pencil out of the pocket of her flannel shirt. "It's not that dire, dear. We've come to discuss some scheduling for the kitchen. We think it's time that you shared your duties."

I blink several times, trying to right myself. It's not easy. A big black wolf and a disgruntled friend almost made our new walls bearable last night, but I didn't get a lot of sleep. "I have plenty of help. More than I can manage, most days."

"Of course you do." Wrinkles pats my knee. "But now that you'll be spending more time in the garden and painting murals and teaching art, we need a kitchen that works when you're not in it."

Her words are innocent enough—but this smells like an intervention. A serious one that got three elders out of their beds and brought them over to my peaceful rock. "Mikayla frees me up plenty."

"It's a start." Myrna's eyes are glinting with hints of her daddy's frying pan. "The rest is up to you."

My wolf jitters. Elders are to be heard. Listened to. Respected. I clutch my mug more firmly. My human knows just how much trouble these particular elders can cause, furry or not. "I don't know what you mean."

Her eyes don't leave mine. "Yes, you do. Samuel as good as locked you away in the kitchen. You made it work for you, and you're making it work still, but your heart and your wolf need more freedom than that and you know it."

I don't know any such thing. The kitchen is my happy place, or at least where I mostly manage to keep the things that chase me at bay. It's the place where I best know how to fight. How to protect. How to serve.

Claws close around my throat, vicious and nauseating.

Myrna's eyes soften, but they don't back down.

Wrinkles strokes my back calmly. "We're not kicking

you out, just shifting duties around a little. The garden will be good for you. Your heart sings when you've got your hands in the dirt."

I grab fiercely for the steadiness that has always been my most reliable shield. "Kelsey sings. I just do the work."

She pats my shoulder. "Don't lie to a healer who's mated to an inscrutable bear. And put some mint in your morning tea. It will help with your achy knees."

I turn my head to glare at her. "My knees are fine."

She laughs. "I know. But you should still add some mint. It's tasty."

I scowl. "I hear that most healers are polite and professional and helpful."

Dorie snickers. "The new cat medic gave Reese a digestive that made him fart for three days. She got the recipe from a Whistler Pack healer. They're menaces, every last one of them."

Myrna grins. "Maybe we won't put Wrinkles on the kitchen schedule."

Wrinkles snorts. "Because you're so much more orderly and reliable?"

"I can manage stew." Myrna makes a note before she looks back up at me. "Today's menu is pizza on the grill for lunch and stew for dinner, right?"

My heart tries to thump outside my chest. I don't know how to fight the big fights. I never have. "Mikayla and Ravi are making the pizzas. Dorie was going to send down a couple of helpers."

More scribbles. "Good. I'll see if Reuben can handle

the stew. He's got a good hand with spices, and Cheri might drop by in the next day or two."

My jaw drops. Maneuvering Reuben and Cheri into the same building might end with my kitchen in flames.

Myrna nods at her notepad in satisfaction. "We'll get this on some kind of chart that everyone can see. We can rotate the meals between those of us who are decent cooks. You can keep making cookies and birthday dinners because otherwise there will be mutiny. I'll tell Cleve that he's on muffin duty."

I gulp and pick the one battle I might win. Or not, but I need to try. "Cleve isn't ready for that." He guarded the bread dough well enough, but he hasn't been back since.

Something fierce flickers in Myrna's eyes. "He can manage muffins."

My gaze darts to Wrinkles. She's not always the most gentle of healers, but she would never let someone get pushed too far on her watch.

She just looks at me, straight through my human layers to where my wolf lives. "Trust the elders of your pack, Shelley Martins. Go stand on the floors that you helped make warm with your own two hands. Fill a planter box with dirt and seeds or get your ass in gear and design the mural for that big, beautiful, empty wall."

My heart stutters. I've tried. I can't even figure out where to begin. "The wall isn't ready yet."

Her hands are warm and steady as they take hold of mine. "It will be. And so will you."

LISSA

I yawn and lean against my alpha. "Told you they were up to something."

Hayden chuckles and kisses the top of my head. "So you did."

We watch the four women up on the big rock, three of them very pleased with themselves and one who looks like she just ran into a wrecking ball. My wolf has her suspicions about what they're up to, and she very much approves. Shelley walked into hell of her own free will to try to keep the remnants of our pack breathing. She so deserves to walk all the way out.

Even if it requires a little help from a wrecking ball or three. I'll find her in a bit and commiserate.

Hayden nuzzles my cheek. "Is she going to let her alpha be her soft place to land, or do I need to let you do that job?"

I smile. She'll need a little space first. She always does. Some of us think our way to solid ground. Shelley drinks tea or runs in the woods or bakes. Or helps someone else. Kind of like a certain alpha I know. I kiss his scruffy chin. Last night filled his heart, but it also clawed at it some, and he's not so quick to tuck that away these days. "Kenny stayed the whole night."

A grimace. "Only because Rio put a big-ass paw on top of him."

He did. Half a breath after Kenny rolled over and

discovered Stinky sound asleep and curled up against his ribs.

I breathe into the crisp morning. Pain like that isn't something that ever truly ends or goes away or gets all the way better, but he didn't push Stinky away. "Ghost and Eliza are leading the window crew this morning, right?"

A nod into the top of my head. "That's the plan. Do we need to change it?"

He asks that so very easily. "I don't think so." I thought Eliza might miss her wayward son last night, but enough of Dorie's strays came to cuddle with her that she fell asleep smiling. "Ghost is worried about the windows. She saw how much they cost in one of my spreadsheets."

Hayden chuckles. "They're triple-paned glass designed to cope with Canadian winters and shifter shenanigans. But I'll tell her that she should be careful anyhow, because the cats are definitely going to need all of the spares that Ryder brought."

I grin. The cats sent another video of their build in progress. Yesterday's antics included three sets of bandaged toes, one wall panel that got sprayed by a skunk, and a teenager who managed to dip herself in wet concrete. "Being a HomeWild employee is not for the faint of heart."

He snorts. "Ryder would be bored out of her skull here. She probably poked the skunk just to stir things up a little. Or to get revenge for whatever Reese did first."

My wolf shakes her head. Cats are truly strange creatures.

I pat her head. The elder cat up on the rock adores

Robbie and has one of the softest hearts in this pack. "Dorie's going to start rotating her wolves down to the school to sleep. Even the ones who don't think they want to come."

Hayden nuzzles my wolf. "Is there anyone who needs to be pulled out of the way of her bulldozer?"

He makes so much space for leadership styles different than his own—and stands absolutely firm on the right of every shifter in this pack to make their own choices. "A couple of the knitters will likely fuss, but they won't mean it. Her strays will all be fine except for maybe Glow and Molly, and she'll get them sorted."

He chuckles quietly. "She doesn't leave Kel enough work to do. He grumbles."

The man holding me has been acting as both the wrecking ball and soft place for Kel's scars for more than twenty years. "He left early for his patrol shift." He detoured to kiss Kelsey's head as he went, too, but my wolf can't bring herself to share all his secrets.

Hayden rests his head on mine and studies the quartet up on the rock. "Kel and Shelley and Dorie are three peas in a pod."

Smart mate. "They would all hate that you know that." Well, maybe not Kel. He's had more practice at having Hayden see into his soul.

An amused snort. "The whole pack knows it."

I smile. Smart pack. "Wait until the babies get here. They'll have to arm wrestle."

He sighs. "Kel adopted every last newborn in Whistler Pack."

My wolf grins. He'll have his hands full if he thinks he can beat Shelley and Dorie at that game. They haven't had a new baby to fuss over for years.

I sober. The last ones had to be fussed over in secret, stolen moments. Which tore at all of us. Wolves cherish new life, even as our humans feared terribly.

Hayden's hand strokes my back.

I take a deep breath. Last night I got to cherish warm floors. Today I get to work in service of all that they're going to support. "I'm on the window crew this morning. Keep an eye on Robbie?" It's not a necessary request—he will, and so will half a dozen other wolves, officially assigned to the job or not. But watching the two of them curled up together last night melted my heart, and sometimes unnecessary words are the very best kind to say.

Hayden tips his forehead against mine. "I can't remember a time when he wasn't mine, Liss."

I let my hand touch his heart. "Neither can he."

SHELLEY

I walk past my alphas as quietly as I can. Ghost has been working on my woodcraft, and so has Kel, but the lessons haven't covered what to do if your eyes are too wet to see properly.

Three of my closest friends just left bruises on my ribs— and Hayden's softly spoken, reverent sentence chased away every drop of the good bout of self-pity I was about to wallow in, because in the end, it isn't the bruises that matter. It's the belonging. I swipe at my eyes before they spill over and leave embarrassing tracks running down my cheeks.

My wolf bumps me gently.

I smile, even though the world is still blurry. Pushy wolf.

"Uh, oh." An arm wraps around my shoulders. "What did those mean wolves do? Who should I beat up first?"

I make one last swipe at my eyes with my sleeve. Brandy knows what it is to shed tears in solitude. To weep for what is still too fragile to share with pack. "They're just trying to help. Which one of them sent you?"

She snorts. "None of them. Hoot said you might need a friend. I don't think she knew about the elders ganging up on you, though."

Darn Dunn psychics. "They want me to spend less time in the kitchen."

Companionable silence as we walk along, the dew trying to invade our sneakers. It will be time for wool socks and rubber boots soon.

Brandy finally nods. "Good."

I shake my head. "Some friend you are."

She grins. "I have more sketches for the mural for the ravens, but every time I try to sit down with you and go through them, you're up to your ears in cookie dough."

My bowls aren't quite that big, but I was looking at a couple of new ones in an online catalogue. I'm not ordering any, though. Not until Lissa tells me what they cost. "Dorie wants some of her crew to dust off their rusty cooking skills. Myrna just wants to mess with my spice cupboard."

"She's trouble, that one."

I keep my eyes on the forest floor. "She's putting your father on muffin duty."

Brandy's breath hisses out and back in again.

I wait. She's always claimed that her wolf isn't as sensitive as some in our clan, but I've never believed it.

When she finally speaks, her voice is thick with tears. "I miss the ones he used to make. With bananas and chocolate chips."

It isn't the bruises that matter. It's the belonging. I squeeze her shoulders. "Show me your drawings."

She huffs out a laugh. "Those darn birds can't pick one idea. They keep sending me more online messages and the rogue artist inside my head can't seem to stop drawing them."

I used to feel that way once. "They've got a lot of blank walls. They can probably keep you busy half the winter."

She looks at me carefully. "Are you sure that you don't mind?"

I snort. I asked her to sketch some ideas for the nursery mural Tressie wanted. The raven alpha took one look at the black-and-white sketches and fell head over heels in love. "I've got cookies to bake and a garden to plant and a wall or two here to paint if I get the urge.

You're welcome to all the clients who can't make up their minds."

She grins. "Tressie promised to get them into line. It seems to work until Martha pouts or Emma Jean gets a hopeful look in her eyes."

They're Brandy's self-assigned buddies when she visits the raven flock. "How are the visits going?"

She dips her head, but I don't miss her smile. "Good. Fallon is more nervous than I am, and Ben just watches their little chicks fly around and tries not to panic. I had to teach him my breathing exercises."

That warms my belly in a way that the tea didn't. "From the stories Martha tells, you might have to teach them to all of us." I try to imagine Mellie with wings and shudder.

Brandy chuckles. "We'll figure it out. That's why we have teenagers, right?"

They're going to have to arm-wrestle with the elders. "I need to get more lessons from Kel if I ever want to get my hands on that baby."

Brandy smiles and leans into me. "That baby is a Dunn. She's already yours."

I close my eyes as the tears chase me one more time. I came to this pack a distant Dunn cousin. Not a one of them has ever let that mean anything less than sister. Which is why I'll let myself get kicked out of the kitchen and stare for too long at a blank wall and make sure Cleve knows where the bananas and chocolate chips are.

Because I can't remember a time when they weren't mine, either.

8

SHELLEY

Ghost's face is a portrait of relief, tinged with exuberant glee. She's also saying something that's probably important. Unfortunately, three layers of glass is a really good sound barrier.

I look up at Fallon, who's giving us all heart failure as she sits on the top of the wall where our roof will someday be. Taking it easy, bird-style—and also providing critical communications support.

She grins and pops the dried cranberries that she's chewing on into her cheek. "She's got an idea for how to grow more watermelons in with the green beans."

Bailey and Hoot, who are on window-propping duties with me, look at each other and snicker.

I shake my head. Now is not the time for revising the garden plots. "If we don't get these walls up before winter, there will be no green beans or watermelons."

This is the first one made of glass. It's an interior wall that runs the full length of the school and separates the greenhouse space from the room that will house students and laptops and other things that shouldn't be misted on a regular basis.

Ghost makes a hand signal that we actually understand, and we all step back. Gingerly. This particular wall is a whole new level of terrifying. The sheets of glass are more than twice as tall as I am, and if we drop one and it breaks, we'll probably have to eat rice and beans for a year to afford the replacement.

Bailey shakes out her arms. "These suckers are heavy."

"You could always go help Reilly set up the new school tablets," says Fallon cheerfully. "I hear that teachers get fancy ones."

Bailey scowls up at her. "Aren't you supposed to be napping or something?"

Hoot snickers. "You might want to be careful. The last wolf who asked her that is missing part of his tail."

Poor Hayden. He's such a good, respectful, enabling alpha who knows all about giving us space when we need it, but his wolf is obsessed about the new babies and entirely freaked out that one of them is currently living inside a shifter who can fly.

Fallon makes her way along the top beam, her bare toes casually gripping the steel, and does whatever magic locks the top of the huge window pane in place. Ryder sent a fancy harness and ropes for that job, but Rio just grinned at Fallon and left them in the box.

My wolf grumbles. She knows that she has packmates who like being up high. She's even climbed a tree or two herself, and she understands that Fallon has wings and can shift in an instant. None of that will make her any less uneasy until the raven she loves puts her feet back on solid ground.

Bailey shakes her head, her wolf commiserating with mine. "We've got three more to go, right?"

"Just two." Ghost pops through the opening that will eventually be a sliding door. "This one in the middle gets filled in after we have the roof on and some of the pipes run."

I smile. She's been this clear and confident and bubbly all morning. A wolf who can't quite manage to contain her pride. "Then let's get our part done so Eliza and Danielle can get to theirs."

Hoot takes some jerky out of a snack jar and hands it out. "Have you seen the really big pulleys they're going to be using to lift the roof panels?" She waves the jar in Fallon's general direction.

Our pregnant raven wrinkles her nose. "No thanks. That stuff smells like dead shoes."

"Good." Cori grins as she walks in. "More for me."

Ghost shoots her a look that she absolutely learned from Kel.

Cori rolls her eyes. "I ate all of my breakfast, I feel fine, and I promise not to run under any falling windows." She looks up at Fallon. "I'm so jealous that you get to hang out way up there."

"Only for a couple more months." Fallon makes a

face. "Then it will be my turn to be jealous because I won't be able to shift anymore and Ben and Wrinkles will swaddle me in blankets until this baby comes."

They won't need to use blankets. Every knitter in this pack is currently making oversized sweaters. Mine is a pretty green that matches Ben's eyes, and so soft.

Bailey hands Cori the jerky. "You both know where I live. If you need to escape, I can hide you where they'll never find you."

Hoot giggles. "Ghost can find anyone."

I pat her shoulder. "Ghost knows that sometimes wolf packs can be a little overbearing where pregnant mamas are concerned, and they might need a few hours to themselves."

She sobers instantly. "I know that." She looks at Fallon and Cori. "I do. I know some good hiding places, too. A couple are really close to the den."

I smile. "You let me know if you need tea or cookies for any of those places."

Bailey frowns at her jerky. "Why are we eating this instead of cookies?"

Ghost reaches for the bowl of dried cranberries. "Why are we eating instead of putting up windows?"

Hoot rolls her eyes. "Go easy, boss lady. Even Kel lets us take snack breaks. Some of us are growing wolves, remember? And others of us are growing an entire new person in their bellies, and if we don't feed them often, they get kind of cranky."

A pinecone narrowly misses her nose.

Bailey grins and tosses the pinecone back up to

Fallon. "Never taunt pregnant mamas. It never ends well."

Cori wraps her arm around Bailey's waist. "Never eat the last of their special cookies, either. Because they know where you live and they can find ways to get even. Like making sure the grocery deliveries to your baby pack get extra lettuce and no marshmallows all winter long."

Ghost grins. "I think Braden ate a whole bag of marshmallows while Stinky was supervising yesterday. Hayden made him go look up *in moderation* in the dictionary."

Braden has talked marshmallows out of far tougher wolves than Stinky Dunn. Including the one who happens to love the same cookies that help to settle Cori's belly when her morning sickness lands every afternoon like clockwork. "I'll go put another batch of gingersnaps in the oven."

Cori leans over and kisses my cheek. "My fussy pregnant stomach thanks you. After you finish building this wonderful wall of glass, of course."

My wolf isn't at all sure that's the right order of business. She doesn't like cookies, but she knows that they should never, ever run out.

Cori pats my arm. "You can't use your oven right now, anyhow."

My wolf can suddenly see an awful lot of complicated feelings in Cori's eyes. Maybe she didn't just come in here to steal our snacks. "Why not?"

She takes a deep breath and lets it out again. "Because it's full of muffins."

RIO

I rest my cheek against the soft, warm one of the four-year-old who just hurled herself into my arms. "I know, sweetheart. I can feel it, too."

Kel dials down a notch from the red alert he hit the instant Kelsey started running. Ebony, over by the school house, takes a few seconds longer. I throw her a fast, imperative hand signal. Kel's brand of warrior won't affect the submissive wolf who's struggling mightily in the kitchen, but Ebony's will. All dominants need to get themselves under control immediately.

She repeats the hand signal for two wolves I can't see. I don't need to. I can feel them—and the abrupt easing as Kenny and Kennedy get their shit together.

I shake my head and nuzzle Kelsey's hair. I wonder if she has any idea just how many dominants in this pack have handed her their nuclear codes.

She rocks herself in my arms as another wave hits, her small body desperately trying to process the flood of pack emotions that are landing as one wolf after another gets shaken by the earthquake currently happening in our kitchen. My sentinel holds her as gently as he can and lets her rock—and tries to do the terrible math that will tell him if the man in the cook shack needs him more.

Kel's hand lands on my shoulder, a soldier ready for whatever I need him to do. Hayden materializes from somewhere with a bristling white pup in his arms and alpha steel in his eyes, and I can feel more wolves on their way.

Kelsey whimpers in my arms.

"I've got you, sweet pea." Shelley reaches in and scoops up a small girl, her eyes calmly telling a sentinel to go stuff himself. "Remember the breathing that Brandy does when she gets a little anxious? Do you think you can do that with me?"

Kelsey sucks in a wobbly breath.

The pack of wolves on her heels glares at me like I was about to light a match and toss it at their favorite four-year-old.

I manage to suck in a breath of my own as I drop down and put my palms on the ground, trying to get a better read on the guy in the kitchen.

"He'll be fine." Shelley's tone brooks no argument, and the undertones tell me that if I don't stop scaring my pack, I'm going to find out just how much it sucks to have her truly mad at me. "Grandpa Cleve hasn't made muffins for a while, so it will be a little bit of work, but he'll manage."

Spoken like someone who has done a whole lot of her own healing work with a mixing spoon in her hand. I take another deep breath. My sentinel knows how to do hard things and how to walk with others who are doing them. He just has some very sensitive triggers where Kelsey Dunn is concerned.

Along with every other wolf in this pack.

Hoot takes a breath, just like Kelsey is doing, and holds one side of her nose the way Brandy does when she needs extra focus. Ghost leans against Kel, which annoys the hell out of him because he fucking hates it when anyone can see his scars bleeding, and Cori and Fallon bracket Hayden to help settle the small baby alpha in his arms.

My wolf shakes his head wryly.

Oops.

Shelley sits down on the grass and settles Kelsey in her lap.

Our tiny pack psychic takes a far steadier breath than mine and looks up at the brisk, wonderful woman who just pulled us all back from the brink. "He mixed up the flour and the eggs and the milk, just like you do. Then he used the silly muffin cups with the kitty ears on them because they made him smile."

Shelley chuckles. "Reese will be glad to hear that."

Troublesome cat. He delivered several thousand of the damn things a couple of weeks ago.

Kelsey's eyes are pensive. "I was going to go help with the muffin cups, because I like that part, but his wolf was worried. The dark claws inside his heart don't like it when pups get too close."

Every dominant within earshot makes a desperate leap for their shaky nuclear codes. My sentinel tries not to freak out. Cleve was fine right up until the moment he closed the oven door.

Shelley just nods calmly. "He has some bad memories about that."

Kelsey's quiet hum of sadness cracks every last one of us.

Shelley strokes her curls gently. "Remember when we talked about seeds and how they feel when they start growing?"

Puzzled wolves tilt their heads, mine included. Gramma Shelley tells lots of stories, but I haven't heard this one.

Shelley's voice calmly speaks to all of our ears. "The seeds lie in the ground in the dark and soak in the water. Then they start to grow inside, but the outside of the seed isn't soft enough to crack for a while." She smiles at the listening girl in her lap. "How do you suppose that feels for the seed?"

Kelsey wrinkles her nose. "Cold and squishy."

My sentinel blinks. Most of the other reactions are noisier.

Shelley just keeps calmly petting a small, psychic wolf and offering a story for her heart. "Exactly. And what do good gardeners do when a seed is in that cramped, uncomfortable place and not quite ready to reach for the earth and the sky?"

Kelsey beams. "We sing them songs and wait until they're ready for more water."

KEL

There's a man less than five hundred feet away in a desperate struggle with his wolf, lying in a puddle of shivering gray fur and waiting for the timer on the stove to demand that he once again have hands and memories and a human heart.

I know that much because I saw Cleve's face right before he shifted—and because I've been that man more times than I can count.

Shelley Martins has been there, too.

I suck in a ragged breath. My respect for her just found an entirely new level, and I didn't think that was possible.

Hayden stares at me long enough that I finally give him the eye contact he wants—and the answer he doesn't. I have no fucking clue what to do. This isn't the time or place for the skills of war, and I don't trust the other ones I have. The ones that know about shivering and timers and wounded human hearts.

My wolf shivers. He hates this particular weakness more than any of the others.

Alpha eyes keep drilling into my head.

I ignore them. This isn't about me. I spend way too much time being a seed who's not ready for more water, but I'm also a fucking beta in this pack, and that means I need to help tip the watering can over the seeds who are struggling mightily to crack themselves open.

I glance at Rio, just in case he's got opinions. Then I look at the pup who is one of the very best reasons a shaking Cleve Dunn stood naked in the cook shack and carefully mixed up sugar and flour and eggs and milk. "I like banana muffins."

Kelsey smiles at me, amused pup to silly beta. "You have to let the belly babies have the first ones."

They would be the second and third reasons that Grandpa Cleve is trying to walk through culinary fire. I tip the watering can very gingerly. "I wonder if he knows that Fallon really likes butter on her muffins."

Shelley sucks in a breath.

I meet her eyes and hold out the watering can to see what she thinks.

She exhales slowly, pondering in the way of a friend of very long standing, and finally nods.

I contemplate our limited options. It's entirely possible that we're both wrong, which means there's no chance that I'm letting a four-year-old touch the watering can, and Rio is likely the only one who can keep Kelsey out of the kitchen. Hayden will strike me dead with alpha lightning if I send one of the pregnant mamas in there, and Cleve hasn't let me get any closer to him than bare glimpses. Hoot, maybe, but if we're wrong, it will tear her tender guardian heart in two.

Shelley smiles faintly. Then she pats the ground beside her. "Why don't you sit here, sweetie. I'll go get us some milk to go with our muffins and tell Cleve about the butter."

Kelsey tips her head, considering.

Nine wolves and a raven wait silently for her to render a verdict.

When she finally nods, we all start breathing again.

Shelley gets to her feet. Then she looks at me, a fucking brave plea in her eyes. She's walking in there alone—but she wants to feel us at her back.

Damn wolves who insist on being heroes. "I guess

that means the rest of us need to sing a song about banana muffins."

There's no confusion. We all heard the story, so pack just nods and hums and looks to a four-year-old girl for our starting notes.

Because this is what we do while we wait for seeds to be ready.

9

HAYDEN

I make my way in the dark cautiously. Not because it's hard to see. The moon is waxing, gathering its sharp hold on our wolves and illuminating the night more than well enough.

It's feelings that I'm worried about tripping over.

Whistler Pack has a few shifters like Kelsey, deeply sensitive in their human forms or animal forms or both, sensing the emotional landscape as easily as my wolf reads the scents of the forest. This pack has an entire family of them—and most of them are so mauled that I only know them as faint traces on the back of my eyelids.

My wolf growls. They're his, no matter how faint they are.

Damn straight.

He makes his way along a small stream. It worries him. The water smells of ice to come.

I pat his scruff. The school will be done in another day or two, and it will serve as a passable den. Small and squishy if we try to fit everyone in at the same time, but it will be safe and warm.

He grins as he runs. Squishy is good. More pups will come sleep on his belly.

I roll my eyes and try to convince him that a tent and some privacy with a green-eyed wolf could be good, too.

He snorts at my foolish human ways. That's why we take nice walks in the forest. Well, for that and to hunt tasty rabbit snacks.

Dumbass. I scent the air again. Kel told me where to head, but the stream is screwing with my nose, and there are enough baby packs in this part of the territory that if I miss Shelley's trail, someone will likely be nearby enough to witness the ignominious sight of the alpha who got lost in the woods.

My wolf's ears perk up as I catch a faint whiff of Ghost. She doesn't leave those by accident, so I veer away from the stream and make my way up a channel of moss-covered boulders. The moss rebounds under my paws, oddly resilient for this time of year. My wolf pounces on a particularly thick patch, always happy to be a goofy, silly pup.

I shake my head and guide him back to the task at hand. Gently. He's had a long day. His wolves kept eating banana muffins and hugging each other and crying, and I wouldn't let him snarl at the bad muffins even once.

The mossy rocks give way to forest floor again. I pay attention. Ghost has decent respect for my tracking skills, which means the trail markers she's leaving me likely won't be all that obvious. I still almost miss the next one, mostly because I'm busy trying to keep my ass from falling into an unexpected crevice.

My wolf grins. Shelley chose a wild run. A brave run. He approves.

Definitely a dumbass, but at least he's a loyal one. I work my way along the edge of the crevice as it grows into a ravine and do my best not to turn into a wolf land-slide. This was part of Bailey's turf until her baby pack moved closer to the den, so I'm still learning my way around.

I catch another one of Ghost's scent markers and leave the rim of the crevice that tried to eat me. The trees open up, casting odd shadows that grab at my wolf's instincts. I run faster, playing with the forest, letting the night tug on the primal parts of my soul.

I assume that's why Shelley is out here, too.

When I finally cross her trail, it's fresh and obvious and so close that I crash to a halt so I don't accidentally mow her down. Ghost nearly drops down on my snout instead, which causes my wolf to growl and glow with pride at the same damn time.

She's calm and alert and wearing a sweater that I've never seen before. She tosses a larger version at me. "Ebony brought me a bag of stuff. I ate all the soup and cheese, but there's some snacks if you want. And tea."

I look her up and down as I shift and get dressed. She's had a very long day. She competently shepherded her emotionally wobbly building crew through the several hours it took to finish erecting all the glass walls, and she didn't let banana-muffin aftershocks cause any more of an issue than tired arms or pups who came to peer at the work in progress or lurking betas.

I dig into her supply bag and start with the easy stuff. "Thanks for letting Kel be a pain this afternoon."

She shoots me a look that says I don't get to pick on Kelvin Nogues tonight.

My wolf grins. Ghost was never scared of him, but she's gotten downright feisty lately. "You did a really excellent job of giving everyone's wolf the hierarchy they needed today, including him. That's not an easy thing to do when you're a submissive and a teenager."

My mother would roll her eyes at the wild understatement in those words, but she's not here, and I handed out the biggest compliment that I think Ghost will allow. She's plenty used to being confident and skilled, but she's still feeling her way into her alpha noticing.

She shrugs a little. "We all hold steady when it's our turn."

That's something that Lissa might say, or Shelley. Neither of them take alpha compliments worth a darn, either. "You held steady while a retired Special Forces soldier crowded your show and muttered under his breath. I get to outvote you on that being a big deal."

She rolls her eyes. "Kel's a sweetie. He was just worried about Fallon."

And Hoot and Shelley and Bailey and all the dangers in the world that he can't defuse no matter how hard he tries, but Ghost already knows that. "I think you should call him a sweetie where he can hear it. I'll take video."

She punches my arm. "Brat."

Kennedy is so damn good for the submissive wolves of her baby pack. "Whatever. I didn't nearly install a window upside down just to see if Rio would turn green."

He was up on the highest, farthest ledge with a still-trembling gray wolf. The window fiasco almost killed him until he figured out that they were doing it just to mess with him.

Ghost's lips quirk. "That was an honest mistake."

I bump against her hard enough to make her scramble for balance. "I hear that only betas are allowed to lie to their alpha."

She goes absolutely still.

I sigh. She isn't actually the wolf I came out here to deal with, but apparently the universe didn't check in with my plans. "Your wolf is ready, Ghost. More than. If we don't give her what she needs, it's going to twist you up. There's no need for that. I know how to work with a beta wolf who shares a brain with a human teenager, and so do Ebony and Kel."

She shakes her head mutely.

I study her. It's not panic in her eyes—it's sheer stubbornness. Which is a character trait that good alphas feed and water. "Okay. Why not?"

Her arms cross. Silence.

Right. Because just one moderately tractable beta would be way too much to hope for. "Be nice to me. I had to eat almost half of Kelsey's banana muffin."

Her eyes soften. "You had to. She needed you to. We all know that."

I let my wolf growl a little. "I know, but still. There were only twelve of them." A dozen slightly undercooked treasures that emerged on Shelley's tray along with several tumblers of milk. Some got crumbled, and some were reverently eaten, and more than one got drowned in a waterfall of tears. "Bailey only ate a nibble."

A snicker. "She's tougher than you are."

I sigh. "Duh."

Ghost dips her head, smiling. When she looks back up at me, her eyes are those of the shy, quiet teenager I first met. "Shelley is just up past the spiky boulder—the one that looks like Braden's hair after you feed him pancakes."

I'm being dismissed. By a fifteen-year-old who doesn't want to finish our conversation about whether it's time for her to be an official beta of this pack. That my wolf is going to let her get away with it pretty much makes my point. "I don't feed Braden. He feeds me. That's our deal."

Her lips quirk. "Go find Shelley."

I reach out and tug on her hair. "I convinced Kel, you know."

She scowls—but her eyes only make it up to my chin.

SHELLEY

I hear him coming. He's loud, far louder than he needs to be. Definitely trying to make sure I don't get surprised by his presence in my woods. He stops when he's still far enough away that his face is little but shadows. "May I join you?"

I somehow wasn't expecting politeness. I check in with my wolf. She just settles her head back down on her paws. It was a long run to get here and the moon is pretty.

I snort. She's a foolish wolf and I'm going to be stiff as a board in the morning. "If you promise to leave when I get cranky."

Hayden chuckles as he crosses over to my small puddle of moonlight at the base of a scraggly tree. "That's fine. You let me know."

"You have a mate. If you don't know what cranky looks like, you'd best be getting yourself some lessons."

He eyes me. "It's that kind of night, is it?"

My wolf blinks.

He smiles a little as he settles on the ground beside me. "I just told Ghost that it's time for her to take on official beta duties."

I huddle a little deeper into the soft sweater Fallon dropped from the sky. It's light as a cloud and warm as an oven, but it's not nearly enough protection from the intent notes in my alpha's tone. "She's already taken on the duties. It's her choice whether she wants the title to go with it or not."

He leans against me gently. "Agreed."

A word I never heard from my former alpha, not once in six years. I have no idea why that makes my claws want to rake this one. I breathe quietly and don't try to hide it from the wolf next to me as completely as I once would have. Progress, of a sort.

He holds out a travel mug. "Tea. I gave it a good sniff while I was still in my fur. It smells like Mikayla, not Wrinkles."

He never lets my brisk words chase him away, or the sharp currents that sometimes come after them, either. "Thank you."

He smiles somewhere above my head. "That's my line."

My wolf tenses. The intent notes are back. She likes her alpha's approval. She doesn't like it when he tries to go deeper. Her human is skittish. Fragile.

I grit my teeth. It's true. And still.

His hand strokes my arm over the bulky sweater. "I'll stop if you need me to. But I have some things I'd really like to say."

I take my time. Watch the moonlight. Take a sip of the tea. It's Mikayla's evening blend, cheerful and warm and surprisingly sturdy, just like its maker. "You didn't send Lissa or Kel or Kennedy to say them this time."

He huffs out a laugh. "Am I that obvious?"

Only to one who still can't stop herself from tracking her alpha's every mood and whim. "You're that persistent."

"I could have sent someone else, but these feel like things that you deserve to hear from your alpha." His ribs move against my arm, rhythmic and easy. "You might feel differently, and you absolutely have that right. You can hold up your hand anytime, including now, and stop my words dead in their tracks."

My wolf is almost alarmed enough to do just that. These are big words. Serious, intent, powerful words. Words that are hunting.

I hold very still. I learned long ago not to cringe, not to cower. Prey doesn't survive if it moves.

Every molecule of Hayden Scott freezes.

My wolf snarls at me. *Not. Prey.*

No, I'm not. Not anymore, and I've just utterly panicked a very good wolf and a better man. I hold up my tea and gulp it right down to the dregs. "I don't need hand signals. I know all the people who make you cookies."

They're shaky words. Woefully wobbly ones. He lets them be the right ones. He exhales like a man who just got airlifted off a mountain of lit dynamite, and shoots me a wry grin. "Good threat."

Very carefully, I lean my shoulder back against his. Then I put both hands on my wolf's scruff and hang on tight. "You can say what you came to say."

He doesn't speak for a long while. He just leans against me, two wolves in a small puddle of moonlight. When he finally begins, his words are almost a meditation, slow and calm and somehow talking to the forest instead of to me. "I tell some people in this pack that they're heroes, but I don't think that's what you need to hear, even if it's true. So I'm just going to tell you what I see when I look at you."

Those words would terrify Shelley Martins.

The forest just listens.

"I see someone who left everything when she was young enough to maybe not know quite how hard that is to do, and then did it anyhow. Who found her place in a new family and figured out how she could contribute and where she could love most usefully, and she made herself a part of the very bedrock of that family and that pack."

My wolf stares.

"I see someone who understands beauty and treasures rituals. Who wields watering cans and cookie sheets and all the details she remembers about those she loves as if they're just everyday tasks instead of the breath that fills the lungs of her pack."

The forest breathes. I can't.

"I see a woman who held on tight to those things when she made a choice that I can't even fathom, and she made it sincerely, and she planted herself in evil's garden to see if she might help it grow into something good."

The tears don't ask for my permission. They cascade in silent, unstoppable waterfalls down my cheeks.

"I see the wolf who stood warrior strong inside that woman's heart, who remembered the moon and ran in the forest of her own soul and somehow, some way, kept you alive."

I shake my head, flinging tears.

My wolf trembles, utterly naked before her alpha.

He reaches out infinitely slowly and touches my hair. "I see the woman and the wolf who went through all of that and still lets me know every day how I can be better. Who got shaken by her friends this morning, and then took her shaky heart and tired arms and raised windows for hours so that our new den will let in more light."

A pause—and then almost whispered words, spoken only to the moonlight. "Who allows her pack to water her every day, even though she's not really sure that there's enough of her left to be a seed."

A river of tears inside me joins the ones on my cheeks.

He doesn't wipe a single one of them away. "You're wrong about that, you know. You reached into your entire pack today and told an earthquake to stop, and it did. You're not a seed. You're a stunning, majestic, old-growth tree."

10

SHELLEY

I stick the big wooden spoon into my bowl and stir fero-
ciously. My whisk would be better, but I can't seem to
find it. I stab at the egg yolks that float by in the sea of
milk, taunting me with their round, cheerful wholeness.

They clearly have no idea where they're headed.

"Want some chives for those? Or fried onions?"

I raise an eyebrow at the woman brave enough to
breach my privacy this morning. "I'll handle breakfast.
I'm too cranky for company."

"So I heard." Myrna pulls open the door of the fridge.
"There are a lot of leftover onions. They'd be good in the
scrambled eggs."

There are a lot because Mikayla made an enormous
batch and forgot to tell Brown, who made some more
because he considers onions the only vegetable worth
eating. "Save them for the soup. They'll add nice flavor."

Myrna's head emerges out of the fridge long enough to peer at me. "You're not supposed to know what's on the menu today. You're supposed to be playing in the dirt with Kelsey and Moon Girl and making sure that Ghost doesn't do anything harder than sneezing until at least lunchtime."

I chuckle. Ebony has some very clear thoughts about wolves who are so tired that they fall asleep in their salad bowls. She also has thoughts about who should be in the cook shack this morning, but I'm not as easy to maneuver as a sleeping teenager. "If I don't keep an eye on the menu, we'll be having hot dogs six days a week and vegetables exactly never."

Myrna lays an enormous handful of chives on top of her cutting board. "There's tomato soup for lunch today and roasted carrots for dinner. That's two whole vegetables in a single day. Three if you count the chives."

She clearly hasn't taken a good look at my tomato soup recipe. "Any idea what happened to my whisk?"

"Science experiment." She pulls a big knife out of a drawer. "You might get it back by tomorrow. Don't ask where it's been."

Darn bear cub. "Didn't we buy all those nice school supplies for a reason?"

Myrna hacks at the chives with an abandon that should lose her several fingers but somehow never has. "Beats me. Do I look like the teacher?"

That would be the stubborn wolf we're all working on herding. It will take a while, yet. Bailey has good reasons for keeping all of the gravity beams in her hands far away from the den. I stab at an egg yolk with my wooden spoon.

"You got in late last night." Myrna's voice is casual, but her words aren't. "Hayden, too."

Troublesome wolf. "I don't have a curfew. Neither does he."

She snorts. "That tone worked on Samuel and his lieutenants. It doesn't work on me."

It didn't always work on them, either. I stab another egg yolk. "I went out to the forest for a bit because my wolf needed a run. Hayden showed up, we had a chat, and now I'm making breakfast for my pack like I usually do."

Myrna tips a cutting board full of chopped chives into my bowl. "That's nice, dear. Now tell me the version that bears some resemblance to the truth."

I sigh. My wolf isn't feeling very feisty this morning, and she's never been a match for Myrna on a tear. "He said some things about me. Nice things." Things that kept me up half the night with my face pressed against one of the new glass walls.

She sets down her cutting board with a *thunk*. "Oh, hell. Do I need to work up some good insults?"

I add more pepper to the milk and eggs than I probably should. "For me or for him?"

She chuckles and starts chopping more chives. "Either."

For six years, we did this for each other. Nudged and cajoled and bullied our feet back to solid ground so we could be ready for the next battle or packmate in need or abysmally tiny act of resistance.

I swallow. I wasn't the only one who felt invisible during those years. "He knows that we fought."

Her knife whacks onto the cutting board. "Of course he does."

I'm not doing his words justice. He was so clear last night. Alpha poetry under the light of the moon. "Not just that we tried. He thinks that what we did mattered."

A long, fierce silence. "Do you believe him?"

I close my eyes. He called me bedrock. Breath in the lungs of my pack. A majestic, old-growth tree. "It made so little difference."

Her fingers whiten around the handle of the knife. "I was there. I know exactly how much difference you made. How much difference you still make, every damn day."

I shake my head as I carry my bowl over to the stove. "I came in here so I could work in peace."

She snorts. "You came in here because it's where you stash all of your weapons."

I add a pat of butter to each hot frying pan. "You're the one holding a big-ass knife."

"Shelley Martins. Such language."

I look for my best spatula, but it's nowhere to be found. Probably off doing science with my whisk. I grab an ancient flipper instead. "I learned it from somewhere. Can't quite remember where, but it will come to me."

"Memory loss is one of the first signs of elderhood." She joins me at the stove, a container of shredded cheese in her arms. "I'll tell Wrinkles to switch you over to the old-lady tea."

If there is such a thing, Myrna surely doesn't drink it. "Don't use up all of that. I'll make some cheesy garlic bread to go along with the tomato soup."

"Bread's my department. Finish your eggs, and then I'm kicking you out of here. With my big-ass knife if you don't go quietly."

Annoying wolf. I lean against her shoulder. I don't know what Hayden imagines when he thinks of bedrock, but my version is small and feisty and can curse in eleven languages.

RIO

I stifle a laugh when Kennedy nearly trips over a rake as we sneak away from the kitchen. It's not all that easy. The open walls mean that two people standing around like eavesdropping dumbasses are kind of hard to hide.

We didn't mean to eavesdrop, exactly. I was following some disturbances in the sentinel force when I literally ran into Kennedy, who was doing the baby-alpha version of the same thing.

My stomach grumbles. It was hoping for cookies.

Kennedy giggles. "Remind me to feed you before I have you on my team for pinecone wars later."

I eye her suspiciously. "That's not on today's schedule."

She snorts. "Did you check the school calendar?"

I didn't. I'm a terrible third-grader. Fortunately, Stinky is a somewhat better student than I am, and he usually keeps me informed. "Exactly what will we be learning by throwing pinecones at each other?"

Kennedy shrugs. "Physics, I think."

She has at best a very passing acquaintance with that particular science. Chemistry is more her style—she likes blowing things up. "You know that physics is math, right?"

She grins. "I know that I'm supposed to have a team ready to go in two hours. Kel says we have to pelt Ebony until she agrees to teach the geography lessons for this week, because he read the unit materials and they make no sense. Something about mountains a gazillion years ago with really bad tempers."

Kel is a geek who could probably teach any science unit under the sun, but if he's trying to make Ebony do it, he's got reasons. Either that or he just wants to mess with two of his favorite warriors. Bored dominants make the little hairs on the back of his neck itch.

I eye the one teasing me. "How's Ghost?" Her baby pack swooped on her when we finally got everyone herded back home last night, but she passed out before I could sweep her with my sentinel wand.

Kennedy makes a face. "Are all betas like that? She totally ran out of gas, and she just kept going. I don't think she even noticed."

I wrap an arm around her head. "That's why they have packmates."

She snickers into my ribs. "Duh."

I grin and let her go. "Yes. The good ones are all like that."

She sobers. "Is that why Kel got so messed up when he was a soldier?"

She's a goofball teenager, right up until she isn't. "That's a big part of it. Add submissive wolf tendencies to beta ones, and a whole bunch of bad situations that can't be fixed, and you have a hot mess waiting to happen."

She shrugs. "Yeah."

I wince. She knows all about war zones and their traumas.

She elbows me. "You're allowed to say smart stuff when I ask, even if I already know most of it." She cocks her head to the side, thinking. "It's a good reminder that we aren't just dominant or submissive wolves. It's more complicated than that."

This is so not a conversation to be having before coffee and breakfast. I dig a few of my brain cells out of overnight storage. "Tell me what you mean."

She shrugs again. "Well, Shelley and Myrna, for example. They're both submissives, right? But they don't fight for pack the same way. That means they got hurt differently, too."

I nod slowly. I definitely wasn't the only one smelling things in the ether this morning. "Yes."

Kennedy leans against a tree, her eyes really far away. "Myrna stood her ground and defended her turf and dared anyone to mess with it, and Samuel kind of respected that, even though he didn't want to."

I hate that a fourteen-year-old understands that. And I'm pretty sure I'm going to hate what she's about to say next even more.

She exhales slowly. "Shelley invited hell to come for her instead of anyone else. She protected us by making herself the target. By letting the awful stuff into all her safe places. Samuel didn't respect that at all."

I wait for her eyes to meet mine, because I can hear the guilt and fury and pain of a baby alpha who learned the limits of her claws and teeth far too young—and I can hear the extraordinary choice she forged out of those feelings. "He didn't. We do."

"Yeah." She looks over at the cook shack, and the love in her eyes is as big as the mountain behind her. "That means Myrna needs to be on my team this morning, because turf matters and we are totally going to win this pinecone war."

My sentinel could not agree with her more. "And Shelley?"

She looks at me, and suddenly she's a juvenile with uncertainty written all over her. "I'm not sure. I don't think pinecones will help her. I think that maybe she needs to invite something even scarier than hell into her safe places."

HAYDEN

Wrinkles pats my knee. "Don't think that you can get away with only drinking half of that, Alpha. My patients have been trying that for longer than you've been alive."

Robbie, who is sitting in my lap with infinitely better-tasting hot chocolate, grins.

I scowl at my mug. It smells like fetid socks. "I'm fine. Really."

"Of course you are. This is just a little booster. Nothing that should scare a big, strong man like you."

I roll my eyes. "It's not my masculinity that's scared of whatever you put in here."

She chuckles. "That's because you're a wise alpha who greatly respects the gifts of every wolf in his pack, even if he maybe used an oversized hammer in communicating that fact to a couple of them last night."

I eye her over the top of my mug. This visit of hers isn't about doctoring me with stinky tea. It never was. "I blew it, huh?"

Her eyebrows slide up. "Not at all."

Confusing wolf. I shake my head at Robbie. "Next time, we're staying asleep until we smell the bacon."

He makes the hand signal for scrambled eggs.

That might be the official breakfast menu, but I'm a hopeful guy. "If we stayed asleep and looked really sad, someone would probably make us bacon."

He giggles.

Wrinkles grins at him fondly.

He makes more hand signals. Love. Helping. Smelly stuff.

She nods. "I'm making some new infusions after

breakfast. You're a great helper for those. You can measure out the ingredients and mix them up nice and slowly before we add them to the oils."

He sips hot chocolate, his eyes gleaming happily.

I know this is how healthy pack works, but my heart still squeezes fiercely. He's not just pack. He's mine.

Wrinkles chuckles quietly. "That way you feel right now? That's how Ghost and Shelley felt last night. Sometimes a big hammer can get to a place that gentler approaches might not."

Wrinkles is a delight—and a very scary healer.

I cuddle the not-so-small boy in my lap.

She looks down at him and then up back at me. "The hammers will come for him, some day. When they do, he'll have a father's love behind him."

I somehow manage not to drop the mug on Robbie's head. The last thing the poor kid needs is to smell like fetid socks for a week. I do glare at Wrinkles as I try to mop up the mess she just made of my insides.

She chuckles and pats my knee again. "I like a good hammer, myself."

I shake my head slowly. "Am I even kind of in charge of anything in this pack today?"

She grins. "I hear you're carting around bags of dirt. That sounds like an important job."

Robbie makes more hand signals. None of them are about bags of dirt.

Wrinkles chuckles. "That's right. First the infusions, then the roof. Fallon says it might rain tonight, so we need to make sure the school is warm and cozy and dry inside."

Robbie's face shows the clear disdain of a wolf pup for a little sky water. Then he spies Stinky, who's stirring on the other side of the fire pit where he slept next to Brown and Mikayla.

My wolf cuddles him tight one last time and lets him go.

Wrinkles watches him as he runs off. "Shelley came here when she was about Mikayla's age, looking to be useful because her wolf has a fierce need for that and her old pack didn't truly need her. Aaron Dunn loved her, but he never really understood all of what she gave to us. Samuel never even tried. Last night was the first time in her life that she was truly seen by her alpha. Give her a little time to let that sink in."

Last night was pure instinct. The signals aren't so clear this morning. Generally that means I shouldn't try anything fancy. "I'll go move dirt."

Wrinkles smiles. "You grew up seen, Hayden Scott. You have no idea what it feels like to be invisible. Which means that Shelley isn't the only wolf in this pack who sometimes badly underestimates her own value."

I blink.

She pats my cheek. "Keep seeing clearly. And drink your tea. It's got lots of good things to help your eyes."

11

ADRIANNA

I'm not surprised to find my daughter sitting at my desk. It's a little unexpected to find her staring intently at my computer screen, though. "My budgets are far messier than yours, dear. Don't fix them. I like them that way."

Jules grins, but she doesn't take her eyes off the screen.

I haven't survived as her mother by being slow. There's only one online event worthy of that much interest today, and it's not my annual budgets. "Are they putting the roof on?"

She nods. "I want to see how well the new pulleys work."

She never would have released them into the wild without putting them through their paces hundreds of times first. This has nothing whatsoever to do with hardware. For Jules Scott, founder and stubborn, visionary

CEO, HomeWild has always been about stoking the fires of belonging—and a small shifter pack in northern British Columbia is live-streaming proof of that out to the entire, engrossed shifter world.

Ghost Mountain's video feed the first day was afterthought, a small side project meant to placate Ronan and Ryder and Jules. Silly wolves. There are so many of us who love them—and so many more who are enchanted by the story of their rising.

I pull up a rolling chair and scoot my daughter's over some so I can see my screen. "They've gotten fancy with the live feed." There are two camera angles this morning, one giving us a panorama, and the other one zooming in on various faces as the team installing the roof panels gets themselves sorted.

Jules chuckles. "Myrna is doing live chat commentary, too. I don't think Hayden knows that."

Alphas miss very little unless they think it serves their purposes. "It's not going to hurt HomeWild to have half the shifter packs on the continent watching a bunch of women and juveniles assemble one of your building kits."

The glare I get is a reassurance. I raised her right. "This isn't marketing."

That's the very best kind. "Of course it is. And you'll be able to explain it just that way when you give them a nice discount on their next delivery."

She shakes her head wryly. "Dammit, why didn't I think of that?"

She would have. "Because you've been working

around the clock to get their new den through manufac-turing." With Ronan and his team up north, HomeWild has been more than a little shorthanded. Which will stop my daughter from keeping her promises exactly never.

She rolls her eyes. "I slept. Some."

I consider the contents of the plate in front of her, which was obviously filled by someone who knows her penchant for eating dinner for breakfast. I pick up a spicy meatball. "Open up."

She snickers. "I didn't come in here so you could feed me."

I don't believe that for a minute. "It's handy that they have two bears."

Jules opens her mouth, temporarily distracted by the antics on the screen. Reilly and Brown are being hooked into two harnesses that will allow them to power the system of ropes and pulleys which will lift the roof panels. I can see the temporary tracks for the first one in place, and two women conferring off to the side in the universal pose of consultative leadership. "Danielle looks much more confident than she did when they got started."

Jules's eyes gleam. "She sent me a couple of suggestions on how to improve the wall-panel installation."

I laugh at my gorgeous, lying fiend of a daughter. "She did not."

Jules grins and scoops up another meatball. "Fine. She said a couple of things under her breath while they were assembling the walls. Her team wrote them down and sent them to me."

That, I can entirely believe. "She'll be horrified when she finds out."

Jules shrugs. "She's a pragmatic geek like me. She'll deal. The kits will be better, and that will matter."

I weigh what I know of Reilly's mama. It might work. If it doesn't, the guy lazing around on the ground with a couple of pups will have to earn his keep.

I grin as Mellie tries to swat her alpha's nose. She's getting so big. I need to visit soon. She needs some grandma attention before the babies arrive so that she doesn't feel displaced.

Jules snickers and pokes me in the ribs with her elbow. "Mom. Focus."

Oops. I steal one of her meatballs and pay more attention to the wider action on my screen. Danielle and Eliza have stopped conferring and are running through the instructions with their team. Jules leans in, listens for a moment, and jots down a couple of notes.

My curious wolf gets the better of me. "What are you noticing?"

"Tweaks to our instructions, mostly. These two are largely sticking to what we sent, but Ghost does a lot of rewording. She's got a knack for simplifying the geeks-peak while still keeping the details right."

I smile. I suspect Ghost has spoken more in the last three days than in the previous three years, and she's done it with a quiet confidence that I would bottle if I could. "They'll be making her beta, soon."

Jules pouts as she surveys the contents of her plate. "When did you talk to Hayden?"

I chuckle. "That's not inside information, it's alpha intuition. I might be wrong."

She snorts. "Not likely."

My wolf leans in and nuzzles her cheek. She's all grown up now, and just as fierce, demanding, insightful, and loyal as she was the day she pulled her tiny self up on two handfuls of Hayden's fur and wordlessly insisted that he teach her how to walk.

She's not sitting here to watch a building rise.

She's sitting here because that day, and all the ones that followed, he was the brother she needed. Which is so much of why she's spent the last few months absolutely dedicated to sending him a building that his pack can put up without any hands holding on to his fur at all.

That fierce, demanding, insightful, loyal pup grew up into a woman who understands her big brother very well.

I study the screen. They're almost ready to raise the first roof panel. They'll install the solid ones over the school side of the building, and then the finicky, tricky glass ones over the greenhouse. The HomeWild team put in a very long week figuring out how to make the field installation of those work. Even Ronan tried to argue for sending a couple of experts along with the delivery. Jules never wavered—because HomeWild isn't, and never has been, about the hardware.

I smile as I steal another one of her meatballs. There's enough food for two on the plate. I'll have to stop by the kitchen later. Good alphas don't miss details unless it serves their purposes. "Have dominant male hands done anything more than pull on a few ropes?" I've seen most of the footage, but Jules has probably watched it all a dozen times.

The satisfaction in her eyes is almost feline. "Kel caught a teetering wall panel once, and Brown rounded up a couple of missing bolts. Other than that, they've been chasing pups and fetching sandwiches."

Hayden has always been a master of that kind of hiding in place. "Rio did well to pull that off." He would have been the most obvious expert for his pack to lean on.

Jules sighs happily. "They've hardly even looked at him."

She's put countless hours into the design, execution, materials, and instructions that are making such breathtaking independence possible. She's watching it happen from afar because it's the right choice—but it's also nearly killing her. I wrap an arm around her shoulders. "There was no one better at putting power in the hands of submissive shifters than your father. He would be so proud of you."

She leans her head against mine. "You don't exactly suck at it, either."

I don't. But he was the one who taught all of us just how much it matters.

SHELLEY

It almost looks like a building. I peer up at the first roof panel, just settling into place after its run up two gigantic, triangular tracks. Ghost said the tracks are a safety feature, a way to get the roof in place without needing a whole bunch of ravens to help.

Danielle is staring intently, too. She grins at Eliza as we all hear several loud *clink*s. "That sounds right, doesn't it?"

Even my wolf knows the answer to that. She listened to the video of the music that the roof panels make when they install correctly. It's a simple song and a pretty one.

Eliza nods diffidently.

There's no doubt in Ebony's chuckle. "Excellent. Let's get the rest up before Brown decides to wander off and catch a fish."

The smaller of the two bears in harness shoots her a dirty look.

She smirks at him. "Not that Reilly seems to need your help."

Tricky beta. Reilly is the primary lifter. Brown is on the secondary safety rope, just in case he's needed. And however growly he might be pretending to be, I saw the proud gleam in his eyes when that first panel rose into the air.

The big, strong men of this pack want so very badly for us to do this without them.

Danielle nods at Kennedy and Hoot, who are captains for the team of youngsters moving the roof panels into position at the bottom of the tracks. I'm pleased to see Mikayla with them. She's a wolf who blooms wherever she's planted, but she loves being right in the thick of things. Today, that's not in the kitchen. Indrani is tucked in beside her. I don't know if most packs pay their visiting engineering interns with cookies, but this one absolutely will. She's worked at least as hard as the rest of us.

Hoot adds fancy trills to the call signal for all hands in position. She guides the cautious, steady lift as they ease a roof panel off the pile and carry it over to the tracks. Those have already been repositioned by Reilly and Stinky, which seems like something that pups shouldn't be able to do, but all it took was flipping a couple of levers and pulling on a rope.

That hasn't stopped either of them from grinning like loons.

I spare a thought for the painstaking work that must happen in the HomeWild offices in order for them to send out tools that can be so easily used. I know how to structure the making of cookies so that pups can help, or walk beginners through a batch of muffins from start to finish. I can't fathom what it must take to do that on this scale—to let every last shifter in this pack, right down to the tiniest pups, contribute to the making of home and den.

Lissa dusts off her work gloves and steps into place beside me. "Ready?"

We have an easy job this morning. We're assembling planter boxes, or the frames for them, anyhow. They'll move into the greenhouse once the watering pipes are in place. I study the pile of steel and bolts that Hoot and

Kelsey and Robbie unpackaged earlier. "We might need to move a little further away. I don't want to end up underfoot."

Lissa grins. "That would be Hayden and Kel."

Hayden scoops up Mellie just before Kel intercepts her. "We can't be held responsible for what happens when we're chasing pups."

Mellie holds up her arms imperiously. "Ride."

He grins at her. "You can have a wolf ride, cutie. Or a bear ride if you wait. But nobody gets to ride on the roof panels."

I watch the second one on its slow ascent up the tracks and hide a grin. It does look a little bit like a roller coaster.

Kel scrubs his knuckles on Mellie's belly. "How about we help Shelley and Lissa build some planters for the greenhouse?"

The dominant toddler wolf regards him suspiciously.

Hayden wraps an arm around Lissa and kisses her. "I like this idea."

Mellie settles, as all dominants do once the hierarchy of the day falls into place. She reaches out to me. "Cookies?"

Kel chuckles. "Work first, kiddo. Then rewards."

She frowns at him.

He frowns right back, which is good. She's been trying out her bossy powers on Robbie and Stinky lately, and they're both good-natured enough to let her get away with it most of the time.

She decides Kel is a tougher nut than she wants to try

to crack this morning and turns her imperious gaze on me.

Lissa and Hayden snicker silently.

Kel rolls his eyes.

My wolf snorts. Lazy pack. I tap Mellie's nose. "Did that work the last time you tried it, missy?"

She considers my question and shakes her head.

It's a start. I study her a minute. Dominants need a task they can own, even the smallest ones. "I think Grandpa Cleve is in the kitchen making some muffins. Can you use your best manners and ask him to put a few cookies on a plate for us?"

Her eyes widen.

So do the eyes of a couple of alphas and a beta.

I ignore the lot of them. We've been working hard on good pup behavior around the shadow wolves, the same as we do for babies and submissives and our wild cousins in the woods. Mellie can do this, and that imperious stare of hers will help keep Cleve grounded.

And if it doesn't work, it will give Hayden and Kel something useful to do.

HAYDEN

Mellie strides off, a toddler on a mission. It feels enormous, but she's the one pup that Cleve can sometimes handle having nearby. Which surprised all of us until

Shelley pointed out the obvious. Not a whiff of Mellie is fragile.

It wasn't dominance that broke Cleve. It was failure—the bone-deep belief that he didn't protect a pup when it mattered.

Kel watches Mellie, looking for signs of a toddler about to reshape her task or a guy in the kitchen about to run for the hills. "You must really want a cookie."

Shelley pointedly keeps her eyes off the cook shack. "I want to get these planters built. Danielle said they'll have the roof done by lunch, and we'll still be sitting here with a pile of parts and nowhere to put the dirt."

Kel grins. His wolf adores pragmatic, bossy Shelley.

Mine wonders if she has any idea just how world-class her steadying skills are. She headed into the kitchen earlier this morning hiding tears and growling at anyone who came near her. A couple of hours later, she's so easy and solid that she's stirring up pack trouble almost as an afterthought.

Carefully measured, nuanced, brilliant trouble.

I sneak another look at the cook shack. Most packs would see Mellie as a dominant toddler who needs some help on her manners. Shelley just sent her off on a far more complex task, one that isn't about restraining dominance in the interest of good pack relations—it's about channeling it. Judiciously applying it. Being a responsible dominant with integrity and good judgment.

The kind of delicate, fiercely important work that a gentle, submissive grandfather wolf probably used to do on a very regular basis. Shelley isn't asking Cleve to protect Mellie. She's asking him to nurture her. To water her and guide her and to also let himself be of service and face the exuberant gratitude it will bring.

Which is a breathtakingly astute read on two complicated wolves, an excellent way for them to lean into each other's strengths to shore up their own, and a side project for several pack leaders in case we're bored. All casually sorted while Shelley pulled on her work gloves.

Kel shoots me a look that says it's time to stop thinking big alpha thoughts and get my ass in gear.

I take a look at the jumble of square steel tubing, helpfully unboxed in no particular order by our cookie fetcher and her helpful minions, and sigh. "Someone knows how this goes together, right?"

Kel picks up two pieces that would need a blowtorch to connect. "Absolutely."

Shelley rolls her eyes. "I saw you rescuing the directions, Kelvin Nogues."

My wolf wrinkles his nose. Something's up. Kel never makes a mission error this obvious.

Shelley pats his knee. "We promise not to be daunted by your skill and big muscles."

Kel picks up some tubes that look like they might actually join together. "Excellent. My muscles have been feeling sorry for themselves."

My green-eyed wolf snickers quietly.

I shake my head. That little performance wasn't for her, or for Shelley. It was for me. Kel's muscles are happy to hibernate in service of his pack. Mine have been more cranky. Dominants tend to develop some skewed notions about why we matter, and lifting heavy things is on that list. Watching an eleven-year-old bear build walls like a boss was a pretty convincing reason to sit on my ass and stay there, but Kel never leaves residual cavewolf dust lying around if he can help it.

Another roof panel clicks into place with the distinctive song that delights every wolf in hearing range. I hope the live feed is picking it up—Jules used to sing that song in her sleep.

Shelley smiles. "Would you look at that."

She's not looking at the roof. She's gazing fondly at the people on the ground. The ones with proud, satisfied looks on their faces and easy confidence in their stances. The ones who have morphed the hopeful jitters of the first day into well-oiled, competent teamwork.

Pack at its best.

Eliza points at the dwindling pile of roof panels and the teenagers groan in unison. She laughs and says something I can't quite hear. Hoot throws up her arms and mimes some kind of horrible death involving armed squirrels and rogue spaghetti. Mikayla throws a pinecone at her head. Kennedy doubles over laughing.

Eliza says two quiet words and the entire team snaps back to attention.

Kel's grunt is laced with approval.

My wolf can't make a sound. He remembers the casually slapped order from Eamon the day we got here that literally drove pancake-carrying, deeply submissive Eliza to her knees.

I let him remember. This is the grown-up version of

the lesson that Mellie just got sent off to learn. Dominance needs to be channeled and used judiciously and held in balance, because when it is—this is what rises.

"Oh, and look at that."

Three sets of eyes track to where Shelley's have gone. Over to Cleve, who's standing in the doorway of the cook shack wearing an ancient t-shirt and a raggedy pair of sweatpants, looking every kind of awkward and terrified and resolutely waving at the small girl leaving with a plate of cookies.

Shelley calmly waves back, just like she might to any other helpful wolf in her kitchen.

Cleve gulps hard and nods before he vanishes back into the shadows.

12

SHELLEY

I round the bend of the stream that leads to Bailey's camp. My wolf is glad for the run, even if she wasn't expecting a romp in the woods today. I watched the last of the glass roof panels settle into place, hooted and hollered along with everyone else, and then we all got summarily shooed out of the den by the interior decorating crew.

It wasn't the plan, but when Moon Girl and Kelsey and Ravi all look that fierce, a smart wolf knows to scamper.

I stop by a tree that's got a stash of clothing for those of us who run deliveries out this way and try to shimmy out of the bags on my shoulders. It's not all that easy. They're bulky and oddly shaped and my wolf isn't as young as she used to be.

The bags lift up suddenly. "If you wait two damn seconds when you get here, someone will come help you." Bailey scowls as she gives my fur a scratch where the straps used to be.

My wolf leans into her leg.

She snorts. "I can pet you and tell you that you're a pretty wolf later. Teesha and Elijah are here, and he's got about three more words in him before he's done for the day."

I shift and eye Bailey as I pull on baggy jeans and an old flannel shirt. Moon Girl usually comes to these meetings, but this one didn't happen with a lot of notice, and she's part of the decorating crew. Elijah is likely here to speak for her baby pack. The power of sat phones and teenagers who know how to use them. "I brought some of Myrna's fiery chicken wings. He likes those."

She eyes me wryly. "Do you ever forget what any of us likes to eat?"

Food preferences are like names or fingerprints or smells. They tell the story of a person. "I might have forgotten to bring gingersnaps."

She picks up my bags, chuckling. "Even my human nose knows that you're lying."

Troublesome wolf. "There's tea in there for Tara. If she doesn't drink it, two cups every morning and evening, there will be hell to pay, including something about teaching Kelsey how to quiver her lower lip."

Bailey's eyebrows go up. "Wrinkles isn't messing around."

She rarely does when it matters. "Tara has a hard head." One that got encased in concrete after her mate and son were murdered. "Is she here?"

"Nope." Bailey ducks under a branch that's just the right height to whack her in the nose. "She went to Dorie's camp. Something about knitters who can't tell the difference between lavender and violet and need to grow eyes in their heads."

Tara Dunn never says a gentle word when a pointed one will do. Aaron called her the tip of his spear. He was also smart enough to know that she used it in service of what mattered. He was a better alpha with her at his side —and nearly took her with him when he left us.

I will never forget the look in her eyes as she held his head in her lap and watched his blood pour into the earth.

A spear, breaking.

Bailey glances over at me and says nothing.

I swallow. She's the one who tied a makeshift shaft onto Tara's arrow and somehow managed to keep her mother from killing herself on Samuel's claws. Bailey doesn't need my harsh memories. She has plenty of her own. "We're running out of purple yarn. She might have to take the closest thing to violet that she can get."

Bailey snorts. "Tell that to Tara."

"Awesome." Teesha steps out of the trees, gives me a quick side hug, and shakes her head. "You just got here and she's already trying to get you killed."

I stick my hands into the pockets of jeans that are at

least two sizes too big so that I mostly keep them to myself. Teesha is one of my favorite people. No nonsense and a heart as big as the moon, but she doesn't like touch as much as most wolves. "I knit what I'm told. The rest of you should try it."

Teesha hoots with laughter. "Oh, Shelley came feisty today."

I came jumbled, which is the last thing this meeting needs. I look over at the solitary wolf sitting by the fire. He's in pants as oversized as the ones I slipped on and a shirt that blends in with the rocks at his back. Borrowed clothes, more than likely. Moon Girl's baby pack spends most of their time in their fur.

He watches me, his eyes more those of a hunter than a guy who got sent to a pack meeting about logistics.

Teesha sits beside him with the matter-of-fact calm of a human who has spent years in the company of troubled shifter wolves. "I managed to dig them out of the woods before they ate all the good snacks." She waves at the bags on Bailey's shoulder. "Hand them over."

Bailey sets them down easily—and at about half her usual speed. Hunters startle easily. "The gingersnaps are mine. You can fight over the rest."

Elijah grunts.

Teesha grins as she elbows him. "Yeah, yeah, I know. You have big teeth and claws, so you think you'll win."

He looks moderately horrified before he catches on to the joke, which is lovely and human and the old friend I remember. I'll tell Myrna. She knows all the reasons he stays out in the far orbits, but she misses him fiercely.

Teesha unbuckles one of the bags and reaches into its depths. The gingersnaps and chicken wings come out first because I've learned a thing or two about packing bags for the woods. She laughs at the pillows that come out next. Six of them, covered in paw prints and secret messages and silly drawings. "These are adorable."

Elijah side-eyes the bags like they might suddenly disgorge pillows at him, too.

I shake my head. We're smarter than that. His baby pack has a base camp, but most of them rarely use it. I unbuckle the second bag and pull out six leather thongs long enough to go around a wolf's neck. They're simple and sturdy, with a carefully drilled, polished rock anchoring each one. I lay them over my palm and hold them out.

He eyes them, not quite certain what I'm trying to give him.

"They smell of pack," I say quietly. "They've hung in the kitchen while we baked, and gone swimming in the river, and slept in the pup pile."

His eyes soften.

I won't make him speak words that I already know. "The blankets and such are useful, but you can't easily keep them with you in wolf form. These, you can. They're sturdy, and easy enough to repair or replace if they get snagged on a rock."

He studies them, blinking thoughtfully.

I wait. He's a smart wolf. He'll see what we're asking to drape around their necks. He'll also know whether we're stepping wrong. With wolves as uniquely and fiercely damaged as our woods-dwellers and ghosts, several layers of weighing and measuring are necessary.

He finally nods. "The forest will smell less of pack in the winter."

My wolf exhales, relieved. The pendants were her idea. We know the ghost wolves follow our scent trails in the woods, especially after big pack runs, but the coming rain and snow will chase those away more quickly. This scent trail can be carried with them. A gentle, persistent reminder that we're still here and they still belong.

I swallow and offer the rest of the gift. "We're making another set. We're hoping that in a month or two, some of you might be willing to trade one that smells of winter and friends in far orbits for one that smells of the den."

Teesha sucks in a quiet breath.

Elijah shrugs, in the way of a wolf who doesn't make predictions. "Perhaps."

That could mean a lot of things, but my job isn't to try to make any of them happen. I give the simple strands of leather one last squeeze, because several of the ghosts in the far orbits are particularly precious to me. Then I lay them on the ground beside Elijah's knee. "I've got food packets and the last edition of *GhostPack News* for all of you, and a second sat phone for Teesha."

Her grin is a little surprised. "Really?"

She has the ghosts who spend most of their time human. "We had room in the budget." We did after Lissa got a scouting report from Kennedy, anyhow, about heads crammed together trying to see one small screen. "There are some interesting lessons coming up in the online classroom."

Bailey groans. "Do I want to know?"

Sometimes it's not entirely safe to be the messenger. "You might. You're teaching a couple of them."

Elijah huffs out a laugh.

She scowls at all of us.

Teesha throws up her hands. "I'm innocent. Bite someone who isn't."

She's about as innocent as Myrna, and nearly as tricky. "How's your baby pack? Any needs?" That's the primary purpose of these meetings. Other minds in the pack do the fancy thinking about how to tend to hearts and souls. We take care of the logistical wrinkles.

She tilts her head side to side for a minute, clearly debating. "We watched the live feed of the new building going up. I don't know whether to ask for more of that or tell you to shut it down."

Some logistical wrinkles are bigger than others. I look at Bailey.

She rolls her eyes. "Of course we watched it."

Meaning she and Tara watched it with whoever else from the den was hanging around. Her ghosts don't do business with laptops and tablets. They barely do business with breathing.

She shoots me a look that's just a hair too casual. "Cleve's been spending a lot of time at the den."

He's technically in Moon Girl and Elijah's baby pack, but every Dunn belongs to Bailey. "He's been assigned to muffin duty."

Three sets of eyebrows go up. They're prelude to a long list of objections, if my reading of them isn't faulty.

I throw my best friend under the bus. "Myrna did it."

Teesha chuckles. "Right. Good. I like muffins."

Bailey frowns. "Is he ready for that, or does someone need to come and bust him out of cook-shack jail?"

She's never understood that jail and freedom are sometimes found inside the same cage. "He seems to be managing. His banana nut muffins are just as good as I remember." The bits that weren't drenched in tears, anyhow.

My exhale wobbles more than I mean it to. I do my best to shore it up. The den has the luxury of wild feelings. Out here, those are weapons, and they can be just as fierce as teeth and claws. I look at Teesha. "More video or less?"

Elijah clears his throat. "More."

Teesha blinks at him. "You guys watched?"

He shrugs. "Mostly we listened."

I try to imagine what the live feed must have sounded like without visuals to interpret the cacophony of noise. I can't even begin to get there, but I know my job. Get details. "Was there something in particular you liked hearing?"

Elijah's forehead wrinkles. He sits in contemplation for a long time. "Pups. Laughter. Call signals."

The first two I could have guessed. The last is more mysterious. "The owl hoots?"

He nods silently.

Bailey looks as consternated as I feel.

My wolf scratches at the mystery, trying to make sense of it. We can send more audio of owl hoots, but that doesn't feel right. I'm missing something. Then it hits me. "We used them to coordinate the teams."

Bailey's eyes clear. "The sounds of pack working together."

Elijah smiles faintly.

More than that. "Pack working together and succeeding." There's nothing more precious to the soul of a wolf.

Elijah nods. "When we turned it on the second day, there were more listeners. And they came closer."

"That makes sense." Teesha's words are quiet and tinged with pain. "The newspaper is great, but it's a human way of telling stories. The audio told a story to their wolves."

Which we've been trying hard to do with food and things that smell of pack, but this is so much richer—and a lot more complicated to get right. I try to think. "Would visuals help? A bigger screen, maybe?"

Teesha snickers. "Sorry. It's just—wolves watching TV in the woods. That's so weirdly human."

Bailey rolls her eyes. "Says the human who helped me chase the confused yearling bear out of our camp last night by growling at him."

My eyebrows go up. We've made every effort to keep the satellite camps safe for and from the local wildlife, but the young ones can get frisky in the fall. "Do I need to send Brown out?" He's our expert at thwarting hungry bears.

"Nope." Teesha grins. "He wasn't coming for our

food. He was following a girl. The cute one with the wrinkly ear who lives over by the rogue cats."

She's been the star of several episodes of FollowThe-Cats's new bear video channel. I pat Teesha's arm. If either wild bear was at all dangerous, Bailey would have tied her to a tree and chased the poor things into polar bear country. "You growled at young love, did you?"

Elijah's eyes glint with quiet amusement.

Wolves love silly stories. We need to work on that. Winter has a lot of long, dark hours. "We can do more audio recordings of the den. And perhaps you can record some of your howling." His baby pack often sings to the night sky, and lately, it's been sounding less fragmented. "What I've heard is beautiful."

Elijah looks unconvinced.

He hears the fragments that remain. My wolf hears the tentative beginnings of something different. "They're the songs of pack."

Teesha nods firmly. "Send those to us, too. Blaze and Terrence spent half of the last pack run furry. Our wolves are listening, even if we're crap at howling."

Pack songs matter, even to those who can't be in wolf form. I eye Teesha, thinking. "Do you have anyone who might want to learn to play guitar?"

She makes a thoughtful face. "No idea. I can ask."

I smile. She's not the right messenger for that question. "Don't. I'll send Ravi and Kelsey out with a couple of extras. We just got a small shipment of beginner guitars for the school."

"Those will need to be kept warm." Elijah seems surprised that he's spoken. He shrugs. "I remember Ravi saying that his didn't like the cold of winter."

A memory from before. I hug it tight to my chest. "The cats sent over a few of those silly solar tent heaters that made us all laugh. If you had one for each camp, you could use it to keep things like guitars warm." Or video screens. Or tiny visiting babies.

Teesha looks cautiously intrigued. "We could try."

I make a note in my notepad. I've come back from these meetings with far stranger requests than heaters in the woods. Not once have Kel and Ebony ever done anything other than deliver.

I look back up at Teesha. There's a detail that's unsettled, yet, and those are almost as irritating as forgetting to add baking soda. "You weren't sure whether you wanted more live videos or less."

"I'm still not sure." She makes a face. "It was hard to know exactly what we're missing."

That's the kind of complicated that exceeds logistics, and we worked out what to do with those long ago. "I'll ask Hoot and Rio."

Several nods. No one in this group trusts easily—not with the ghost wolves we protect. But Hoot has always been their guardian, and Rio simply walked in and made it very clear that they now had two. Which might have gone badly, except that every single one of us can feel the absolute faith inside our wolves for what lives in him. Even Bailey, and I wasn't sure she had any faith left.

I try to keep my next question casual. "Do you and Tara need anything?"

Bailey sighs. "You could convince more people to have babies. Tara won't stop knitting tiny hats and leg warmers and sweaters."

The ravens are putting in orders and so are the cats, but this isn't really a logistics problem, either. Tara Dunn is out here because she's standing watch over wolves she considers her babies, even though most of them are fully grown. But I also saw the hell she lived through when Kelsey was at the den, too far away for Tara to love her properly or shred the monsters under her bed.

I write another note.

"Lissa could have babies." Teesha grins. "She and Hayden would make really cute ones."

Bailey rolls her eyes, but there's a glint in them that she doesn't quite manage to hide. A sad, helpless one, because the thought of her best friend having babies without her being able to see them every minute of every day has just stabbed her right in the gut.

I don't dare write that down. I just edge gently by it, because that, too, we worked out how to handle long ago. Logistics startle a lot of deeply emotional bunnies out from under the bushes. We don't chase them. "Anything else?"

"A pack run would be good." Teesha looks over at Elijah and gets the nod she's expecting. "The building project has cut down on the foot and paw traffic out our way. We miss it."

So does my wolf. She took the long way here, hunting

scent trails of precious hearts. "There's a full moon in a night or two."

My packmate who should have the least instincts for howling at the moon grins. "That works. I don't trip over nearly so many tree roots when the sky gives me a nice flashlight."

Teesha runs through even the darkest nights with a proficient elegance most of us can't begin to manage without our fur. "I'll let Hayden know."

She smiles down at her knees. "Thanks."

My wolf cocks her head. There's something else there, but this packmate is tricky. A human with a heart that howls, but she has no wolf. I wait. Bailey always leads with her most important request. Teesha sometimes finds hers as we're getting ready to leave.

When she finally looks up, it's so very obvious that's happened again. "Would you plant some dandelions? In the greenhouse?"

We put out a garden request list weeks ago. Ghost also visited every baby pack and made sure we knew what they wanted, and then visited again with the finalized plans of all of the bounty we hope the greenhouse will produce over the winter. There were no dandelions —those are on the list for the spring garden when we have more space.

It doesn't matter. There's only one answer to give to the eyes looking into mine, even if I have to drive into town and find an empty lot and dig some up myself. "Yes."

Bailey bumps against her shoulder. "You want to grow weeds? Seriously?"

Teesha sticks out her tongue. "Weeds are just flowers that someone isn't smart enough to appreciate."

I blink—and then I smile.

There are no weeds in this pack. Not anymore.

13

HAYDEN

I roll over in my sleeping bag, a little startled to discover that I'm in one.

My wolf snickers and tries to pretend that he's been awake for hours.

Liar. I convince enough of my neurons to fire to get one eye open. It promptly gets distracted by Robbie's grubby, sleeping face, so I pry open the other eye, hoping my brain can belatedly sort out where I am.

It doesn't take all that long to figure out. I apparently conked out at Dorie's camp, which is technically part of the main den—or this is what Dorie's camp looks like when a couple dozen shifters invade for the night. That wasn't in the plans, but Kel got a text as the sun was setting on our impromptu hot dog roast. He read it, left with Brown, and came back a few minutes later with all of our sleeping gear.

After three days of chaos and heavy lifting, nobody had any complaints about sleeping wherever they happened to be lying at the time.

I raise my head cautiously, but no one is stirring yet. Not even Shelley, who's usually up with the dawn. That might have something to do with the two hard nights she had before this one. Her wolf has a problem with walls. She clearly doesn't want me to know, but sadly for her, Rio and I can recognize that particular affliction at a hundred paces.

My wolf shakes his head. Too much thinking. It's a pretty morning. He looks around for his green-eyed wolf.

She's down with the interior-decorating crew. Which I'd be worried about, because there's no sign of any of them, but Rio is with Lissa, and so are Myrna and Kelsey and Ebony and Hoot and Reilly and Brandy and Moon Girl and Eliza and Ravi, and there's no way they aren't inside the garden school creating absolute magic.

My wolf pants into the crisp morning air. He likes it when his pack does magic. He could go catch them tasty rabbit snacks as a reward.

I remind him that bunnies are our cute, inedible friends, at least the ones close enough to the den to possibly be related to our garden marauders.

He has opinions about that, but he keeps them to himself. He's seen the pups sit and watch the garden marauders with happiness in their eyes. There are other ways to be proud of pack.

I advise him against early morning howls, too, and try to slide out of my sleeping bag without rousing any of my neighbors. Robbie opens one eye, yawns, and goes back to sleep. Kennedy is a different kettle of fish. Alertness snaps into her eyes.

I use hand signals. They're quieter.

She fires off one that I don't know before she plunks her face back in her pillow.

I shake my head. The hand signals are rapidly evolving into full-blown sign language. Reilly found some videos online, and when Robbie and Kelsey had an entirely silent conversation the rest of us could barely follow a couple of days later, Ebony contacted the SchoolNet resource center. Lissa just giggled helplessly as she added the spreadsheet line to trade sign-language lessons for cookies.

I need to practice. And check in with Reese to make sure we're not triggering a regional shortage with our ridiculous consumption of butter and eggs. Not that he'll protest anything that might threaten his cookie supply, but maybe we need to have a chat with some of our local farmers about increasing their cow herds and chicken flocks.

Wolf shifters are good at many things, but we tend to panic livestock.

I manage to tiptoe most of the way through my sleeping pack before I wake up anyone else. Kenny is already glaring at me from on top of a boulder, but he doesn't count. The groggy raven at my feet does. I squat down beside Fallon's head and try the same hand signal I used on Kennedy.

Her lips quirk as she cuddles deeper into her sleeping

bag, probably mostly to avoid waking her mate, who has two pups curled against his belly. They've been sleeping there a lot lately, drawn in by the new life growing in Fallon and the eternally patient kindness that lives in Ben.

My wolf pouts. The pups are spreading their napping places around a lot more these days. He rarely wakes up with every last one of them piled on his head.

I scratch behind his ears. He'll just have to play with them more when they're awake. I leave Fallon and head for a mossy rock with a nice view. Dorie's baby pack chose this spot for its relatively flat tent sites, but it has some nice perches for a cat or an alpha who woke up early and needs to think far enough away from his sleeping pack that he doesn't disrupt their dreams.

My wolf mutters. Too much thinking. It's a pretty morning.

I smile as I take a seat on still-damp moss. He's got a point. It's a gorgeous, clear morning, the sky still showing off the oyster-shell colors of the sunrise. Wispy pockets of mist hover over patches of green here and there, and the silence feels sacred.

I breathe into the stillness.

Three days of hellbent teamwork. It's been a ride. One full of some wolves stepping into boots they didn't think they could fill, and other wolves discovering just how capable their pack is when they take several large steps backward. A reimagining of the power in this pack that's no less spectacular than the building that rose from a pile of gorgeously engineered parts and faith stretched right to its limits.

Today I suspect we begin to learn what we've actually built.

RIO

My paws touch the earth. Listening. Measuring. Hearing the sound of a heartbeat that hasn't happened, yet.

Our pack waits. We sent them all away yesterday. That wasn't planned, not until I saw the first of the boxes come out of storage nooks and crannies and began to understand what the decorating team truly intended.

I don't issue sentinel edicts often. This one was worth it, and not just for the judiciously offered handful of gummy bears I got from Kelsey after everyone other than the decorating crew left. There isn't a wolf in this building who got more than snatches of sleep last night, and most of us have walked into a wall at least once, but what we've brought to life inside these walls is priceless.

Up the mountain, I can feel Hayden sensing the moment that's building. He won't have the details, not yet, but he'll roll with them when they land. He's an alpha born and raised for days like this one.

My paws move on the earth. Circling. Honoring. Adding what a sentinel can offer to what has already been built. I don't know if the building needs it, but I do.

I take a moment to be with the stretch and tilt of my

own soul, and then I check in with those who are walking the same circle in my wake. Reassurance comes back to my paws, and solidarity. We are eleven wolves greeting the morning with weary, victorious hearts. There was doubt in the deep of night. There isn't any now.

The smallest wolf in the circle turns, tracing a path in the dirt just inside my larger one. Each larger wolf she passes nuzzles her cheek, adding their blessing to whatever it is that moves her paws.

My sentinel isn't sure, but he trusts her absolutely.

Kelsey looks at him as she approaches, her eyes firm and bright.

He begins to understand her intentions.

He wavers.

She taps her paws lightly on the earth. Silly sentinel.

He answers slowly. With respect. It could be done in parts. In stages. In careful steps. Perhaps later, when the bigger building comes and the pack has had time to adjust.

She stops and tips her head, watching him. Waiting.

He looks inward, asking the hard question. The one a healer must always ask. *Is he the one who hurts?*

Her eyes glow. I see in their depths the most profound truth of the last three days. The wholeness that came in the midst of, and because of, breathtaking speed. I tremble. Souls don't come with detailed instructions and exquisitely engineered parts.

Gentle, bubbling laughter from the earth, and from the small red wolf standing light on its surface.

Oops. I exhale my need to hold, to steady, to control. To engineer.

A small red wolf nuzzles my cheek. I am sometimes silly, but she loves me very much. She turns, walking in front of me this time, her paws making a promise in absolute silence.

I place big black paws in her footsteps and use what I was given to be her megaphone.

14

SHELLEY

I expected this morning to be chaos, but it isn't. It tried to start that way, as groggy wolves with sore muscles began to greet the day in our usual manner, but there is something tugging on all of us.

A silence. A solemn stillness.

I drink deeply of the remaining coffee in my mug. It's warming the nooks and crannies the oatmeal didn't reach, fortifying more than just my belly. This silence doesn't hold the murmurings of evil—but so many silences that came before this one did. Their echoes are reaching for me.

A warm head settles on my shoulder. Kennedy holds a mug of her own, filled with steaming milk. She says nothing, just leans against me as she offers her own strength, giving to my wolf and taking at the same time.

The echoes recede. Not their time. Not their moment.

I breathe into the stillness. Let ribs that carried wall panels and lifted windows into place and readied planters for dirt be my answer to the silence.

Kennedy nuzzles my shoulder with her cheek.

Sweet pup. My hand strokes her hair, knowing that she isn't a child and honoring the one that still lives in her anyhow. I see glimpses of her more often these days, and I'm glad of it.

A sound from over by the trail that leads down to the main den has eyes sharpening all over Dorie's camp.

Kennedy's head stays on my shoulder.

My wolf belatedly does the math. A mug of warm milk. Soft cheeks seeking snuggles. The oversized hoodie that comes out when a baby alpha most wants to shield her pack from what lives inside her.

Kel closes in on her other side. He catches my eye, shoots Kennedy a measuring look.

My wolf finds her feet. She knows how to steady little girls and nearly grown baby alphas, even when they share the same soul.

Kel smiles faintly and moves away.

Kennedy turns her face into my chest, sheepish.

I run my fingers through her hair, something she rarely lets anyone do. Robbie trots up, a small white wolf checking on his packmate. Kennedy bends down, scoops him up, and deposits him in between our chests. We stay like that, our three hearts together, and wait.

It doesn't take long for the newly arrived sounds to

make their way over to us. Kelsey arrives, a small girl in purple rain boots and a bright green puffy jacket, walking with joy in her eyes as she collects a parade behind her.

We fall into line, or the best approximation of one that wolves can manage when the ground isn't level and some of us haven't had quite enough coffee and Kennedy isn't the only one with her head on someone's shoulder. It's a scraggly parade, and a quiet one, but we make our way down the rocky, winding path that connects Dorie's camp to the school well enough.

The walk is a reminder of just how short that distance has become.

Kennedy is still cuddled into my side, but her head is up. Scanning. Sniffing. A baby alpha who took her moment of comfort early, knowing that her pack might need her.

I look around. Sometimes cookies and brisk words are needed, too.

Kenny isn't overly pleased to be here, but some of Dorie's strays are herding him. Jade is complaining because she can't find her new rain boots, but Hayden lifts her to his shoulders and takes care of that. Bailey's wolf has a wired energy that gets my attention, but she won't miss this day, no matter what torments await her once the doors of the school open.

All in all, a calmer pack than it could be.

I take in the school as we approach. I saw it finished yesterday, but it had to share space in my tired brain with a packing list for Bailey's camp and a mad rush to find the leather thongs that we had made and somehow lost in the bowels of Stinky's sleeping bag. Now it stands alone.

I'm somehow surprised by how beautiful it is. The metal-and-glass walls of the greenhouse shine in the early morning light. The cheerful red siding on the school is exactly right, warm and inviting and nothing like the bright eyesore Kenny muttered about under his breath.

He obviously didn't see some of the other siding color choices.

Kelsey steps up onto the small deck in front of the main schoolhouse entrance. "You can stand on here and take off your boots, or wash your paws if they're muddy."

Kennedy grins. "Are you teaching today, cutie?"

Kelsey shakes her head solemnly. "I'm just inviting you inside."

We follow instructions, a few wolves at a time, and make our way in the doors. Instead of the big room I was expecting, we run into a big gray curtain that's hiding most of the space. There are ten wolves standing in front of it looking nervous and gleeful and like they haven't slept for a week.

Ravi clears his throat. "The curtain is just temporary. We wanted everyone to see what we've done at the same time, so please, if you could put away your boots and jackets. There are hooks for each of you."

There are quiet murmurs from those nearest the walls, and then louder ones. Hands reach for me, guiding, gently pushing me to where I need to go. When I arrive, I stare at the small stretch of wall in front of me. It's a simple setup. Three bright red shelves, the bottom one running at about eye level, with baskets on top. Underneath my stretch of shelf is a hook for my outerwear and a place for my boots. It's cheerful and orderly and my wolf entirely approves.

There's a pencil drawing on the basket with my name. I lean in to take a closer look. It's one of Brandy's clever sketches. She's captured the early morning when I sit on a rock with my cup of tea, right down to the sturdy lines of my favorite mug.

"That looks just like you." Hoot's grin is a little watery. Her basket is nestled on the shelf just under mine. Brandy did a sketch of her wearing Myrna's army boots and driving Rio's truck.

Kel leans in, studying our drawings, his face that of a man who just tried a new food and isn't at all sure that he likes it.

Hoot elbows him. "Brandy wanted everyone to have a good moment to look at every day. A hopeful one. I think the one she did of you is awesome, and it made Rio go all soft and gooey, so you have to keep it."

His lips quirk. "Yes, ma'am."

My wolf cranes her neck to see Kel's drawing.

He grumbles and pulls the basket down so I can see it.

It's a fine drawing. A beautiful one, even. Brandy captured Kel in a moment of laughter that's coming right from his toes, the lines of the sketch nearly alive with it. I want to reach out and touch it, but I know why it's got him all bothered. She might as well have drawn him naked.

I look back over at the sketch of me, sitting on my rock with my mug of tea. She was gentler with me, but no less clairvoyant.

A Dunn who feels with her sketching pencil.

I exhale slowly. This is only the entryway.

KEL

Some of the worst days on the battlefield are the ones that come after the fighting, when the rush of adrenaline recedes and soldiers start to process the changes that landed while they were fighting.

This isn't a battle and we aren't soldiers—but whatever's hiding behind that gray curtain is at least as fierce. I take one last look at the meticulous, skillful drawing that just put several new holes in my gut, set my basket back up on the shelf, and try to pull my shit together.

I don't know if I'm going to be needing my pack or they're going to need me, but either way, it will be less of a disaster if I'm paying attention.

Hoot and Shelley bracket me and we face the curtain together. The rest of the crowd slowly starts to orient, quite a few still distracted by the pieces of their souls that the decorating team casually taped to some bright storage baskets. I imagine that wasn't an accident, and if the quivering of the teenager on my left is any indicator, it was just prelude.

She knows what's behind the curtain.

Myrna, standing stage center in front of us with Ravi and Moon Girl and Ebony, clears her throat. "Close your eyes, please. We'll tell you when you can open them."

The emotion in her voice tries to reach out and strangle my wolf.

I know why. It isn't that he doubts his packmates. It's that he trusts them. The eleven wolves who did this all have impeccable instincts for what home needs to be— and home is a place he's been trying to make awkward peace with for twenty-two years.

Shelley pats my arm.

Fuck. I hate it when they see right through my tough-guy routine. I lean against her shoulder, though. I'm not the only one standing here with home-and-hearth issues, and she doesn't like wearing hers on her sleeve any better than I do. Unfortunately for both of us, I don't think the team that did this has any intentions of letting us off their hooks.

There's clinking over by the curtain, along with muffled giggles and a few stray curses. My ears strain for more information, but other than being pretty sure that the curtain landed on top of Moon Girl and Ebony, I don't get much. More shuffling, some nudging as the waters part in the waiting crowd and one gray curtain gets summarily dumped outside the doors.

Excitement ripples.

The footsteps cease.

A collective, indrawn breath.

Myrna lets hers back out again. "Welcome to the

beginnings of the new Ghost Mountain den. You can open your eyes now."

She didn't call it a school. That's my first and only thought as my eyes open.

Then I can't really think at all. I can only feel.

HAYDEN

I thought I was ready. I should have known better, because that kind of arrogance is just daring the world to kick me in the pants, and I already saw the shelves and the drawings and the hooks with a place for every shifter, even the ones who might take years to have a jacket to hang up.

I'm absolutely not ready. I know that even as I make my way through packmates who are turning in circles and walking forward in a slow daze and clutching the hands of whoever happens to be closest, their faces slack with shock. The eleven who did this get enveloped, instincts far older than either gardens or schools making sure that no one greets this moment alone.

I find Lissa.

She smiles up at me, and I can see the wild, uncertain joy in her eyes. "What do you think?"

Thinking is going to be hours, yet. I wrap my arms around her and turn us in a slow circle. The room is still open, but it's divided into nooks and crannies by low shelves that I somehow never saw Brown make. They're filled with books, and bright containers of art supplies and science experiments, and tablets showing off enticing screens that make even my dubious inner student curious.

There's an area with mats on the floor, a play nook for the smallest pups, and pillows and blankets tucked away in cozy spaces for anyone who needs a nap or a cuddle or a quiet place to read. There's a two-tiered table in front of the long glass wall that separates the school from the greenhouse, with a lower level neatly laid out with paper and crayons and an origami project that's clearly meant to break alphas, and a higher level that's got six laptops connected to SchoolNet ready and waiting.

My heart stutters. We have a school.

The far short wall is a searing lime green, with neat rows of words running from the ceiling all the way to the floor. I squint, trying to make them out.

Lissa's body goes still in my arms.

My wolf nips at me in case I missed the obvious.

I didn't. The words matter.

I shuffle us closer. When I can finally read them, my nose buries in Lissa's hair. I swallow twice before I can get the words out. "You're going to kill her. You know that, right?"

She chuckles quietly against my shoulder and says nothing.

I read the words again, all the way to the bottom this time. They're familiar ones. They should be. They're from the preamble to the Whistler Accord, the guiding document of the shifter world. The part of it where my mother laid out, in clear, small words for idiot dominants, just why submissives matter.

I rest my chin on Lissa's head. Very little can make Adrianna Scott whimper. This is going to make her bawl like a baby—and possibly her son, too.

"You need to tell them that it's okay," says my green-eyed wolf, very quietly.

I have no idea what she's talking about for at least a solid minute. Then some of what's going on around me finally makes it through my skull. It's not fear, not quite. But my pack is paying an awful lot of attention to their alpha, given how many wildly more interesting things there are in this room.

Fuck. They've put the core truth that needs to live at the very center of our pack right on the damn wall—and they're worried that I might not understand why. I look over at the wall again and pitch my voice loud enough for everyone to hear. "That's my favorite part of the preamble, too."

Rio shoots me a look that says I'm not entirely useless.

That's not good enough. They put the words on the wall. My job is to live them. I grin at Kennedy, who's always happy to help me demonstrate appropriate dominant behavior. "I think that means you're the assistant dishwasher from now on."

She shakes her head primly. "Nope. I have physics to learn."

Bailey snorts.

Excellent. Two sidekicks are better than one. "Bailey,

care to explain for the class why that quote from the preamble is about all of us and not just the submissives?"

She shoots me a truly dirty look.

The submissive wolf in my arms straightens and glares at her best friend.

Bailey doesn't whimper, but it's a close thing.

Her alpha is smart enough to keep his snickers to himself. He's been on the receiving end of Lissa's looks a time or two.

Everyone helpfully swivels to face the packmate who absolutely wants to be their teacher in every part of her except her brain.

She sighs. "You all know the answer to that."

Reilly shrugs solemnly. "We might have it wrong."

I do let my wolf snicker at that one. Smart bear cub.

Bailey scans the room, looking for someone to take the heavy bucket out of her hands, but she knows that it needs to be a dominant, and they all manage to look suitably stubborn or uninterested.

Her sigh is mostly a growl. "Submissives are the center. They define a pack, shape it. Without that, dominants are just a collection of teeth and claws, but if we're smart and hold space for submissives to be who they need and want to be, then they shape us, too. It takes all of us to make the whole—but it has to begin at the center."

My mother might wordsmith that a bit.

Her son hasn't got a single word left.

SHELLEY

I know all of them. Lissa and Myrna and Kelsey and Ebony and Hoot and Reilly and Brandy and Moon Girl and Eliza and Ravi and Rio. I know all of them, each individual ingredient of what went into this, and I know what can happen when the right ingredients find each other and make a whole from their separate parts.

I know all of them, and I somehow expected to walk into this room and feel comforted and warm and relieved. Instead, my poor body is trying to shift into a shape it can barely remember, and my heart and soul have no idea how to help.

"Breathe." Lissa drapes a blanket over my shoulders. "Then go fold a flower or read a story or make a baking soda volcano with Stinky. Rio was saying something about using fizzy water instead of vinegar, and that seems like it might be a bad idea."

Air somehow finds its way into my lungs. I can fold flowers. "The fizzy water will be fine."

Lissa's smile is wry and lopsided. "We maybe got a little carried away."

My wolf shakes me by the scruff. "You did exactly right. Did any of you sleep?"

She shakes her head. "Not really. I kept expecting Kelsey to fall over where she stood, but she had to arrange everything on the shelves just right."

I can manage the shelves. I let my eyes wander along one of them, falling in love each time they discover something new. There are some of Kelsey's flowers in a pretty glass, and a book of poetry, some shiny rocks next to a math game and blocks of modeling clay in every color of the forest and sky, and that's just a single shelf. "I didn't know we had so much."

Pride gleams in Lissa's eyes. "We raided your art supplies. You can probably see that."

They were never mine. I've just been their caretaker. My wolf grins as Layla reaches for some of the modeling clay. "How are we possibly going to keep all of the adults from going to school?"

"We aren't," says Bailey dryly, joining us. "Reilly is already enrolling everyone. I think you're in eighth grade."

Lissa chuckles and wraps an arm around her best friend. "The real students need to spend plenty of time outside and off in the woods, so it will work out. We might need some more teachers, though."

Bailey growls, but even my wolf doesn't believe her.

I look over at the glass wall, the one that's bathing the entire school in bright morning light. There are shifters on the other side touring the greenhouse and touching the overhead hoses and pipes and putting their fingers in the dirt. "We'll need plenty of hands in the garden, too."

Lissa's smile matches the morning sun for brightness. "Kelsey and Moon Girl planted some seeds already. Lettuce and dandelions and watermelons."

Dandelions. For Teesha. My heart squeezes.

Bailey shakes her head. "Does anyone remember that we're wolves? I keep expecting to find cows or chickens the next time I show up."

Lissa grins. "I'm pretty sure Shelley considered it."

Only the once, when I saw what we spend on milk and butter and eggs.

My wolf tugs on me.

I keep staring fiercely at the wall of glass with all the conviction of a lesson learned in six years of fire. Look at what you can handle.

Bailey leans into me, sighing. "It didn't kill me to read it. It won't kill you."

Lissa rolls her eyes. "Way to be subtle there, B."

"Your mate used a hammer on my head. You didn't tell him to be gentle."

Lissa sticks out her tongue, but she doesn't offer the objection that would have come, once. The one declaring that she hasn't yet mated herself to a yellow-gold wolf.

My fingers itch for a note pad. I could start planning a menu. Mating ceremonies deserve our very best.

Bailey tries very hard to hide the romantic that has always lived inside her and nods at the lime-green wall I'm trying to ignore. "Who chose the words?"

Lissa squirms. "It was a group decision."

Ravi snorts behind us. "Don't let her lie. Also, what happens if you put food coloring in vinegar?"

I manage a chuckle. "Nothing terrible, but keep it off anything you don't want permanently colored."

"Noted." He plants his feet as Hoot and Jade try to drag him away again. "How about rubbing alcohol and a blowtorch?"

Bailey looks alarmed.

He grins. "Teacher required at the high table."

She doesn't scurry. Quite.

He grins and lets his captors drag him back over to the art table.

My heart squeezes again. This is what our winter could be like. This kind of contentment and bustling creativity and learning and joy.

Which means I can't be scared of what lives in here. I nudge my eyes over to the words on the lime-green wall. They're written in pretty handwriting that looks like Eliza's work. It doesn't make them any less searing.

Even my wolf knows these words. They're the ones that saved us. The ones that Lissa read to us on our very darkest night and on so many of the nights after that. The ones that somehow held the evil at bay just enough that we could keep breathing.

Lissa tips her head against mine. "I wasn't sure they belonged in a school. I got outvoted."

I stare at the words a very long time. "They belong in ours."

"Good." She smiles, and turns me, ever so gently, to face the long wall that runs the entire length of the school. It's blank, empty, white. "Now imagine what belongs on this one."

15

RIO

I glance over at the greenhouse windows and then back down at what I'm doing, so that I don't accidentally grate my knuckles into the growing mountain of cheese. I'm on lunch duty, along with a bunch of teenagers who are preparing the rest of the quesadilla fillings in the cook shack. I should probably be in there supervising, but my sentinel wanted to keep a line of sight on a different wolf.

I'm not alone in that.

Myrna, who joined me shortly after I sat down, follows my gaze. "She's stubborn, that one."

That describes most of the shifters in this pack. I dump a plate of grated cheese into the big bowl. "I'm not sure it's the easiest way to arrive at artistic inspiration." Shelley has been sitting in there, unmoving, for a good two hours. Ever since Lissa gently steered her smack into a blank white wall.

Myrna picks up a stray bit of grated cheese and deposits it in the bowl. "You set her up for this. Now you need to let her walk through it in her own way."

I glance again at the back of Shelley's head, which is all we can really see through two walls of glass and the people who are in the greenhouse helping Moon Girl and Kelsey plant seeds. Myrna isn't wrong. We absolutely set Shelley up. In the dark of night, it rang resonant and clear and true. In daylight, things are a little muddier.

I sigh and line up a new block of cheese against the grater. "I was hoping it was going to feel like an invitation."

Myrna pats my knee. "Even sentinels make mistakes, dear."

My wolf winces. This isn't a mistake at its foundations, but he did allow me to layer some wishful thinking over what he knows to be true. The blank wall *is* an invitation—it's just a really uncomfortable one.

Which the woman calmly grating cheese beside me clearly expected, and she was there in the dark of night when the setup happened. My wolf might have let lack of sleep addle him a little, but he wouldn't have missed an elder's disapproval, and she wouldn't have let him overlook it. "You didn't put a stop to my nonsense."

She shoots me a look that says I'm a grown-ass adult, even if I am making us all eat fancy cheesy sandwiches for lunch. "Nonsense is sending four teenagers into the kitchen and believing they won't put zucchini in your quesadilla. Shelley is something entirely different."

I'm pretty interested in what she thinks that might

be. But for all that she's an open book on some subjects, Myrna knows how to keep the tender and wounded and private very well hidden. Hers, and those she loves. "The more I know, the better I can be of service."

"I'm not sure that's true this time." She keeps calmly grating cheese like a boss.

I watch her technique. I throw brute force at the problem. She does something far more elegant.

Her lips quirk. "It's all in the elbows. Our old graters would have just given you bloody knuckles for trying, but these ones are fancy."

I grin. "How do you think I convinced Shelley to buy them?"

Myrna rolls her eyes. "Lissa would happily give you some of the pack discretionary funds. You don't actually have to convince someone else to do your dirty work all the time."

I do if I don't want Hayden to chew on my ass. Besides, it's more fun to do it my way—a truth that applies to both fancy kitchen tools and my sentinel homework. I angle us back to where I was trying to head before I got distracted by cheese. "You think I'll be more useful to Shelley if I don't know what your thoughts are?"

Myrna scowls at her grater. "Troublesome wolf."

I wait patiently. She came over to sit with me.

She finally sighs. "Most of us are on a journey to find our place in this new pack."

My sentinel's ears perk up. "You're not one of them. Neither is Shelley."

Her smile is slow and a little surprised. "You know that already, do you?"

I borrow Hayden's poetry. "You're bedrock, both of you. You were before Samuel and Eamon showed up, and after they came you gave everyone in your pack solid ground to stand on while the storm raged all around you."

Her eyes drop to the block of cheese in her hand. "Damn. You hand out pretty compliments."

I stare at her pink cheeks, really annoyed that I haven't been handing them in this direction more often. "You're the spine of this pack, Myrna Landon."

Her exhale is shaky. "I leaned on the woman who is watching that wall every damn day."

Of course she did. Myrna is the spine, Lissa is the heart, and Shelley is the breath. Hayden got that part exactly right. The problem happening inside our new schoolhouse is that someone as essential to the pack as oxygen also has a right to just be herself. Which I arrogantly thought I understood how to encourage. A big, naked wall seemed like an excellent playground.

Except that's not what we've done. Shelley is in that room literally sitting on our new foundations—and I'm the idiot who didn't realize what that would do to the bedrock of this pack.

I lean gently against the shoulder of the small, wiry elder who is more than capable of holding me up. I came here for Shelley, and so did she, but my sentinel suddenly and belatedly has a different scent teasing his nose. "Tell me about your boys."

Her block of cheese lands on the plate with a *thud*.

I very gently offer to stand in her mighty shoes in case the spine of this pack needs to curl up and be something other than defiant and strong for a while.

When she inhales, I understand just how big a job that might be. "You know that my oldest is working on the wind project in Montana. He found himself a lovely mate down there. She's got a big family and they adore him."

Her pain shimmers in the air. "Does he know how much *you* love him?"

Her fingers grip each other in her lap. "It was best that he stayed away. I let the distance between us grow. Encouraged it, even."

I know six years of reasons for that, but I also want to take Gregory Landon's head and crack it up against a hard rock. Which can't happen. Gregory is only the tip of a very painful iceberg, one that Myrna has never let me anywhere near. "And your other two boys?"

She swallows a lump as big as a boulder. "Milo and Xander are hiking in the Andes. They're off the grid, have been since the spring. They'll likely visit their brother in the next month or two."

Samuel was still alive in the spring. I take a deep breath. I'm missing so many pieces, but one of them is blindingly obvious. "When they do, you'll go see them."

Her arms wrap around her ribs. "I'd like to. I haven't asked for the discretionary funds, yet."

I keep my words casual, which is a hard fight. "You'll

go. It won't cost the pack a thing. Ames will take you to Whistler, and Adrianna will make sure you get to Montana. There's always someone headed in that direction." If there isn't, Jules and Ronan can always arm-wrestle for the privilege.

Myrna's fierce independence tries to rear its head.

My sentinel doesn't hesitate. Power snaps out of him.

Her eyes widen.

Choices. I believe in them, deeply. I manage to find one to offer her, over my wolf's loud protests. "You'll go, or they can visit you here."

Alarm leaps into her eyes.

Fuck. I reach out and take her hands off the grater and wrap her fingers in mine. She's a packmate who leans into touch, always.

She grips my hands. "I'll go to Montana. I don't want them to come back. It would torture Milo."

I know some of the story, but not nearly all. "He's a ghost." Hit by the same blast that took out half the Dunn family.

Her whole body shakes. "Xander says he's getting a little better, but yes. Not quite as bad as Ruby, but close."

Ruby is nothing but a ball of rage on our far border. When dominants break, they don't break gently. "When did they leave?"

A helpless shrug. "A few hours after Eamon murdered Cody. Xander took Milo away. His wolf was shredding him from the inside out. It was the only way to save him."

I thought I knew what she'd sacrificed. I didn't have a

fucking clue. These women who fought for their pack from the inside of hell learned to conceal themselves so deeply that even a sentinel can't see unless they permit it. "You didn't go with them."

"I couldn't." Sadness and grief flood her eyes—but no doubt. "An old woman would have only slowed them down, and the pack needed me. There had to be enough of us here to distract Samuel and Eamon from the ones who needed to disappear."

The horror of those sentences lashes at my skin, along with the murk under the words. Her sons left and stayed away, which means she hid the depths from them as well as she's hidden them from me. "They didn't know how bad it was here."

An almost silent whimper. "If I'd told them, they would have tried to come home, all three of them. And then I wouldn't have had any sons at all."

I breathe. Spines, even temporary ones, need to do their jobs.

She turns her head to gaze in the greenhouse windows. "Eamon got wind of Milo and Xander about a month after they left. He was going to take a group and hunt down my boys. Shelley started flirting with Samuel as a distraction."

I begin to understand why Kel still has nightmares. "How did she manage to fool him?"

"She didn't." Myrna's words are quiet and oozing with pain. "She wasn't a good-enough actress for that, and she knew it. She honestly tried to love him."

My sentinel chokes.

Myrna looks at me, her eyes unfathomably sad. "She tried to change him. She couldn't because he never let her become necessary."

The anvil she came over here to drop on me finally lands. "She thinks she failed. She thinks she failed because she wasn't enough, and I just handed her a paintbrush and told her to take some time off from being bedrock. Which she'll take as a message that she isn't necessary."

Myrna looks at me for a long time before her lips quirk. "Do all sentinels have such big heads?"

I have no idea. Mine is currently under an anvil. "What did I get wrong?"

She pats my knee. "The kind of art that Shelley Martins will do might not be bedrock. But it is absolutely essential."

I glare at her, because spines are handy like that. "I know that."

She smiles. "Once she stops chasing her tail in there, so does she."

SHELLEY

It's the biggest stretch of white wall I've ever seen. So far, that's all I've managed to figure out. I scowl at the notepad where I jotted down my mural ideas. I even did some rough sketches of a couple of them. Kelsey's flowers. Pretty rocks in a stream. Paw prints meandering through alphabet letters.

All fine ideas for a school.

Except that's not what this building and this wall are. We'll learn here well enough, and there will be lessons, and we'll probably even call it a school. But I just stood in here with my pack and felt the truth.

No matter what else we build or where we hang our jackets or lay out our beds, this first set of walls and a roof will remain something at the very center of who we are. Something that isn't a shelter or a cocoon or a den. Despite the warm floors and slanting light and beauty—or perhaps because of them—this is our seed. The place we'll always be able to come for sunlight and water and the courage to grow into who we're meant to be.

Which means that the last thing this long, blank, white wall needs is a pretty painting meant to amuse the eyes of small children.

My wolf nudges me cautiously. Too much thinking. Maybe I need a cookie.

I gulp down laughter that tastes like tears. Poor sweetheart. She understands everyday tasks and runs in the forest and tending to packmates. My artist has always bewildered her. Art is entirely human.

My fingers crinkle the pages of my notepad. I tried to share my art with Samuel, once. To reach across the divide between us with something of my heart. A pen-and-ink drawing because I didn't have proper supplies, but I worked on it for three days, struggling to capture the bend in the river that was his favorite spot.

I wanted him to look at it and see home. Something to be protected.

Instead, he saw the reason that his dinner was late.

My wolf nudges my fingers. Paper is precious. Don't scrunch it so.

I look down at the mess I've made of an innocent notepad and sigh. I know better than to let the memories out. The healing books Cori and Eliza are reading say that we should, but it only works if you can bear to look at them once they escape.

I ponder the wall.

My wolf stirs, restless. All this sitting can't possibly be good. Leaves are falling in the valley and the pups love how they crunch underfoot. We could take them to the ridge that smells of wind and snow and the foolish skunk.

My shoulders shake with laughter. That poor skunk accidentally wandered into the middle of a pinecone war, one where some of the combatants promptly sprouted wings when they discovered it wasn't a packmate they were pelting. The ones who could only turn into cats or wolves had to show a lot more creativity to evade a very riled skunk.

My wolf wags her tail. She doesn't understand this throwing-of-pinecones business, but she's happy that I've stopped thinking so hard.

I scratch behind her ears, grateful as always for her fierce resilience. Today is a wonderful day, and the last thing I should be doing is sitting here feeling sorry for myself. The work of a pack never ends. If a run with the pups isn't needed, there are always cookies to be baked or a grocery list to be made. Or I could head up to Cleve's ledge and have a chat with him about what might have happened to my jar of cinnamon sticks.

This business of having other people in my kitchen is complicated.

My wolf rolls her eyes. The kitchen is for pack. The basket is mine, though.

I smile at the cheerful basket beside my knee. Stinky's is already filled to overflowing, and Braden was unhappy that he couldn't fill his with berries, and Kelsey moved hers over by the window so she can grow some flowers. Mine is empty, waiting for me to figure out what I want to do with this small space that's entirely mine.

It was so very wise of the decorating crew to understand just how much that would mean. My fingers run along the rim of the basket, both daunted and enchanted by its possibilities.

I used to feel like that about painting.

Some of the chaos inside me abruptly settles. Maybe an empty basket is an easier place to start than a blank wall. I pull my knees up to my chest and wrap my arms around them and consider what might go inside it. My cinnamon sticks, perhaps, but it's more sensible to leave those in the kitchen.

Memories scritch at my skull, the ones where none of my small treasures were safe from Samuel's need to hunt and seek and destroy.

I push them away. This is a basket for new memories,

not old ones. I reach into the pocket of my flannel shirt and take out a shiny nickel. My bank-robber loot. I set it gently in the bottom of the basket. It looks up at me, a little lonely in its newly palatial surroundings.

Fizzy bubbles rise in my ribs. I know what else to add now that I've begun. The new book Wrinkles found for me in town on the history of recipes. The hat with wolf ears that I'm knitting for Teesha. The small, lop-eared bunny Brown carved and threw onto the kindling pile.

I breathe into the strange mix of feelings inside me. Some filled their baskets easily, but mine isn't the only one that remained empty.

It feels audacious to claim space.

My wolf nuzzles me. All the pups claimed theirs. The rest of us will learn.

Wise wolf. I climb to my feet, patting the warm floor as I rise. I'll be back. For now, I've a hat and a book and a bunny to collect, and likely other jobs will come to find me, too. It's the way of pack.

I touch books and flowers and half-done drawings on my way out. I smile at Kenny, who has somehow ended up asleep in the corner with two pups and a stack of board books as high as my knees. I bend down to set a lump of clay that might be a dinosaur back on a shelf, and then I detour past the neat rows of baskets, smiling at the faces and hearts of my pack.

By the time I get to my jacket, I feel very much like a student. I'll learn in this place. We all will. I slide my coat off its hook and put on my new boots. They feel big and sloppy after a summer in sneakers, but my toes are cozy in my new knitted socks.

I put my hand on the door knob and take a deep breath. I turn and take a last look at the long, blank, white wall.

I wonder what the inside of a seed looks like.

16

KENNEDY

The grown-ups in this pack are working through some stuff. Which means that the teenagers who listen to Ghost, which is pretty much all of us, have jobs to do. I walk into the cook shack, peering around for Cleve to make sure I don't step on his tail.

Mellie grins from her stool in the corner and holds up a beater covered in chocolate icing.

I head her way. Licking out bowls so the dishwashers don't have so much work to do is totally an important job. "Hey, munchkin. Got one of those for me?"

Shelley looks up from the list she's writing. "You can help her ice the cupcakes. They're on top of the fridge so they don't get looted by pirates who can't remember how many packmates will be at dinner tonight."

I wince. We only got that wrong once, and we split our cupcakes in half as penance. I pull up a stool next to

Mellie, keeping one eye on her beater. Baking with toddler dominants isn't an entirely safe sport, especially when they get actual weapons to use. "Remember the rules, cutie. No sword fights, and no licking icing off me, even if I get it on my nose."

Shelley's lips quirk as she hands me two big, soft spatulas and the bowl of icing. "If you're doing it right, you shouldn't get any on your nose at all."

I scowl like I'm supposed to. "You're no fun."

She eyes me and nods her chin at the top of the fridge.

Oops. I jump off the stool and fetch two big cookie sheets covered in lumpy cupcakes, some twice as big as the others. I elbow Mellie as I sit back down. Time to work on her sidekick skills. She'll be a teenager one day, and we have an adult to amuse. "I think you should ice all the little ones, and I should ice the big ones."

She looks up at me and scowls.

I grin. Getting the dominants around here to be goofballs can be tricky business. "I'm big. You're little. It makes perfect sense."

She tilts her head and considers me for a long time. "I growing."

Shelley chuckles. "Growing pups do need plenty of food."

I shoot her a dirty look. "Whose side are you on?"

Her lips quirk. "I'd give the same answer if you were in here with Rio."

I ruffle Mellie's hair. "See, this is why we never try to

steal cookies from the kitchen. Shelley is way smarter than we are."

Mellie squints at me in confusion, probably because she was in on my cookie raid an hour ago.

I can't believe we missed the cupcakes. Mission failure. I pick up one of the spatulas. "Think we're smart enough to use these?"

The enthusiasm that lights up her face isn't exactly reassuring. She picks up the other spatula and scoops it into the icing, coming out with half the bowl.

I get my hand over hers before she dumps it all on some poor, hapless cupcake. "If you put on that much, there won't be enough for all the cupcakes, and Hayden and Rio will be really sad."

She stops growling and listens. Mellie might be feisty, but she loves those two big dorks, and she knows exactly who would make sure they got the naked cupcakes.

I set her spatula back in the bowl. "See how much icing we have? We have to spread it around so that each cupcake gets some." I don't push for equality. There's no such thing in a wolf pack, and there's always somebody who needs a little extra sweetness in their day.

Mellie stares intently at the bowl, a toddler working hard on pack math, which is the only kind I know how to teach.

Shelley looks up from her list and smiles, a real one that makes it all the way into her eyes.

That means we're not totally screwing up. I pick up a cupcake and drop a cheerful blob of icing on its head. My version of pack math tends to involve a lot of trial and error and eating whatever happens to get left in the bowl.

Mellie watches me intently. Then she picks up the biggest cupcake she can find, sets it down in front of her nose, and digs back into the bowl. She ferries icing over and mashes it on top of her cupcake with lots of enthusiasm and enough skill that it only takes a couple of finger swipes to clean up the mess.

I grin and lick my fingers. "Remember, no tongues."

Shelley snorts. "No licking your fingers and sticking them back in the bowl until all the icing is on the cupcakes, either."

I make a face at my sidekick. "Those are the advanced rules for adult people. I should get the pup rules, right?"

Mellie growls companionably as she lines up a second cupcake next to her first one. Shelley chuckles at both of us.

Good. I have no idea how Shelley sat and stared at the wall inside the school for as long as she did, but teenagers don't have to understand things to help fix them, especially when they have really smart friends who were watching from the greenhouse. Ghost told me to go be a distraction in the kitchen, and that so isn't an order I need to hear twice.

I grin at my sidekick. We're totally rocking this mission. Shelley hasn't written anything on her grocery list for ages.

SHELLEY

I leave the cook shack behind, trying not to laugh. I always make twice as much icing as necessary. This time I'm not sure it will be enough. Mellie's precision doesn't come anywhere close to matching her enthusiasm.

I'll let Reilly know so that he can get us a photo. They're all growing up so very fast.

I spy Mikayla coming out of the greenhouse and head her way. My grocery list is almost done, but I pride myself on getting it just right, and there are a few things I need to check.

She grins and holds up two really grimy hands. "There's lots more planting to do if you want to help. It's my turn in the shower, but I can go hold down the fort in the kitchen after that."

By then, hopefully Kennedy will have rectified whatever mess gets made in the spatula sword fight that almost certainly started right after I left. "I put some of that citrus shampoo you like in the linen closet." The small cupboard that Brown built next to the outdoor shower holds all kinds of wonderful things these days.

Mikayla leans in and kisses my cheek. "Thank you. You always manage to see the little things that matter."

Most are sitting right in plain sight, but it's the ones that don't that are often the most important. "I've got a thing that's perplexing me. Ben headed into town for another hamburger for Fallon. What aren't we getting right?" I've tried to make them as close to the ones from the diner as I can, and she tells me they're wonderful, but this is Ben's third trip in a week. Pregnancy cravings can be strange, but I've never had one entirely defeat me before.

"I'm not sure." Mikayla shrugs. "I have a guess, but I could be wrong. I think it needs a wrapper."

I blink. Of all the things I considered, that never crossed my mind.

She makes a face. "I'm probably wrong. Ignore me."

My wolf doesn't think so. When I was trying to sort out a birthday meal for Fallon, Ben told me that she used to dream about warm hamburgers when she lived on the street. All the ones she ever got were cold or half-eaten.

Wrappers have warm, whole burgers inside them.

I scribble a note on my grocery list. I have no idea where to get hamburger wrappers, but I'll find out.

Mikayla scuffs her sneaker on the ground just like Stinky does when he's not sure about something. "You think that's it?"

I do. I always do up a fancy plate for the birthdays. Sometimes food is just food. Other times, packaging matters. "I think you're a good friend who pays attention. Your baby pack is lucky to have you."

She beams at me. "Thank you. And thank you for the shampoo. I better scoot before Adelina hogs all my hot water."

Rio swears that the hot water will never run out, and it hasn't yet, but we're still struggling to believe him. I watch Mikayla run off and add another note. Not to the grocery list. To the other, uncomfortable one that my wolf made me start in the dark of night. Things that belong inside our pack's new seed.

So far that list is full of chocolate-icing giggles and purple rain boots and friends who know about hamburger wrappers. I have no idea how I'm possibly going to put any of that in a mural, but writing them all down is soothing, just like making a grocery list.

I tuck my notepad into my pocket and keep walking down the path. I pass by the school, even though I'm tempted by the quiet work happening inside the greenhouse and the far less quiet play on the rocks out back. Hayden waves, but he's too busy trying to catch airborne pups to do more than spare me a quick look.

I make another note as soon as I'm out of sight. Dominants who notice and care and never, ever drop the pups belong inside our seed, too.

I flip back to the grocery list. I have two more stops to make before it will feel properly finished. I need to quiz Brown on which honey from the farmers' market he likes best, and Fallon's hamburger wrappers have me thinking about Cori. She hasn't been having many cravings because her belly won't keep down much besides soup and Wrinkles's teas, but when she starts having them, I want to be ready.

After that, I do believe it's my turn in the shower.

KEL

I head over to the art table, which is currently occupied by zero pups and one very intent sentinel, and roll my eyes. "You still get recess in third grade, dumbass."

He looks up and smiles. "Yes, but if I go out there, Ravi will start stuttering through his really great explanation of how glass is strong enough to be a wall."

I looked at the list of today's lessons. Nothing resembling engineering design or the science of glass was on the list. "How did he get there from potato art and testing the best nutrient mixes for baby plants?"

Rio laughs. "No idea. It already happened by the time I got here. Danielle looked kind of smug on her way out the door, though."

I plunk down on a cushion. "It's always the quiet ones."

He snorts. "Tell me about it. Did you catch up with Shelley?"

He tries so hard not to be a sentinel worrywart. "Nope. I found Kennedy and Mellie in the kitchen, though. They gave me a chocolate cupcake."

He carefully runs a razor blade down the side of a ruler, making a precision cut for a scale model he's building for one of his work projects. "You brought me one, of course."

Not today. "I didn't. You have legs."

He looks up at me, his eyes narrowing. "Why do I need to go to the kitchen?"

Smart wolf. "Because Mellie and Kennedy are only half-done icing the cupcakes and Cleve is in the woods behind the cook shack muttering to himself."

Rio scowls down at his work. "Since when did you stop kicking asses for fun and giggles?"

I don't ever kick submissives and he knows it. "I have other things to do." We're still working on chasing down the wolves who think they aren't worthy of this fancy new building.

He looks up again, his eyes sharp. "Need help?"

I shake my head. "No. Ebony's cranky enough as it is. Ghost keeps beating us to the punch."

He chuckles and makes another precision cut. "Welcome to my world."

Kelsey Dunn might be our very best reason to build this into a world-class pack for submissive wolves. I pick up a red crayon. "Shelley's percolating."

Rio just snorts and keeps working on his scale model.

Smartass. "It's like that damn story she told." The one that lit her pack on fire and forced me to sing a song to a freaking banana muffin. "First we plant the seeds, or in this case, build the school. Then we have to wait patiently while the hard work happens underground."

He grins. "You're a real poet today."

I hate it when he notices shit. "That would be Hayden."

He looks at me quietly.

Damn wolf. This is why I hate metaphors. "Do we need to water Shelley more or not?" My radar is usually solid for that kind of question, but Shelley Martins gets into my dark places.

He smiles a little. "You've been teaching her how to

kick and punch. She'll make it out of her seed when she's ready."

Life is about climbing back inside the fucking seed over and over again. I want to bite the assholes who decided that dark, tight spaces are optimal learning environments, but so far they haven't shown up and identified themselves. Which means that I teach everyone how to kick and punch if they want to learn. "She's got a good sense of rhythm and she's persistent."

Rio's lips quirk. "Which of the dominants in town are you planning to have her wallop?"

Any damn one she wants. "I got a good look at those guys on Friday. They're still mostly talking smack and drinking too much, but a couple are starting to squirm."

He stabs a small square with the end of his knife and lifts it out of a miniature wall. "Damien?"

Stupid kid. His mom would walk on water if he came home. "No. He's still got too much hero worship in his eyes." Which is a risk that we took when we hauled Kenny back to the den and left the guys in town to muddle along without him, but sometimes you have to kick asses in the order in which they present themselves.

Rio glances at me again, but he doesn't ask anything else. In the division of labor we've set up, keeping an eye on the town wolves is my job. Which is good. I get cranky if I don't get to infiltrate at least a couple of hostile zones a month, and we're still trying to be nice to the cats.

I need to have a chat with Reese about that. He'd probably like the bandana game, and we're going to have some restless wolves and cats this winter. We could even make all of our lives hell and invite the birds to play. Kendra is on the very short list of people who've ever won, and hawks like flying around in snowstorms.

Rio makes another impeccable, precise cut. "Where are things at with Ghost?"

I sigh. Stubborn teenager. Her alpha has spoken and her wolf knows it and pretending otherwise is almost as foolish as our alpha pair not setting a date for their mating ceremony. We're wolves. Saying words out loud changes very little if the truth has already worked its way into our paws. "I think she's worried that taking on official beta duties will change the human dynamics."

He shrugs. "It will, but less than she thinks."

Wolves have claws. They can bust out of seeds any time they damn well please. Which is the kind of philosophical bullshit that means I need to maybe go sneak up on the guys in town again tonight. "She stepped up when Kennedy needed her. Let's give her a little more time, and if that doesn't work, I'll explain how beta duties can get her out of algebra if she plays her cards right."

Rio snorts as he hooks two walls together and begins constructing his model. "Ghost likes math."

I grin at him. "Exactly. So if she's sitting around in class with her homework already done, who do you think Bailey will assign to help Kennedy?"

He rolls his eyes. "Probably Reilly. He's already done all his math modules for the year."

According to Whistler Pack's math whiz, that happened two months back. Which is fine. Scotty could keep an agile bear cub entertained with numbers for years, and we have an incoming visitor who could easily do the same. "I heard from Ronan. Two weeks until he gets here, maybe three."

Rio pauses his work, thinking. "That should be fine. We'll have all but the biggest rocks moved around for the hot pools by then, and the pipes for those and the main den should be in place as long as Danielle doesn't tinker with the designs again."

Every time she does that, a polar bear up in the Arctic roars with glee. "We need to get things settled down some here before he arrives." Ronan never lands quietly, even when he's really, really trying.

Rio's lips quirk. "That sounds like beta work."

I consider coloring on his fancy new model with my red crayon.

He looks up at me, his eyes softening. "How much did you have to do while this building went up?"

My eyes narrow. I can feel the trap, I just can't see it. "Not much."

He smiles. "Exactly."

I growl.

He grins. "This isn't like math modules. You can't do all your work for the year ahead of time. Go get yourself another cupcake and worry about the arrival of a big-ass polar bear later."

I hate it when he's right. "I'm still not bringing you one."

He doesn't even look up from his model construction. "Yes you are."

17

SHELLEY

I drop to the ground beside Myrna, grateful for the chance to stop moving. Braden helpfully rearranged the labels on several of my spice jars and nobody noticed until the dinner crew turned a simple stir-fry into something only Reilly and Kel could possibly eat.

Making emergency pots of spaghetti didn't take all that long. Calming down the panic of three cooks who thought they'd wasted a huge quantity of food took a lot longer. But what's done is done, and there's a nice stack of very spicy stir-fry packed away in bear-cub-sized servings in the freezer.

Myrna drops her last piece of garlic bread on my plate. "You look like you need this more than I do."

I twirl spaghetti on my fork. My wolf was almost hungry enough to eat inferno-hot stir-fry. "I had to throw Hayden out of the kitchen."

She chuckles. "Good. He would have eaten half of the spicy food just to make people feel better. Since we all have to sleep inside four walls with him tonight, let me be the first to say that I'm grateful."

I don't think spicy food works quite like beans, and I don't want to think about sleeping with walls all around me. "We might need to start having chili a little less often." Sleeping outside has spoiled us in some strange ways.

"Don't you dare." Kel sits down, balancing a plate of spaghetti in one hand and a very full glass of chocolate milk in the other. The pups must be practicing their pouring skills again. "Any wolves who fart because they ate too much chili can go sleep in the tents."

That's going to be happening anyhow. We won't all fit in the school now that the shelves are set up and the greenhouse is misting the planter boxes every three hours.

My wolf's ears perk up. She likes the misters.

I pat her head. I missed my shower today, and she does love her time under the warm rain.

Myrna picks up the garlic bread she gave to me and takes a bite. "This is almost starting to taste like something. Maybe my mouth isn't dead after all."

She was the one who tried to convince the dinner crew that the stir-fry was edible. She changed her mind right about the time it set her ears on fire. I take a bite of the garlic bread, which is delicious. "I'll double-check the spices again tomorrow."

Myrna shakes her head. "We already took care of it.

Wrinkles will be teaching a class in the morning on kitchen smells and their proper identification. No wolf should need a label to tell chili powder from paprika."

Kel blinks slowly, which is as surprised as he ever looks.

She chuckles and pats his knee. "Were you thinking that only betas can solve problems around here?"

He doesn't think any such thing. Which I start to say, and then I realize I'm mixing up chili powder with paprika. Myrna does this when she thinks that some of the pack leadership needs to take a break and eat their spaghetti. Or when she's missing her boys. Either way, my job is the same. "Be nice to him. He ate three helpings of spicy stir-fry."

He grins. "It was delicious."

It made his entire body sweat and his mouth probably won't taste anything for a week. But he's also telling the truth, and once Mikayla figured that out, she turned a whole lot less green. It wasn't all that long ago that ruining so much food would have left us with hungry pups.

Kel sticks his fork back into his spaghetti. "Put that same team back on duty when Ronan's here and have them make it as spicy as they want. He'll be thrilled."

I bump my shoulder against his. "Stop solving problems and eat your spaghetti."

Myrna chortles.

He growls at both of us.

A small hand pats his cheek. Kelsey kisses his nose and then heads my way with her hot-pink guitar.

I make room on my lap. She often sits with me while she sings.

Ravi settles onto a stump across from us, his much-bigger guitar already strumming a quiet tune. "Are we doing old songs tonight or making up new ones?"

I don't cast a vote. Both are wonderful.

Kelsey plays the simple notes that let him tune his guitar to hers. The music lovers of the pack scoot in, which is pretty much everybody. Kel leans against me on one side, Myrna on the other. Kenny walks over with one of the long pillows for behind our backs, and he doesn't manage to escape before he gets pinned into position by a friendly bear cub.

Adelina moves a lantern closer, and Dorie hangs another one from a tree. The teenagers assemble themselves into a pile that manages to capture a couple of wolves who spend too much time on the periphery, and Hayden wraps himself around Lissa and deprives her of her spreadsheets.

The fizzy bubbles in my ribs sway contentedly.

Kel rubs his cheek against my shoulder.

Affectionate, content Kel is the very best kind. I stroke his hair, a gesture my wolf has been encouraging for months and my human has only recently begun to allow.

Kelsey strums in my lap, collecting up our feelings and projecting them into the chilly night. The fire isn't doing much to warm most of us, but there are sleeping bags and wolves in their fur who are happy to warm their neighbors.

I look over at the horizon where the moon is just coming into view. It tugs on the primal places inside me. The wild ones. The ones that Samuel never touched.

My wolf shivers.

I stroke her fur softly, with gratitude. She kept those parts of me safely out of his reach. She knew, far earlier than I did, that he would never earn them.

Kel and Myrna stir on my shoulders, both of them sensing what stirs in me. Or perhaps the moon tugs on them, too. Kelsey's simple, little-girl melodies pick up the undertones. Her fingers struggle with anything too fancy on the guitar, but it doesn't matter. Songs aren't about the number of notes. They're about the right ones.

My mural needs to remember that.

Ravi's fingers don't struggle with fancy at all, although he makes it look easy. His notes dance underneath Kelsey's bright ones. Gathering. Building.

I look at the horizon again, at the leading edge of the rising moon. Tonight we work out the notes of our song. Tomorrow night, we run.

HAYDEN

I cuddle Lissa against me. She's up to something again, but my pack is an odd mix of contented and swirling, and I don't have the energy to worry about the mysterious smiles she was casting at her spreadsheets.

She tips her head up to meet my eyes. "You should sing tonight."

I grumble. "Once the others do." There are a whole bunch of shifters in this pack who need time and space to find their voices, and none of them are named Hayden Scott. Which is a steadfast belief that makes perfect sense to me and probably isn't going to survive the hour.

My green-eyed wolf can be fierce.

She turns her attention to our guitar players. "Hey, Ravi—can we do the one you wrote about swinging on a rope?"

Crap, I love that one. It's supposed to be a light and funny song about pack antics on our rope swing at the waterfall, but it's got lines about letting go and choosing not to that slay me every time. And it's got some beautiful harmonies that need to get sung soon or my wolf is going to lose his ever-loving mind. He can *hear* them, and somehow the talented vocalists in his pack are cheerfully ignoring the notes that really, really need to be there.

Which can't possibly be an accident. We're wolves. We can always hear the notes. Our DNA insists.

Ravi strums the opening chords to the chorus, which isn't where the song starts, but it gives the whole pack a chance to sing along with words he wrote one lazy afternoon down by the river when the mamas were reminiscing about our day at Hidden Falls.

Lissa's clear, lilting alto somehow manages to sing the words and chide my wolf at the same time.

I sigh and join in. It really is a catchy melody.

We head into the first verse and most of the pack

quiets. Ravi strums, waiting for volunteers. They always show up. We're wolves.

It isn't a wolf who enters the fray first, though. Reilly picks up the melody, cheerfully out of tune and smiling in happy memory of one of his favorite days ever. Kennedy joins him, gently herding him onto the right notes so that three dozen wolves don't need earplugs.

I blink. There aren't that many wolves at the den.

My wolf snorts. There are now.

I carefully don't look up at the ledges or over at the rocks or into the shadowy trees. If he's right, we have a lot of company tonight.

Somebody elbows Brown, and he adds a growly low harmony. Miriam comes in on top, softly, but with a quiet smile into her lap that slays my wolf. Layla leans against her and whispers something that causes Miriam's singing to wobble, but when she steadies, her head comes up, too.

I beam at her mate. Good wolf.

Layla turns tomato red, but she doesn't duck her head.

Lissa pats my heart. Good alpha.

Smartass mate. The chorus comes through again, and most of the pack joins in. When verse two arrives, every head that I can see swivels to look at me.

I know a setup when I see one. Especially when the green-eyed wolf at my side is snickering and not even trying to hide it.

I sigh. If I have to do this, I'm not doing it alone. I look over at another wolf who usually needs stiff encouragement to add her pretty harmonies.

Shelley scowls.

My wolf grins. He likes feisty Shelley.

I roll my eyes. He needs to get her to sing with him, not bite his tail. I keep my eyes on her and the guitar-strumming small girl in her lap. Ravi and Kelsey are calmly circling on the chords before the second verse, waiting for pack math to do its job and produce some singers.

Shelley shoots Hoot a pleading look, which is a good play, because Hoot loves to sing, and also a really dumb one, because Hoot has no intentions of setting foot in verse two alone and her spicy grin makes that perfectly clear.

My wolf lolls his head. He likes feisty Hoot, too.

Dumbass. Feisty Hoot would definitely bite his tail.

Kel keeps leaning against Shelley's shoulder like he somehow ended up there totally innocently. It's possible —she's one of his favorite people. Myrna on the other side definitely isn't an accident, and if there's a ringleader of this little verse-two showdown, she's my bet.

Kenny watches from Myrna's other shoulder. Weighing. Measuring. Deciding whether this situation needs his teeth and where he might use them.

I hide a grin, even though my ass is on his list of considerations. Whistler has to work hard to nurture enough wolves with beta tendencies for leadership roles. In this pack, they can't figure out how to hide themselves fast enough.

My wolf preens. Good pack. Strong pack.

He's not wrong about that. I wrap my arms around

Lissa and wait. I'm in no hurry. Verse two will happen when it's ready.

SHELLEY

I consider just sitting here and listening to the music. The few bars that Ravi and Kelsey are playing on repeat are a pretty waterfall of notes, and they're bringing soft smiles to so many faces.

My wolf nudges me with her cold nose. Songs are for joining. Listening without singing is human silliness.

I've done it often enough. But the moon tugs on me tonight, and so do the faces of three cooks who thought they had done harm to their pack. This next verse has some sweet lines about letting go even though you're not ready. Perhaps it can serve as gentle medicine for their lingering worries.

I look over at Hoot. She'll sing with me.

She replies with a couple of owl calls that make present and former sentries all over the pack giggle. A few mimics take up the hoots, adding them to the music, and if my ears don't deceive me, Robbie has found something to use as a drum.

I take a moment to remember the words. Then I look at my alpha. I haven't forgotten. He doesn't get to sit quietly and pretend he didn't get me into this.

His eyes turn the yellow-gold of his wolf.

My wolf shrinks. Tries to hide.

His eyes change abruptly back to deep brown, his hands signing quickly. *Sorry. All good. Just happy.*

I don't even know where I learned that last sign. Probably from Robbie. He's happy a lot. I sigh. The moon is calling Hayden's wolf out of him. If anyone should be able to understand that, it's me. I sign back. *Pretty eyes.*

His cheeks turn pink.

Kel snickers quietly beside me.

Troublesome wolf. I start humming along with the guitar players, finding my place. Hoot launches into the melody, which surprises Hayden. She changes up the words, which makes Ravi laugh and guarantees that we'll be doing verse two more than once.

Kelsey stands up so that she can see me, playing her notes without even looking at her fingers. The woven strap that Wrinkles made to hold her guitar does its job, even when she lifts her hands to her mouth to hoot along with the owls.

I should go high with my harmony and leave Hayden more room to wander in the low notes, but that isn't what comes out when I finally begin to sing. My wolf picks a tight and tricky harmony that weaves around the melody, just above and below it.

Ravi's eyes widen.

I tell my wolf to stop being such a show-off, but she's far too caught up in the music to notice. Hayden has joined us, and he's taken her dare, finding the notes that bunch up against mine—snug, resonant harmonies that make the small hairs on my arms stand on end.

My human protests. Too difficult. Too much.

Hayden signs, his eyes shining. *Beautiful.*

Ravi tugs us back around to the beginning of the second verse, and one more time we swing out on the rope, watching the water below us, dizzy and drunk on sunshine and not at all sure how to let go. Kelsey's guitar sings the invitation of the water. *Come on in. Play. Let go.*

I'm not at all sure I'm ready for tonight's metaphorical water, but my notes are moving in lockstep with Hayden and Hoot, and my entire body vibrates with what we have made. We go through the verse once more, and this time, Robbie signs the words, a pup who never did let go of the rope and somehow feels our joy, anyhow.

My wolf sniffles and holds one last pretty, crunchy, complicated note. The next verse is his. Time to let him have it.

18

SHELLEY

The low shelves inside the school taunt my woefully inadequate human eyes in the dark, but I don't dare shift. My wolf would never let me slink out of here with my tail between my legs, even though there are dark claws raking at the feeble bravery that foolishly tried to spill over from a few lines in a song about letting go of a rope.

I rap my shins against one last shelf and then I'm finally at the door, my hands fighting to release me into the night. I close it silently behind me and lean against the outside wall of the schoolhouse, sucking air into my lungs. My heart beats against my chest, a fast, helpless flutter.

Of all the things I hated about life with Samuel, and there were so very many, this feeling is what haunts me most. Helpless. Trapped. Weak.

My arms wrap around my ribs. I stepped into that

cage of my own free will. I thought I could hold on to enough of who I was to make it back out again. I didn't understand what happens when you get into bed with evil.

I tip my head back. The moon is overhead, so close to full that I want to believe it's all the way there, but the tides inside me say differently. I keep my eyes on the night sky, the pinpoint stars. Tiny beacons in the dark that owe allegiance to no tides.

I inhale. Blow the air back out again. It took three years of weak and trapped and helpless for the walls to start stealing my breath.

A breeze moves in the night. I ignore the big, black wolf. He won't bother me, and he won't try to tell me that the monsters are gone. He knows. Footprints sometimes last long after the feet that have made them.

His silent shadow moves away. Tears spill down my cheeks, the ones I've only ever been able to shed when I'm outside and alone.

The red siding of the school presses firm against my back. I swipe at my tears, impatient and sad. I should go. I'll wake up Kelsey standing here sniffling like an idiot. I touch my fingers to the siding and apologize. I laid down inside the walls tonight and tried to let them be my seed, but the dark claws found their way in, too. Doing what claws have always done.

The hardest truth of the garden is that most seeds never bloom.

I push away from the school. My morning tea will come soon enough, and with it, the reminder of just how many blooms are in my garden these days. In the meantime, the cook shack is far enough away that I won't disturb sleeping pups, and we can always use another batch of muffins.

I don't let myself ask what I'll do when the kitchen has walls, too.

RIO

Fuck. I stand still and at attention, caught between a rock and a hard place. Shelley is behind me and Cleve is directly ahead, and both of them are sending out sentinel-repellent signals that I absolutely need to honor.

Which is going to be damn tricky without a set of wings or rock-tunneling gear. I managed to get myself caught on a short stretch of path that's got cliff on one side and Wrinkles's prized thistle patch on the other, and wolves demanding solitude on both ends.

My wolf curls his shoulders in penance. He was admiring the moon. He got distracted. He's sorry.

I sigh. Not his fault. Not really mine, either. This is the kind of shit that sometimes happens when I have a bad habit of creeping around at night and most of the wolves in my pack are processing so much trauma that I don't know how they keep breathing.

Shelley's lungs had nearly stopped by the time her wolf woke her up.

I take another look at the big-ass cliff to my left.

There's no way I'm climbing that as a wolf, and I'm not sure I'd make it up as a naked, shivering human, either.

I guess I'll be staying right here.

I put sentinel energy into the ground. The earth sends crystal-clear messages to my paws in return. Cleve is nervous. Spooked, almost, in a way that I haven't felt since the day he brought Molly down to Dorie's camp. He hasn't got anyone with him this time, though. Just a firm sense that if anyone so much as flickers an eyelash in his direction, he's going to bolt.

Shelley isn't the only wolf fighting demons tonight.

I lie down very slowly. Sometimes the greatest power of a sentinel is to bear silent, helpless witness.

My wolf snarls silently.

I run my brain in reverse, seeking what yanked on his tail.

Ah. *Helpless*. That didn't come from me. It came from her, from him, from all of them. So many of the very worst wounds of this pack run through that single word.

Ground zero of destruction.

The lands where sentinels walk.

It's why we exist.

I let my nose rest on the earth. I was put in this spot for a reason. Time to earn my keep.

SHELLEY

I'll make zucchini muffins, I think. Reilly and Glow shredded a good batch earlier that I was going to leave for Cleve, but he's not here and my hands need useful work to do. Work that doesn't involve making cookies. Some moods can't be sweetened.

I turn on a light over the oven. I wouldn't need even that much, but this kitchen is new, yet. I reach down to the bottom shelf for the enormous bowls that are the closest thing I have to prized possessions. There are three of them, each large enough for a triple batch of muffins.

I only bring one over to the large island where I do my baking. My bowls might be big enough to feed this pack all at once, but our oven isn't. The old one came closer, but it left us years ago, a shady deal in a back alley that took away my beloved cast-iron monstrosity and replaced it with an oven that I'm pretty sure Fallon rescued from the dump. It's ugly and crotchety and prone to inconvenient temper tantrums, but Danielle has always been able to get it running again, even in the worst of times.

Thank goodness. We all knew that Samuel never would have spared the funds to buy another.

I dig out a wooden spoon and shake my head. Samuel wasn't allowed in my kitchen while he was alive, and I'm a fool to invite in memories now that he's dead.

I walk along the shelves that act as our pantry, my hands reaching automatically for containers of the right size and shape. Flour. Sugar. Baking soda. Cinnamon. Salt. I consider two jars of ground nuts and ferry them over to the island, too. Teesha's baby pack sent them already ground, which is a job and a half, and they're best used fresh.

The light of the refrigerator hurts my eyes, but only for a moment. We're running low on eggs. I count. We'll be fine until the cats deliver more. I set the egg pail on the counter and try to remember to save the shells. Reilly wants them for a science experiment.

I grab the shredded zucchini next, and the bottle of olive oil I like best for my muffins. It's got a nice, nutty flavor, and it saves the butter for the cookies. Reese tells me he can get more butter, but I'm not sure where we'd store it, and olive oil sits on my shelf and doesn't cause a snick of trouble.

I open the bottle and give it a good sniff. Always, smells have soothed me.

My wolf shakes her head. She knows I'll be smelling the cinnamon next, and that one makes her nose itch.

I tell her to make sure that it does. Given Braden's tricks, we want to make sure it's cinnamon and not one of Wrinkles's teas.

She eyes me suspiciously. Those make more than her nose itch.

I chuckle as I mix the dry ingredients. Silly wolf.

CLEVE

She has a skill that I need. I study Shelley from the comforting shadows outside the cook shack. Warm floors beckon, but I worry that they make me soft. Winter comes, and the dark fingers that reach for me are worse then. I won't belong anywhere near a pup.

I'm not sure I belong there now.

I settle my wolf. There are no pups in the cook shack tonight, only Shelley and her baking. She was a friend, once, her competent hands welcome in my kitchen and her brisk, steadfast heart welcome in my family. She found her place in our clan within days, in our pack in just a few more. A wolf who came to us wanting to be useful, and who somehow ended up essential, instead.

My wolf quivers. The essential ones lost so much blood when the darkness came.

I swallow and watch Shelley's hands. She was hurt as badly as any of us, and yet she can stand there cracking eggs and stirring in cinnamon and pouring oil.

She has a skill that I need.

I want to know how she does it. How she carries herself into the morning with gladness. How she fights back the dark, grasping fingers when they come for her. How her wolf stands brisk and steadfast, even when she's human.

She begins to hum, a tune that I recognize from earlier. Molly lay with me a while up on the ledge as we listened. She's finding her place at Dorie's camp, but it still overwhelms her to stay human for very long. When she needs her fur again, she comes to find me.

My wolf sighs. She's young. Strong. She needs to play with the others, not lie beside an old man.

I tell him not to worry. She plays, so much more than

he ever would have thought possible. Kennedy makes sure of it, and Stinky, and Hoot.

His claws scrabble in the soft earth. He doesn't want to think of the pups.

I don't either, but it's the homework I've given myself. To practice saying their names. Shelley can say their names, and she can touch them and hold their eyes and teach them the ways of pack. I've seen her do it, and not once has she ever given in to the shredding guilt and anguish that come to find her in the night.

She dies, just as I do—and she lives.

She has a skill that I need.

SHELLEY

I can sense him out there, foolish man. He'd be better off in here, easing his aching hip in a warm corner or helping me mix another batch of muffins. But Cleve Dunn doesn't deal with floors or wooden spoons any better than I deal with walls in the dead of night, and on this one, I don't have the heart to make him try.

I add a little more oil to my bowl and a sprinkle more of cinnamon. It annoys Mikayla when I do that, because it messes with the recipes and she has to write more notes on them in her careful script. I tell her that she'll get a feel for it, soon enough. She tells me that I'm just being kind.

I'm not. This pack considers her honey berry bars a

complete food group. Those are her own invention, though, and that matters. It's always easier to tinker with your own creations than it is to faithfully render someone else's.

My fingers itch for a pencil. That belongs on my list of what needs to go inside our seed.

I snort. It's dark and I'd just scribble a bunch of nonsense that I couldn't read in the morning and give Cleve a heart attack, besides.

I take a sniff of my muffin batter. Good enough. I move the muffin tins into a stream of moonlight over by an opening that was meant to be a window. It's chilly, but the batter won't mind, and with the warm floors under my feet, I don't either.

I spoon the batter into each spot in the muffin tin, resisting the urge to overfill them. They make lovely, puffy, mushroom-shaped muffins when I do, but they also make a mess of my oven, and the wolves who usually assign themselves scrubbing duty have been giving the kitchen a wide berth of late.

They don't want to alarm Cleve.

I shake my head. Kenny and Ebony and Kel could all have good, useful talks with Cleve while they were scrubbing, about guilt and duty and how failure eats at your soul until all that's left is bare fragments and you're more hole than substance. But that's not a conversation any of us want to have. Living with it inside our own heads is bad enough.

My wolf snorts. Humans talk too much.

Sometimes. I keep spooning batter into the muffin

tin. There are other conversations we could have with Cleve. We could tell him that this pack needs a grandfather—that there's a hole he's allowing to exist in the heart of every pup, and in the rest of us, too. That his family needs him, not to be whole, but simply to be present.

I switch out the full muffin tin for an empty one.

I don't feel like the wolf who can have any of those conversations—but maybe I can put them inside a seed.

19

SHELLEY

I round the corner to the shower and nearly mow down Indrani.

She jumps to the side, a wrench in one hand and a length of pipe in the other. "I'm so sorry."

I reach out a hand and pat her shoulder. We're still learning the needs of this new and temporary packmate, but I see Fallon and Martha touch each other's shoulders quite often. "Entirely my fault, sweetheart. I was reviewing the menus for the week in my head and not paying any attention to where I was going." Reviewing menus and yawning. I tried to take a quick nap as the sun rose, but I was thwarted by sentries who smelled fresh muffins.

Indrani makes a wry face. "I do that when I'm trying to remember which wires need to run to the new node on the heat exchanger."

I have no idea what that sentence means, but I'm glad that she does. "If you're hungry after you get that sorted, there's a fresh batch of berry bars." She's got a fondness for them.

She grins. "Awesome. I just fixed the showerhead, so you should be good to go. It's got entirely symmetrical spray now."

Most of us are still trying to come to terms with a shower that actually has hot water, but she's a meticulous, detailed raven, and even if I don't know a thing about nodes and heat exchangers, I'm familiar with the pleasure of getting the little things right. "We need to come up with some jobs to keep you here a while longer. You've got a knack for making things cozy."

She gulps and takes a tighter hold on her tools. "Thank you. I have so much to learn. I got the pipe diameters wrong in my design yesterday. Rio said I would have made a nice geyser instead of a bubbler for the hot pool."

Rio wouldn't have left it at that any more than I'd leave an aspiring cook staring at a cup of sugar and three cracked eggs. "That sounds far less dangerous than what happens in my kitchen most days."

She relaxes and giggles, sounding like the teenager she was not so very long ago. "He said I would have made quite a few friends with that design, but we should tweak it a little so that we get a bubbler most of the time and a geyser when Hayden is sitting in just the right spot."

She speaks as if she'll be here when that happens. I imagine that's exactly what Rio intends. "Don't tell Myrna and Martha where the controls are." Those two might be elders, but I'm pretty sure they invented trouble.

Indrani laughs. "Danielle is building the control panel. I'm just the engineering intern. I can't be trusted with the really hard stuff."

That's clearly not true, but it's a comfort to her to believe it, and Rio is very good at watering seeds exactly when they're ready. "Go get yourself a berry bar. Maybe steal a few for your team, too."

She nods cheerfully. "If you have time, go take a look at what we've done. The boulders are almost all in place. Eliza's getting set to mix more concrete, so watch where you step."

I've got a few minutes before my turn in the shower, and knowing the two in there before me, I might want to arrive a little late. I pat Indrani's shoulder again. Sometimes a nice morning conversation is as refreshing as a nap.

She heads off down the trail. I walk past the entrance to the small grove where our outdoor showers have been set up. There's new gravel on the path and neat edging holding it in place. Brown's work, likely, although Kennedy has been paying a lot of attention to how the pathways of the den are made.

I smile. That's a job that would be a good fit for both her energy and her heart.

I round the corner and find myself face to face with what will eventually be our hot pools. I scan the rock piles and bags of concrete and the big, natural depressions that are slowly being remodeled into the world's biggest bathtubs.

Danielle looks over from the top of the highest pool and waves. "Hey, Shelley. We need someone your size to sit in a few places and tell us if we've contoured everything just right."

There are several shifters my size within calling distance, including the one standing next to her. I raise an eyebrow at Eliza. "Too good for sitting, are you?"

She laughs. "If I sit, I notice every tiny imperfection, and then I want to bring out my rock-sanding tools and fix them. If you sit, we might finish the pools before the babies come."

Our pack life has been divided into two time periods —before the babies and after. Which is so much better than the old dividing line I was using. I make my way over to them carefully, watching out for loose rocks, stray wrenches, and wet concrete. "Where do you need me?"

"Everywhere." Danielle sweeps her hand grandly. "The water will be at about the level of the white chalk line, so find yourself some nice places to sit and we'll see if we need to install stone booster seats."

That makes Eliza snicker for a lot longer than it should.

I eye the expansive pools and chalk lines and try to make sense of things. I got a tour just a couple of days ago, but so much has changed. "You've moved some of the big rocks."

Danielle nods. "We did. Rio thought we might have to wait for Ronan, but Reilly and Indrani figured out how to use some smaller rocks as wheels and we got them situated."

Her pride in her boy beams sunshine bright. "Those two are good for each other."

Eliza snorts. "Don't get her started. Shoo. Into the pools with you. Brown just finished getting the railing installed on the steps, so you shouldn't have any trouble climbing in."

The railing is a thing of beauty, made from curved tree limbs that look almost as if they grew from the rocks themselves. I walk over, my fingers itching to touch. The wood is warm under my hand and the perfect height for walking into the pools. I try to imagine them full of steaming water on a winter's day, instead of strewn with dust and bags of concrete. There will be three levels, with small waterfalls between them. This top pool is the smallest, and Rio says it will have the hottest water.

I can see the full shape of it now that there are several boulders rolled into place where gaps used to be. There are some inside the pools, too—squat, fat ones that look like footstools, and skinny, flat ones that the baby packs have been scrounging from every corner of our territory under Wrinkles's watchful eye. They've been dragging them back here on a fancy cart that Rio rigged with mountain bike tires.

I point to a flat rock on the far side that has been installed at a slant. "That's the one I found near Shady Creek." It's got a jagged line of white running down it, like it caught a bolt of lightning and didn't let it go again.

Eliza chuckles. "Yup. Brown grumbled about dragging it all the way back here, but it's the perfect size for what we needed. Give it a try. The cement should hold."

I don't ask what will happen if it doesn't. There's too much pride in her voice for that to happen. Too much confidence. It's pure joy to hear it there. She was always such an easy target for Eamon and his lieutenants.

I push those thoughts away. They don't belong in the kitchen, and they don't belong here, either. Not yet. Maybe on a dark night once the pools are filled with water and there are no other hearts nearby to poison with my tears.

I take a seat on a rock that's at just the right height for comfortable sitting and lean back against the one I spied over by Shady Creek. They've both got smooth surfaces and curved edges that make them resemble pretty gray cushions. There's a nice place to rest my head, and a small, flat shelf above the white chalk line for a mug of tea.

I look around me in wonder. I can see it. Water up to my chin. Every inch of me warm. A beautiful view stretching as far as my eyes can see.

There's a duo of chuckles behind me. A third, lower voice joins them. "It's good to know who I'm going to have to arm-wrestle for that spot."

I tip up my chin so that I can see my alpha's eyes. "I don't think this is the right size for you."

He grins. "That can be fixed."

Not so easily, but the big muscles in this pack have been lugging around a lot of rocks, and we have a polar bear arriving in a couple of weeks. I hadn't imagined needing his services, but I'm rapidly changing my mind. "I hear that Ronan likes cookies."

He groans. "Don't bribe him, please. We'll never get rid of him."

Eliza grins and bumps against his shoulder. "If we're going to be ready when he gets here, I need three more bags of concrete over by the new boulder in the bottom pool."

He chuckles. "Yes, ma'am. By the round, fat one, right?"

"Yes." Danielle raises an eyebrow. "Without dropping them so close to my pipes this time."

He slings an arm over her shoulders, looking entirely unrepentant. "Sounds complicated. I might need expert guidance."

I stare as the three of them walk off together. At Eliza, the absolute bottom of the adult wolf hierarchy in this pack. At Danielle, the wolf most perpetually unsure of herself. And at the alpha they're both cheerfully bossing around.

My fingers twitch.

I pull the notepad out of my shirt pocket, but that's not what my fingers are wanting this time.

They want a paintbrush.

KEL

I look over at the big hulk beside me. "It feels too easy."

Rio snorts and repositions his hands on the mammoth slab of rock we're holding up. "The hell it does. It feels like trying to move a mountain. One that's digging in its heels."

Smartass. "Quit complaining. Brown and Reilly will be back soon enough."

He grins at me. "No, they won't. There's a new batch of honey berry bars. We're screwed."

I don't ask how he knows. Even in work boots, he picks up all kinds of crap. "Those should be banned when we're moving heavy things."

He smirks. "I hear that betas can issue edicts like that."

Annoying wolf. I lean my shoulder against the rock that doesn't actually need our assistance to stay right where it's at. Probably.

Rio keeps his hands in place. "Why are you worried about Shelley?"

I always worry about all the things. I would anyhow, but it's also conveniently in my job description. "She was having some obvious struggles and then she got quiet and cheerful."

He grins. "You are always suspicious of both of those."

I am when I didn't see any explosions. That means the struggles have gone underground. "Her wolf feels solid, but that's part of the way she hides."

A small shrug and intent eyes. "Maybe."

Rio knows so much about trauma—but he's never walked in its fiercest grip. "I'm fine with her dealing with this in her own time. We can have the pups finger-paint the school wall and everyone will be absolutely fine with that. Except maybe Shelley, and I can't get a good read."

Rio traces a line in the topography of the slab we're holding up. "There's a timing to these things. There's often a stretch where it looks like nothing is happening."

That's an answer even though it didn't sound like one. "You think I shouldn't push."

"I don't know." He shrugs again. "What I do know is that she sees her own trauma as clearly as anyone."

Getting a straight answer from a sentinel is kind of like asking a healer what they put in your tea. "So you think she's just going to walk in there calmly one morning and start painting?"

His lips quirk. "If you believe that, I've got a nice, docile polar bear to sell you."

According to every polar bear I know, Whistler Pack already bought him. I push off the rock. Rio can stand here and hold it if he wants to—I have beta work to do.

He reaches out a hand and stops me. "I know this one cuts close to home for you."

I scowl. Not the answer I was looking for. "We fell into a pack that's like looking into the mirror at my own shit every damn day of the week. I get that. If I'm fucking up, I expect you and Hayden to sit on me until I stop."

He smiles a little. "You'll notice that neither of us are doing that."

I sigh. "Yet."

He raises an eyebrow—the kind that says I need to stop feeling sorry for myself and doubting my instincts, which tend to travel together. "Keep an eye on her during the pack run tonight. Those usually shake a few things loose, and the submissives are planning something."

I'm in on those plans, and so are a couple of wolves who aren't remotely submissive. Which he'll probably figure out the next time he doesn't have work boots and a big-ass rock screwing with his sentinel radar.

He points his chin behind me. "There she goes."

I look over my shoulder at Shelley's retreating back. "It's her turn for the shower."

He nods quietly. "Good. It's time for a little watering."

SHELLEY

I shiver as the warm water hits me. I got impatient—it's not truly hot, yet, and my puny human hairs are entirely inadequate to the job of keeping me warm.

My wolf pants happily. I could shift. She likes the warm rain.

I shake my head. That might be true, but paws are no good at working up a good lather, and she doesn't want to end up smelling like citrus and vanilla.

She gives that idea more consideration than I expect.

The water warms up some more, and I adjust the temperature a stitch. I look up at the fancy shower head that makes it feel like I'm standing in a rainforest. It isn't the sensible one that Danielle bought off the discount table at the hardware store. It's the one Rio and Reilly came home with three days later after a visit with the cats.

Which smells of all kinds of nefariousness, but Reilly looked so proud of himself. And it really is a marvelous shower head.

I turn around, trying to tuck all of me under the hot spray. It's downright cold today without my puffy jacket. Brown offered to build us a windbreak to go around our shower, but so far those votes have all ended up wolves against bears, and I think the only reason that Reilly is voting with Brown is bear solidarity.

I tip my face up, letting the water run down my forehead and cheeks. Much better than the tears of last night.

I stand like that for a long time, soaking in the warmth. I don't need my notepad any longer. My heart is collecting the words.

My wolf eventually nudges me. It's Kelsey's turn in the shower next.

I smile. Most of the pups race in and back out again, half-clean and trailing shampoo bubbles, but Kelsey spends every minute of her allotted time in here. She comes out with raisin fingers and a beaming smile, and she always smells of roses.

I sniff the shampoo I brought in with me, making sure I didn't accidentally pick up her shampoo, or Reilly's that smells like honey, or Ebony's with the avocado on the front of the bottle, or Kel's that seems like it might just be dish soap. They would all happily share, but when I smelled the citrus and vanilla in the store, I had trouble putting it back down again.

It wasn't on the discount table, either.

I sigh and squeeze out a dollop for my hair. Rio is a terrible influence and he somehow almost always goes along on the shopping trips.

The shampoo lathers under my fingers. I stick my head out of the shower spray so that it doesn't get washed away until I've managed to get my hair clean. A chill wind bats playfully against my cheeks, but the rest of me stays toasty and warm. I smile and tip my face up into the warm rain again. Rio thinks we'll eventually give up this shower in favor of one that isn't surrounded by snow.

Silly wolf.

20

HAYDEN

Some pack runs are informal fun, a ragtag band of fur and legs on a playful night ramble through our woods that tires out the pups and nurtures our connections and drives those of us with overprotective wolves a little nuts.

This one is something else. It has a heartbeat.

My wolf circles around to the back of the pack, nudging pups closer to the center and rolling his eyes at the teenagers who are working at cross purposes with his best efforts.

Rio bumps my shoulder. *Leave them.*

I growl. Pups belong in the center.

His answer flows crisp and clear. *Not tonight.*

My wolf jerks his head around, trying to figure out what he needs to bite first. I grab his scruff and remind him of the plan. The one Lissa told me about shortly before we left the den—and she did it with her hands on alpha gravity beams. We want the pups more seen. More visible to the ghost wolves who follow their scent trails in the forest and sleep with pillows and blankets that smell of pack.

My wolf grumbles. He doesn't like this plan. He hates it, in fact.

I try to distract him with the shiny full moon so that he doesn't think too hard about the second part. The pregnant mamas. Cori is with her mate on the far edge of the running wolves, and only the fact that Kel is stalking her got either of us anywhere near to agreeing with this insanity. Fallon is flying, which mollifies my wolf slightly, but he worries that this might be the day she can no longer take to the skies.

Suggesting that nearly lost him an eye, however. Fierce raven.

The big, black wolf of death bumps into my shoulder again.

I growl. It was my green-eyed mate who master-minded this idea, but Rio had her back, which means he's fair game if my teeth and claws decide they need a target.

A herd of teenagers, half in their fur and the other half in sneakers, runs between us, knocking me off my alpha high horse and nearly braining me on a tree for good measure. Kennedy snickers as she swings off a tree limb. "Stop sulking."

My wolf skids to a stop and growls. *Respect, baby alpha.*

Her eyes widen. Then they soften. "I bet this feels a lot harder in your fur, huh?" She bends down and nuzzles her human cheek to mine. "This really smart guy once told me to trust my pack."

She's gone before I can snarl the wolf equivalent of *that guy's a flaming idiot*.

I start running again. I need to pull my shit together. The heartbeat of this night is growing louder, even with teenage hijinks running through it.

I let the forest speak to my paws. The smell of dying summer is faint, giving way to the cold, slow, deep work of winter. Leaves crunch, stirred by the wind of a wolf pack traveling through, and pebbles skitter, the work of a mountain slowly turning to sand.

Instincts buried deep in my wolf rise. Winter is danger. Winter is threat.

The earth speaks. *Not this year*.

I look over at Rio, but it isn't his sentinel messing with the pack airwaves. I shiver. My mother tells stories. I'm not sure I'm ready for casual chats with the forest floor.

My wolf snorts. He is alpha. He will listen.

Right. I roll my eyes and speed up. If I make it to the front, I can circle back at least once before we get to the ridge.

Kel body-slams me hard enough that I nearly get turned into pancake wolf. He docsn't even look back as he angles off toward the run perimeter, but his message is clear. The alpha stays in the middle where he can't cause a ruckus and scare whoever might be creeping closer to howl with the pups.

I growl long and deep at his retreating gray backside. He's supposed to be glued to Cori.

The answering growl isn't from Kel. It's from Bailey. Which means I need to be on my very best behavior, because something in our plan must be working or she'd be out in the far orbits of this run instead of here harassing me.

Fuckballs. I must have been drugged when I agreed to this.

A green-eyed wolf bumps against me far more politely than Kel did, her amusement clear. My head manages to screw itself back on a little. I have absolute faith in Lissa's instincts, even if they're tap-dancing on the grave of mine. I stay at her side, holding tight to the one gravity beam I can lean on without scaring anyone. She's a swift, surefooted reminder that the answer, almost always, is to trust the submissives of my pack and give them more room.

Even if it kills me.

She slows.

We've reached the ridge.

SHELLEY

So much grief. I lean into the wolf beside me. This isn't the ridge where Jason died, but the human keening inside Kenny's wolf doesn't care. He was fine just a moment ago. Now he's a geyser shooting a hot mess of torment into the sky.

Ravi and Eliza find us, gathering around him. They

were pups together. Friends. Whatever came after, we will not let him weep alone.

His wolf resists.

Mine snaps her teeth. He will not do this alone.

The grief pouring out of him blurs, joining with primal instincts that hold tight to the earth and reach up to the moon. More wolves gather around us, some in their fur, some in their winter jackets, some with feathers and cat tails and bear claws.

It matters not. We are wolves.

Kelsey's snout tips up to the moon, and in her first undulating notes, I can hear our wailing. Eliza's grief for the son who won't come home and Kenny's for the one who can't. Pain from the wolves who can't get close enough, but who also can't stay away. Wretched holes where anguish should be inside wolves who are here only as whispered remnants.

Cori shifts and touches her naked belly, tears streaming down her cheeks. Blankets find her, a sweater, wool socks. Ebony, who shares her shoe size, strips down and leaves her boots at Cori's feet before she shifts into her rangy gray wolf.

Hayden and Lissa lean against each other, their alpha strength blazing out into the night.

Rage answers.

Bailey stiffens.

The pack goes utterly silent.

It comes again. Incoherent fury, great jostling waves of it from the far orbits.

Kelsey trembles.

I try to go to her. My wolf holds me in place and tips back her head instead. She knows rage. She can answer what speaks from our far reaches.

My throat closes as the human inside me cowers. No. Please, no.

My wolf's answer is gentle and relentless. *Not that rage, love. This one.* Fury lashes out from somewhere deep inside her—vicious anger, born from cruelty and injustice. She hurls it at the moon, a howl more shriek than song.

Voices join mine. Ugly ones. Rending ones. A cacophony of feral rage and fury and dark, violent grief.

RIO

My wolf braces, trying to hold his ground as the sentinel inside him reacts from pure instinct. There isn't time for anything else. This pack just exploded.

His paws reach deep into the earth.

Not for comfort.

Not for containment.

Not for peace.

For righteous, holy anger.

SHELLEY

There are wolves pressed into my shoulders, their lungs heaving along with mine. Fiercely connected grieving as we take some of what poisoned us and puke it out of our organs and heave it out of our souls.

It won't last much longer. Moments of violence rarely do.

The wolf beside me shudders. Eliza, remembering.

Kennedy wraps ferocious, tender arms around her neck.

Myrna trembles, unable to hold back a whimper. Lissa nuzzles her cheek in the way of a pup who loves the one who has mothered her since the day she was born. Robbie walks over solemnly and stands guard for them both.

Danielle's snout rests on the head of a gangly bear, and Wrinkles does the same on the head of a bear who isn't gangly at all.

A yellow-gold wolf stands shoulder to shoulder with Bailey, facing the far orbits where Ruby lives, the air around them still crackling with the lighting bolts of her rage that set off the storm. Tara is wrapped around Stinky, but her eyes are on her daughter, meeting the rage as she has always done—and this time, Bailey's pack didn't let her do it alone.

Ben and Fallon and Brandy and Hoot grip each other fiercely, completely enfolding a small, red wolf.

I suck in a breath. Release it.

I need to go back. I need to paint.

I don't know where the wall ends—but I know where it begins.

21

SHELLEY

I open my eyes, which are gritty with sleep, and blink at the sunbeam. It must be morning, but I have no idea why I have a pencil in my hand.

Then I remember.

My eyes dart over to the wall. It's still white. Blank. Empty.

That can't be right.

I rub the grit out of my eyes and look again. This time I see the light lines, the rough sketching I do before I begin a mural. A guide, not necessarily for the paint, but for the artist wielding the paintbrush.

I didn't finish. There are barren patches and places where only a line or two suggests what I didn't dare put on the wall in the dark of night.

I push myself up on my elbows, wincing. My left arm is fiercely tired. I don't know when I finally laid down amongst my paints and went to sleep, but it wasn't until hours after we returned.

I gingerly push myself up to sitting. A couple of paintbrushes roll out of the way. I shake my head. So many brushes scattered amongst the small cans of paint— the really good kind that turns a wall into a canvas and a mural into art. It seems like I shouldn't have this many paint cans or brushes, but when I opened the cupboard where the most precious art supplies are stored, this is what emerged.

Many hands helped carry them here.

And then I sent them all away.

I look around, wincing again. I could have waited until morning, let them sleep on warm floors and begun my mad drawings when I had enough light to actually see.

Rio's words emerge from the fog of last night—the ones he spoke quietly from the doorway as I clutched my pencil, wild with the need to draw. My packmates are fine. Some went off to sleep in the kitchen and some found a convenient tent, but most ended up in a big pup pile with Lissa and Hayden.

My wolf nods complacently. They needed their alpha.

Bossy creature.

She nudges my hand toward a paintbrush.

I pick up the pencil, instead. She doesn't get to win all the battles, and I've some detail work to sketch in, yet.

KEL

I tiptoe inside the greenhouse with Rio and Ghost. We carefully keep our backs to the glass that divides us from the school. We won't look, but we have plants to water. Kelsey worries, or she will when she wakes up. Most of the pack is still snoring.

Rio picks up the watering can that's used for the youngest seeds. The rest are watered by the misters overhead unless one of the gardeners stages an intervention. Ghost picks up a second can and heads for a planter with sturdy vertical scaffolding. I have no idea how that's supposed to help us grow more watermelons, but its design involved more research and engineering than most spaceships.

I walk along a different row, touching random patches of dirt with my finger. I'm not in here because I'm a gardener. I'm here because Ebony told me to get my ass over to the greenhouse.

I look over at the guy who I assume sent that order.

Ghost peers at me through an opening in the watermelon scaffolding. It doesn't surprise me that she's awake. Kenny is as well, even if he's trying to pretend that he isn't. Beta wolves might not have sentinel radar, but we know what's coming.

Rio calmly pours water on some seedlings that are barely tall enough to peer over the edge of their planter. "Do you think these need some of that nutrient stuff?"

Ghost walks over and tilts her head in contemplation. "Kelsey's better at figuring that out. Or Shelley."

Tricky wolves aren't made, they're born. I eye her, wondering where she's headed. "Neither of them are here, so take your best guess or Rio will kill the seedlings and Kelsey will cry and then I'll have to kick both of your asses."

Rio chuckles. "That's really helpful, thanks."

Ghost just grins and heads back over to her scaffolding.

I join her. Plants are a mystery, but scaffolding is metal and bolts. I have a decent understanding of both of those. "What are we doing with this?" Other than avoiding the real reason we're in here until the guy with a watering can gets to the point.

She picks up a tape measure, holds it up against a small gap, and squints at the result. "I'm taking the measurements that Indrani wanted for the new rig she's building for the peas and beans. You're standing here looking over my shoulder because you don't know why Rio wanted you in here."

Accurate. I pull up a low stool. "So that you can mess with me, I suspect. He's an asshole like that. Want me to write down the measurements?"

She grins. "Sure. The sat phone is in my back pocket. Just put them in the notes app."

Smartass. "I don't do phones, so either you can talk to the evil spirit voice that possesses the damn thing and have her take notes for you, or I can find paper and a pencil and do this the way that can't get accidentally deleted when Mellie gets the hiccups."

Her lips quirk. "That only happened once, and Reilly

found most of the stuff she trashed. Also, he named the evil spirit voice. If you want to talk to her, her name is Captain Picard."

Of course it is. I sigh and dig around in my pockets for a scrap of paper to save me from Captain Picard. I don't find anything useful, probably because I ended up in Ravi's pants instead of my own. Last night was a little hectic.

I dig out a guitar pick, the very squished remnants of a cookie, and a small rock the color of Jade's eyes. Definitely Ravi's pants.

"Here, catch." Rio tosses me a notepad and a pencil. "Don't screw up the measurements. Indrani is a little obsessed about precision."

I snort. "I wonder who she learned that from."

He eyes me. "Let's see. There's Wrinkles and her ideas about forks and their proper storage, you and your demands that we practice owl hoots until they're good enough to fool actual owls, Shelley's belief that muffins should contain the exact amount of sugar specified in the recipe..."

He's going somewhere with this, but damned if I can see where. "Forks are deadly weapons, and the safety of our pups might ride on the quality of your owl hoots some day." I don't touch the sugar issue. I don't really understand that one, but Shelley is fierce about the proper way to construct a muffin.

He grins and sprinkles water into a new planter. Then he casts a casual look that doesn't quite penetrate the wall of windows into the schoolhouse but comes damn close.

Ghost rolls her eyes. "Sentinels are so subtle."

I snort quietly. Kennedy and Hoot have been doling out some really excellent teenager lessons.

She studies me, a baby beta who doesn't miss much. "I know why he's in here. Why are you still worried about Shelley?"

I wasn't aware that was why Rio was in here. "It's what betas do."

Ghost makes two more measurements and carefully notes them in her phone. "Shelley used to work in the garden all of the time, but she hasn't done anything in the greenhouse. We've invited her to help, even Kelsey, but she's always has something else she needs to do."

I noticed. I also noticed Ghost's gentle, persistent herding. It's been pitch-perfect and it hasn't worked, which means there's something going on that could use the input of a sentinel. I assume that's why we're watering seedlings at the crack of dawn. I sit quietly. Ghost is herding the guy with the watering can just fine.

Rio doesn't look at her. Quite. "You're thinking that Shelley maybe needs a bigger push?"

My wolf cheers when Ghost considers his question carefully. She'll get all the support she needs to become the beta she wants to be, but damn her instincts are solid. She finally shakes her head. "I don't think so. I think it will happen on its own after she paints her mural and whatever else she's doing in there."

Smart, intuitive wolf. "That sounds about right."

Two sets of eyes turn to mine. Which is when I finally know why I'm actually here. It's not to provide reassurance. It's so they can pin my ass to a stool and watch me squirm.

I sigh. "I'm fine." Last night was a riot of shit that I never wanted to hear howling anywhere near my pack, but it happened and we all survived and the furry white pup who slept on my head did a fine job of repairing the shrapnel that hit while I was doing my job.

Ghost tilts her head, studying me.

Fucking beta wolves and their measuring tapes. I let her look. Rio will just sit on me if I don't.

She finally nods. "Do you think Shelley's going to stay in there until she's done?"

Saved by logistics. "What do you think?"

She nods again. "Yeah. Probably. I'll talk to Mikayla about making sure the kitchen is covered."

A beta right down to her purple-and-green sneakers. "We need a better plan for sleeping quarters than last night. We got most of the wolves who landed back at the den situated, but some from the baby packs didn't make it back out to their camps, and I don't think they're going anywhere until she's done."

She considers for a moment. "Hoot will know what to do about that. Tara could use a distraction, too."

Most of the rage that pummeled us last night came from Ruby, but not all. "I'll send her Fallon and Ben." Tara's as cranky as they come, but babies are her kryptonite.

Rio's lips quirk. Beta shenanigans, approved.

He goes back to his watering.

Pain-in-the-ass sentinel. Unfortunately, he's also right. I wait until Ghost's eyes lift to mine. There's a really important mission reg that most betas ignore, and he's making me check in with her so that I don't forget it. Always apply your own oxygen mask first. "How's your wolf?"

She smiles a little. "Fine."

Rio nods almost imperceptibly behind her. Truth.

I frown as the dots suddenly line up. It took me way longer than it should have, but I finally know who issued the order that got me in here. I stand up and look her in the eyes. "Can I stop pretending that I'm helping to water the flowers, now?"

She grins. Permission granted.

RIO

I walk a little further along the row, adding water to seedlings that probably don't need it. Ghost trailed out after Kel, leaving my bare feet to do their thing in silence. It's not all that easy. The messages coming from the schoolhouse are muted. Quiet. And the ones coming from outside are jittery and loud.

The pack is waking up.

I sigh and gently touch a sprouted seedling that's barely more than a stem. Last night gave voice to the unspoken, and that never greets the light of a new day without some adjustments. Which this pack will make, because that's who we are and who we intend to be, and that groundwork was laid long before I arrived. But it isn't going to be easy.

My toes scrunch, logging their complaints. The warm concrete floor might be practical for gardening, but it isn't all that great for sentinel eavesdropping.

The tiny green shoots that I'm watering laugh quietly.

I roll my eyes. This is hard enough without adding talkative plants to the mix.

They don't say anything else, which is a relief to my wolf. He likes the greenhouse. It's strangely configured, but it's warm and smells of happiness and pack.

My sentinel cocks his head, intrigued by what my wolf sees and what he misses. To sentinel eyes, this is a space for composting trauma and harvesting beauty and standing in the very brightest sunlight while water mists your face.

One of the worries niggling at me settles. That's why Shelley hasn't come in here yet. She's gathering up her trauma, her beauty, and her light. She needs them for her work.

My wolf dissents. Loudly.

I pat his head. He hates this part. In the language of Shelley Martins, there's the busy beginnings when the seed is planted. Then the watering, which starts off looking like nothing is happening and builds into the increasingly uncomfortable pressure of contents squished into a container they no longer fit. Which any self-respecting wolf wants to help along with a well-placed claw, but that isn't his job. Last night poured a volcano of rage and grief into our seed, and I need to let myself be squished and wildly uncomfortable.

We all do. Especially the artist in the room on the other side of the glass wall. Gardeners stand outside of the seed and pour the water, but art doesn't work that way. Artists have to be what they paint, just like sentinels have to be the wounded heart that they seek to heal. I don't know how to reconcile that with the quiet, muted messages passing into my toes from the floor, but I don't have any doubt about what's happening inside our school.

I've always known what it would mean when Shelley picked up her paintbrush. I just didn't expect to be crowded inside a seed while it happened.

22

HAYDEN

Thank fuck. I take the coffee from Lissa with whimpering gratitude. We still don't have a good way to make it in bulk, and a whole lot of wolves needed caffeine this morning.

She gives me a quick snuggle as she steals a sip. "Are you heading out to check on Bailey?"

If I don't go, my green-eyed wolf will, and I can literally feel the ghost claws and teeth in the morning wind. I take a big glug of coffee, even though it's still way too hot to drink that way. "Yes. What do I need to know about Ruby?" I only have whispers. The alpha wolf who mated into the Dunn clan and felt her mate die as she raced to save her pup.

Lissa shakes her head sadly. "She's not who she was. I don't know if anything that I remember matters."

That's been the answer from everyone I've managed

to corner since last night. Which eviscerates my wolf. He refuses to believe that Ruby Dunn is nothing more than a rage-filled husk with violent teeth and claws who can't even remember her own pups. He wants desperately to reject that such a possibility exists.

Except I remember the day my mother stood on the brink of that very same hell. She didn't quite fall in—but it took a whole pack to save her. Ruby didn't have that. Too many of them were breaking at the same time.

It takes a moment to register Lissa's fingers, gently tracing the lines of my face as she looks up at me with steadfast gentleness. "It doesn't have to be you who goes out there."

She knows. There's no way that she doesn't. But I would go even if I didn't owe the universe an absolutely unrepayable debt. "I need to go, and you need to stay here. In case any of the others need their alpha." So many did, in the night—and more of them sought out her wolf than mine.

She nods. "Kenny's going to watch Robbie."

Poor pup. His baby-alpha instincts are going haywire, which involved a lot of sharp teeth before Ebony got to him this morning. He needs a dominant babysitter, and Kenny is good with him. "Is your wolf okay with that?" There's so much history we're still working through. I'll find another way if it's going to hurt Lissa to invest that kind of trust in a guy who was on the asshole side of the fence not that long ago.

She manages a smile. "My son bit him twice over breakfast. He was wonderful. He growled just enough to help Robbie's wolf remember his manners, and then he cuddled him."

At some point, when the chaos settles, I need to have a chat with a wolf who still thinks he's a fuck-up. "If that changes when I leave, you tell Kel. He'll figure something out." Tara could handle Robbie, maybe. Or Dorie. Although they have their hands full at the moment, too.

Lissa pats my cheek. "Drink your coffee and go. We've got this."

I drink and refrain from mentioning that Brown could probably also handle Robbie. Or Kennedy once she gets back from Dorie's camp. Her wolf is going a little nuts, too, but I only know that because I saw her wake up. She slammed down titanium walls of control less than a heartbeat after her eyes opened.

That's not a permanent fix, but the whole point of that kind of discipline is a day like this one. It also means we'll be sending her out on the one job that might be even more delicate than mine. Running the territory with Rio, looking for furry explosives. He wasn't out there defusing them last night, and he didn't let me go, either, which tells me just how much Lissa is going to be holding in her hands.

So much rage hit the den wolves. And so much rage inside them answered.

My wolf tries to bite my coffee mug.

I sigh. His two most primal urges are currently at war with each other, and he doesn't know the half of it. He's reading the wolves of his pack, not our humans. He's barely registering that the woman who chose to stand at the center of the storm last night is in our schoolhouse wielding a paintbrush.

He ignores me. Brushes with funny fur on the end are not a threat.

I'll just let him keep believing that.

I finish my coffee. It's going to be a long, scary, really important day. Or several of them. Rio doesn't think this storm is going anywhere until the woman with the paint-brush finishes.

KEL

I swing up onto a ledge that isn't anywhere a pup should be and crouch down. Dorie watches from a short distance away, her face lined with worry. I eye the pup wedged in between two rocks. Mellie's eyes look bright enough.

She snarls at me, which explains why she's still stuck between two rocks.

I snarl back companionably.

Dorie eases closer. I wave her back. It's not the rocks that have Mellie riled, it's the storm of dominant rage that hit last night. For the first time in her short life, our fear-less dominant pup is a little afraid of what lives inside her. When Robbie growled from the other end of a sock after breakfast, her wolf skedaddled.

Unfortunately, somewhere in the skedaddling, she forgot that she isn't a hawk. This ledge was a challenge for Dorie. I needed a rope.

I reach out my hands, holding Mellie's eyes with enough sternness that she doesn't try to nip my fingers. If I had more time I'd let her snarl at me for a while before I extracted her, but I need to get back to the den. She isn't the only wolf struggling to keep it together—she's just a more reckless climber than most.

I get a hand on her scruff, which goes a long way to reminding her that she's a pup. "How's your baby pack doing?"

It takes Dorie a moment to realize that the question inside my soothing tones is aimed at her. "Fine. We've done this before."

That's a lot different than being fine, and I need her to keep talking to me so that Mellie relaxes her muscles and we don't leave a bunch of fur behind on the rocks that have her pinned. "Care to give me some details? We've got a little time."

Cat eyes squint at me, and then they put the pieces together. "Plenty of disturbed sleep, but we've been handing out tea and making sure everyone stays buddied up."

She's matching her tone to mine. Smart kitty. She's taken in strays with backgrounds that likely included plenty of sleep disturbances. "We appreciate the help you sent this morning."

She pauses a beat longer than I expect. "How's Myrna?"

Wrecked. Her youngest son picked today to check in, which almost certainly isn't accidental and says volumes about his lingering pack sense. It also touched down a cyclone of Xander learning that the asshole who broke his brother is dead and Myrna getting the details on everything from the health and welfare of her boys to a recipe for spicy Andean chili. "There's been a lot of yelling and cursing and some tears. Lissa's on it."

"Good. That's good." Dorie's hands twist together in her lap.

Fuck. Rio says this is the inside of a seed and it's not supposed to be comfortable and we're supposed to keep everyone safe and not try to fix too much, but that's easy for him to say. He's off running around in the woods. I'm watching the women who hold this den together tremble.

I do a quick assessment. Mellie's muscles are relaxing under my hands. She'll be unstuck shortly, and she'll think that monkeying down a cliff is fun. I nod my head at the only way off the ledge. "Go. I've got the munchkin."

Dorie's hands stop twisting.

I'm not an entirely dumb beta. She needs a reason to leave, or maybe more than one of them. "Check in on Myrna and poke your head in the kitchen while you're down there. Reilly is in charge of lunch."

Her eyes soften. "He'll be fine."

It's a really good thing that she isn't my first cat rodeo. "You don't know who's helping him."

She shakes her head, but I've managed to amuse her. "You're good here?"

I nod at the pup who isn't quite free from her predicament, but will be shortly. "So long as you don't steal my rope on your way down."

She mutters something about insults and wolves with mush for brains, but the words come from an increasing distance. One cat off to hug a friend and do battle with whatever minor disasters she finds along the way.

Unless the den has calmed down a whole lot, she'll be able to take her pick. Ghost and Ebony and Kenny were all busy triaging when I left, and Kenny was doing it with Robbie's teeth in his leg. I look down at Mellie. "Can you squirm out, kiddo?"

She gives me the standard look of toddler dominants presented with a challenge.

I let her wriggle, and chuckle as I figure out which part of her got stuck. Somebody had too many hot dogs for breakfast. I apply judicious pressure and consider myself lucky when it doesn't result in me wearing those hot dogs.

Mellie pants a few times to make sure all of her made it out. Then she turns around and growls at the rocks.

I hide a grin. "Let's get back to the den, tough girl."

She shoots me an almost-cautious look that says she maybe remembers some of what awaits her there.

Smart pup. I pick her up and tuck her inside the front of my rope harness. "You stay put there while I climb down. Robbie's probably wondering where you ended up."

Her ears orient toward my words, a pup not at all concerned that we're about to rappel down a cliff.

I step off and take a couple of test bounces with my feet against the rock, using the guide rope I placed on the way up and keeping sharp eyes on a pup who has a whole bunch of primal instincts that might not be overly excited about this new development.

She cranes her head to peer at the ground below.

I snort. Hawk rides have clearly taught her primal instincts a few tricks. I speed up my descent. I really do need to get back. On top of everything else, the idiot dominants in town are riled, and I sadly don't have time to go kick their asses. I know a cat alpha who might like that job, though. Or some hawks. Kendra hasn't had a good chance to be scary in weeks.

I also need to call a polar bear. If the dominants in Ivan's territory have any pack sense left, their parole officer deserves a warning.

Or I could just let him eat a wolf or two.

BAILEY

Of course he came. Arrogant wolf. I sigh as Hayden strolls out of the trees with a rucksack slung over his shoulder. "Let me guess. You got lost."

His lips quirk. "Not today."

I growl as my wolf takes her first real breath since the sun came up. I hate it when he feels like a warm, comforting hug even when he's staying a respectful distance away from my teeth. "I've got this. All hell must be breaking loose at the den, so get your ass back there."

He raises a silent eyebrow.

My wolf doesn't do a damn thing, traitorous beast.

I sigh. When Ruby's shit hit the fan last night, I wasn't ready. I got knocked on my ass, or I would have, except a massive yellow-gold wolf got to my side first. Apparently that's going to make him hard to bite for a while.

He turns his head and looks out at the same horizon I've been staring at for hours. "How is she?"

Ruby hasn't exactly been a secret, not since Kennedy put her up on the freaking pack whiteboard, but she isn't someone we talk about except in whispers. Until she made a choice last night. One that means she felt safer than I've ever been able to make her feel—and one that means I have an alpha asking me questions that I didn't ever want to answer. "Dangerous. Always."

A long silence. "Yeah. I got that."

She bled off enough of it last night that we probably have a few days. "She's still asleep, I think. I'll know more when she wakes up."

He nods and leans against a tree. A man who plans to wait—and a casual, silent dare.

I don't resist for long. My weaknesses are the same as they were when three-year-old Lissa decided that I was going to be her friend. "How's Hoot?" She jumped in front of Kelsey faster than I did. Mostly because I nearly plowed into Fallon, who was coming in for a landing before Ben entirely lost it, but still.

Hayden's eyes follow a wild hawk wheeling in the sky. "She sent a message. She intends to fully kick your butt at charades tonight, and if you don't show up, she'll put the last photo Reilly took of you up on ShifterNet."

I try not to react, I really do. Sadly, it's an excellent threat.

He glances at me, his eyes glinting with amusement. "It must be really bad."

It makes me look about as tough as a banana muffin —and happy about it. "I'll show up. If I can." It depends on whether Ruby needs a fight and how much damage her claws manage to land if she does. I heal a lot faster these days than I used to, which has a lot to do with the guy leaning against a tree and what he's brought to this pack.

I won't really know until she wakes up.

My wolf sniffs at the horizon again. She's uneasy. The sun has been up for hours. Ruby rarely sleeps this long.

"What's your plan?"

The words are mild. Soft. They don't fool me at all. I also don't answer them. I'll do what I have to do. What I've been getting ready to do since the sun came up. What I've done hundreds of times in the last six years.

His hand squeezes my shoulder. "You'll fight. To help give her an outlet for the rage."

I don't want to say a word, but I have to, because Ruby's rage has never belonged to her alone. "I'll try to hold off at least a day or two. Sometimes she cools down again."

A slow exhale. "Sometimes she doesn't."

That's why I'm out here. I slide out from under his hand. Comfort isn't going to help anything. "If it gets that far, some of the others will feel it. When Ruby fights, she doesn't just want to hurt me. She wants to hurt herself, too. That transmits to some of the others."

His entire body slams into hunter mode. "Who?"

He hasn't got enough bodies to fix this. "Hoot, although she's figured out how to block it some. Cleve. Grady. Ben."

His eyes narrow. "Not Kelsey?"

My wolf shivers under his gaze. Alpha. "No. Rennie blocks it from getting to her." I swallow. I thought I wasn't going to answer those eyes. I was wrong. "She absorbs it into herself."

I see the horror hit him. And the fury. And the aching, devastated pride in a packmate's sacrifice. "She protects her daughter."

I use my claws fast before I lose my courage. "She does it by hurting herself."

He hisses in a sharp breath—and by the time he's done, the hunter is stalking.

My wolf sits up, alarmed.

"You fight Ruby so that she doesn't kill herself." He spins away from me to the horizon, his words calm, quiet obsidian. "You fight her just enough to give her what she needs to stay alive, and you let her tear you up so that it's over more quickly and Rennie can stop making herself bleed."

I have no idea how he knows all of that. I nod, very slowly, never taking my gaze off the hunter. "Yeah."

He turns back to face me, and his eyes have gone entirely wolf. Not angry wolf, although he's furious, and not hurt wolf, even though I can see him bleeding. Resolute, unbending, unyielding wolf. Alpha. "That ends now."

I shake my head, hating every word I'm about to say and what it will kill inside of him. "There's no other way. She won't let you get anywhere near her, and if you somehow manage it, she wouldn't let you lose. You're alpha. It would be a leadership challenge."

I hope he can follow that to its unthinkable end.

His eyes return abruptly to their usual warm brown. "Oh, you can keep fighting her. Or maybe Kennedy or Kenny, if you want a break. The part we need to fix is letting it fuck with everyone else."

I blink at him. "Did you hit a tree on your way here? One full of delusional magic wands?"

He grins. "That's a good one. It will make Rio really cranky."

I snarl, which is the one and only warning he's getting. "Make. Sense."

He looks at me, his eyes solemn and steady and clear. "Sentinels can move gravity beams, Bailey. For a little while, or forever."

My throat closes. Ruby might be dangerous, but when she mated with Cody, she became my sister. "You can't. She'll die."

"Easy." He lifts his hands, palms facing me. "We don't let anyone die around here. We talk it through. After we've done that, if you don't think sentinel woo will work, we find a new plan. I'm not overruling you on the details. I'm overruling you on the outcome. You don't get to keep bleeding so that the rest of your family doesn't. Especially if it's not actually working."

The lashes burn right through my skin.

His entire body winces. "Fuck. That's not what I meant. You kept them all alive, and you deserve a medal for that. A whole trunk full of them."

The words seek their alpha, even as I desperately try to claw them back. "I don't want medals. I want them to remember my name."

His arms wrap around me, fierce and tight and real. "Then we work on that. All of us. Rio's magic wands give us choices. Help me figure out how to use them."

FALLON

I drop down closer to the trees. I'm trying to be careful because Ben will kill me if I'm not, and he has two spies on my tail who will report back to him. But Grady is always really hard to spot, and if that shadow is him, I need to know.

A second raven dives at my side, making it look easy.

She hasn't got a peach-pit-sized passenger riding in her belly. I can't really feel the baby yet when I'm human, but it messes with my flying. Especially when I'm being stupid. I angle out of the dive so that I don't smack into a tree. Whatever the shadow was, it's gone.

A third raven joins us. Martha looks perfectly calm, like

we're out for some kind of sedate flight on a warm summer's day. She circles gracefully, doing something fancy with her wingtips that I can't even begin to copy. She's been teaching me some tricks, but that one must be in the advanced manual.

I skim the trees, following the stream below us and considering where to look next. Grady is the last of the ghosts we're supposed to track down. Rennie was easy, although the way she was pacing in front of her cave worried me enough that I flew back to the den to report it. Kel just fed me a cookie and sent me on my way, so I presume he's on top of it. I can't help much there, anyhow—Rennie never lets me get anywhere near her.

I break off from the stream and climb, gathering altitude on the mountain's updrafts. It's worth checking the ridges. Grady doesn't usually leave the trees, but last night shook up a lot of things.

A raven cry breaks the silence.

Indrani is already halfway to Martha by the time I get turned around. Freaking peach pit. I join the two of them as they spiral, peering into the dense forest below us, trying to get a glimpse of Hoot's twin. Indrani dips down, playing chicken with the trees. Martha moves to block me when I try to join her.

After this baby is born, I'm going on the most reckless flight ever.

My bird makes chittering sounds inside my head.

I don't ask her what they mean. I'm pretty sure I don't want to know.

Something strangely pale flashes in the trees.

My eyes widen. No way. No freaking way. I fly closer

to Martha, trying to nudge her away. She doesn't speak wolf, and I have no idea how to herd a raven, but hopefully she'll get the message.

Indrani flies up from the trees, looking panicked.

I make shooing motions with my wings, which isn't in the flight manual either.

Indrani instantly arrows away, Martha following her more sedately. I watch as the two of them become dots in the distance. Then I aim straight for the trees. I pick one that's old and dead and lightning-struck, which means I have a fairly clear flight path in to a branch fat enough that even a pregnant raven can probably stick the landing.

Unfortunately, when I get there, it's obvious that the branch is still way too high to get a good look at what I need to see. I hop around like an idiot, and then I consider shifting, which is an even dumber idea. The branch isn't that wide, and it doesn't have any nearby friends.

I crank my wings into gear again, aiming for a different landing that probably won't go over well at the campfire. It's worth it, though. When I turn around, blinking to adjust for the sudden shadows, I can see exactly what I came to see.

Grady Dunn, human for the first time in six years—staring right at me and saying something I can't quite hear.

I hop, trying to ease closer in the entirely ungainly way of a raven who isn't using her wings. He jumps to his feet, pacing in random directions, his arms gesticulating wildly as he screeches what might be owl hoots into the hushed silence.

He looks like the dictionary definition of crazy, and I have no idea what to do. I only know that he's Hoot's brother and Ben's nephew and kin to the peach pit in my belly, and if there is anything in my power that will help him in any way, I'll do it.

More cries into the silence. Definitely owl hoots this time. None of them mean anything to my ears, but I put every bit of my raven's ferocious memory into remembering them. Whether there's a message in there for Hoot or not, she'll want to hear them.

He slows, staring at the ground. Watching his feet. Less owl hoots, more murmuring. He circles, his fingers tugging on his hair trying to soothe his wolf, but he doesn't shift back into his fur.

My raven leans. Listens.

He comes closer, nearer to my tree. I hear a word. Two words. Another.

My heart catches.

He's not talking.

In his harsh, guttural, unused voice—he's singing.

A song about letting go of a rope.

23

RIO

My wolf peers up at the stars. The moon is at his back, hidden behind a rocky crag, but it isn't what calls him tonight. Here, in this place of wind and vast dark skies, he seeks to slow down. To process. To feel.

I smile. Those are human words for his need to be what he has always been—the bridge between man and sentinel. The man would appreciate the stars and be shivering in his boots. Winter comes to the high mountains, and he knows he doesn't belong in its fierce winds. The sentinel was born for fierce winds, although not usually the kind that come with the turn of the seasons.

The wolf can be either, and he can be both.

I set my nose down on my paws. It's been a long day, for man and wolf and sentinel all. I spent most of it in the forest, running alongside a baby alpha's endless energy, and my legs are tired. The rest of me still has ground to travel.

I fill my lungs with the smell of barren rocks and coming winter. Rennie chooses to live up here, away from the trees that shelter most of the ghost wolves, away from a cacophony of scents that might cover the smell of her blood.

I've known shifters who harm themselves. I've walked beside them until they could breathe again, or until the harm became absolute.

The day is coming when it will be time to do that again.

Air puffs out of my nose and is whisked away by the mountain wind. There are places with more shelter. Perhaps I will seek one out in a while. For now I need the sky and the space that called tired wolf legs up this mountain.

Kennedy wasn't even breathing hard when she peeled off to head back home.

Neither was Kel when he found me later.

I contemplate his messages. A lesser beta would have told me that our pack is fraying, in danger of ripping at the seams. He just filled me in on the day's happenings and asked if it was time to start fixing things yet.

He didn't love my answer. Betas never do.

I sigh. I don't love it either, but we water a garden of complicated and holy seeds, ones strong enough for Ruby's rage and sacred enough for Grady Dunn to sing a song under a tree to the tiny unborn raven who shares his blood.

Kel told me about Grady in a few short words.

They didn't say nearly as much as the tears in his eyes.

Seeds inside seeds, and I am in so very many of them —waiting, cramped and uncertain, just like the rest of my pack. Waiting for each other and waiting for ourselves and waiting for what comes from the woman wielding a paintbrush, because we howled at the moon and put the next page of our story in Shelley Martins's hands.

I look up at the stars and listen to the paws of the wolves making their way up a cold and windy mountain on a dark night.

Some of us are not waiting quietly.

HAYDEN

He knows we're here. He always does.

Rio looms in the darkness as we finally reach the windswept side of a mountain where he decided to freeze his ass off. His eyes watch as the line of wolves behind me spreads out. Ebony. Kennedy. Dorie. Cheri, who was hell to find. Brandy. Katrina. Bailey.

All female. All dominant.

His head swings toward the den.

I wait. His paws will know the truth soon enough. The pups are safe. Kel and Kenny and a bunch of very intent sentries have a perimeter locked down, Reese is watching the male dominants in town, and anyone who gets through all of that is going to meet up with the business end of Myrna's frying pan.

My wolf stands tall. Proud. So much strength, even as we shake. Enough to bring seven wolves up a mountain to see if a sentinel can wave a magic wand.

I don't tell him what we need. He'll work that out, too.

Bailey steps forward. Saying nothing—but finally, also hiding nothing.

Rio jolts, his eyes riveted to hers. Then he turns his face into the wind and stares at the stars, unblinking, while horror writhes in his belly. He didn't know all of why Rennie was suffering.

I hold steady. That's why we're here.

The six others who followed me up the mountain close in. They didn't hesitate when I asked, not a single one of them. They asked smart questions about their own anxieties and trauma and responsibilities to protect pack, but there was no wavering.

Rio scans their eyes, disbelief written in every line of his wolf as what lives inside him hears the plan. Hears their intention. Hears their fierce, implacable gladness to serve in this way. Deeply willing teeth and claws, even if what will be asked of them this night involves neither. They trust, they love—and they absolutely want this fight.

I wait for the inevitable.

The growl that comes out of Rio shakes the whole mountain.

Seven female dominants stare him down.

My wolf keeps standing tall and proud. It's all I've got. I can't do a fucking thing to fix this. I'm just the messenger, the guy who had the big, bold, audacious idea that will put everyone else in harm's way and leave me standing pretty on a dark and blustery rock.

Which seems like exactly the kind of shit that happens inside a seed.

Rio turns his head just enough that I can see the glint of amusement in his eyes—and the uncertainty. He's not sure he can pull this off.

I put the answer into my paws. He was the one who pulled hardest when my mother crouched on the edge of the abyss.

RIO

Damn him.

He's flaming nuts and I should take us all back down to the den and pour some hot tea and calmly explain to seven women that Hayden Scott has lost all of his marbles and they aren't coming back.

Rage isn't like chocolate. You can't just redistribute it.

Except I can hear his conviction and feel his absolute trust. They're blasting right into my center, and I want so very much to match the faith of an eight-year-old boy who felt his mother's soul go up in flames—and the heroics of those of us who managed to get our hands on a fire hose.

He doesn't know that what we did was impossible.

More from Hayden's paws. He isn't an eight-year-old boy any longer. He is alpha.

He is, and his faith matters, and so do the strength and love that followed him up here—and I have no idea if it will be enough. I turn away from the stars that don't have the answers I seek and look at the wolves who are calmly watching their sentinel shake.

If we do this, it's absolutely going to suck.

Seven sets of eyes tell me just where I can stuff that problem.

There are other ones. Brandy's anxiety and Ebony's duties and Cheri's wanderlust. But that's the bold, insane beauty of Hayden's plan. With seven wolves volunteering to be a power grid for rage, I can route whatever Ruby puts out. If someone's having a bad day or teaching a class or holding a tiny baby raven, it can be shunted to the others.

That part doesn't worry me. Sentinels like five-dimensional chess.

The tricky part, the absolutely crackpot part, is getting seven wolves through the eye of an invisible needle and onto the chessboard in the first place.

What Hayden is asking me to build might be possible. I might have the skill, and they might have the willpower and the discipline and the unwavering commitment. But even if all of that fell into line, I couldn't do it without Ruby's consent—and I don't know if enough of her exists inside or outside of the rage to give it.

Something in Hayden eases, replaced by steady confidence. *She is alpha.*

My wolf stills. Considers. Much of Ruby Dunn is beyond my reach, but she attacks only Bailey. Which is a choice. Maybe enough remains. Not enough to choose for herself—but perhaps enough to choose for pack. If she can see the choice.

An unwavering response from a yellow-gold wolf. *My mother did.*

Fuck. Seeds inside seeds.

The eyes of an eight-year-old beg for water.

The eyes of an alpha offer it.

I turn to the seven who wait, the seven imperfect dominants who would do this with one very imperfect sentinel as their guide.

Something inside me stirs. A deeply non-rational sense of alignment. Of rightness. Of fate. Every last one of them carries the vicious trauma of their failure to protect and shield—and Hayden found them a battle they can win. That *only* they can win. Ruby would never allow a male dominant this trust, and these aren't just any women.

These are the old cat who once found her in the cheese aisle of the grocery store and told her about a guy having a burger at a diner down the road who she needed to meet. The sister and cousin she gained when that guy became her mate. The visiting soldier who was once her best friend. The scrappy stray, baby alpha, and fiercely independent daughter of a bear who were her kindred spirits.

Fierce female energy rising up to meet fierce female rage. Not to calm Ruby or restrain her or disarm her. On that, the teeth and claws on this mountain are absolutely clear. We honor her rage and support her where she is and we don't let it keep hurting our pack.

I reach into the earth for a sentinel's tools. Then I gather the strength of seven women and their pain and reach for a heart steeped in rage.

24

SHELLEY

I need tea. And food.

Perhaps some has been left on the porch.

My hands keep moving, wielding the big brushes that are adding shadows to the mountain, layering translucent darkness in amongst the trees.

It's dark outside, too. I should stop, but I can't. I have all of Rio's bright lights, and I use them deep into the night. I can't stop even when I should. I nap, I eat the food left for me on the porch, I talk to the moon. I've possibly gone crazy.

My brushes pause.

The shadows are enough.

It is time for what I have put off too long.

I swallow. The mural is done, except for the center of the wall. I doubted what was meant to go there, questioned it, but the knowing inside me hasn't wavered. Not in days and days of painting, not in a single snatch of sleep or a rambling rant as I blended colors with my tears.

I haven't cried for at least a day.

No more watering. It's time for truth.

Walls have the meaning I give them.

I set down my brushes and walk to the door. A brief walk under the moon, a mug of tea, a meal before my stomach abandons me for a more hospitable host—and I need a raven to steal me something.

Then I will finish.

25

HAYDEN

I manage to catch Braden's hand before he accidentally discovers the fine art of flinging oatmeal with a spoon. That's what pinecones are for. Oatmeal chock full of cream and baked apples and cinnamon deserves to find hungry bellies, and mine still thinks it belongs in that camp.

I lick off his spoon and give it back to him. "Yours tastes way better than mine."

He shoots me the look of a pup who has learned to be skeptical about his alpha's more outlandish claims, and scoops up another spoonful, mostly managing to get this one within reach of his own tongue. Neither of us is very good at being neat, but we're trying. The knitted blanket we're wrapped in is tricky to get clean in the pack's sad excuse for a washing machine. It will be my great pleasure to make sure it dies in a fire as soon as the swanky replacements from my sister arrive.

Braden squirms, his wolf clearly done with oatmeal and snuggles under a warm blanket. He might not need either, since he slept in the cook shack, but I surely did. Last night was cold, and I foolishly fell asleep in my sleeping bag instead of my fur.

My wolf complained loudly this morning.

As he should have. The sleeping bag was meant to have Lissa in it, but she stayed up at Dorie's camp sorting out the new chaos that showed up as the sun went down. Something about biology homework, I think.

It's been a hell of a week. Seven female dominants are learning to balance the new load they took on up on a windy mountain, and the rest of us are overreacting to everything from school lessons and cold nights to the regular kitchen malfunctions that happen when people like me get left on breakfast duty.

I look over at Kel, who refuses to look ragged, and Ghost, who is starting to look a little frayed around the edges. Beta-wolf baptism by fire. She's been incredible. She also needs to take a break. Shelley might be doing her wild-painter routine for another week. Muriel was decidedly unhelpful on when all of this might end. Something pithy about art not being beholden to schedules.

She didn't have to eat any of the breakfasts I cooked.

I set my oatmeal down. I'll go see if I can find a bear cub and talk him into starting a sword fight or something to let Ghost be a teenager for a while. That's my plan until I feel the gravity of my pack tug sharply right, anyhow.

I turn around just in time to see Shelley emerge from the schoolhouse. She walks slowly out onto the deck, blinking like she hasn't seen the sun in weeks and clutching the door handle like her legs aren't precisely sure how to hold her up. Her hair is doing a really excellent impression of a mad scientist and only one of her arms managed to find its way into her flannel shirt.

My wolf stares, and he's not looking at her hair.

For the first time since I've known her, Shelley is so exhausted that she has no filters left, no way to hide behind her brisk, comforting, common-sense exterior. We can see every single thing she's feeling.

Pride and terror.

Satisfaction and uncertainty.

Slowly, awkwardly unfurling joy.

She's absolutely enchanting.

SHELLEY

They're all here.

I don't know where I expected them to be. It's morning and the sun is up and this is when our pack eats breakfast, and I'm somehow still surprised to see them all looking at me with their spoons halfway to their mouths.

My wolf, who has managed to bring me so very far, lies down, tucks her head under her paws, and whimpers.

Something insides me careens wildly.

I clear my throat. I prepared this part. Words that must be said, and I mean them. They're the ones that came to me as I stared at an old photograph for far too long. The words that finally set my paintbrush free. "Some of you saw the mural I had planned. I didn't do that one. I did a different one, and I can paint this one over if it's not right. I had to paint it, but maybe it was just for me, or maybe it was for everyone to see once and then we change it."

Confused eyes. Rebellious ones.

I'm not making any sense. I don't even know if I'm speaking in actual words. I wave a hand at the door. They need to see it. If it's wrong, I can say my piece again. "I tried to put the curtain up like before, but I'm not too steady on my feet and it tried to eat me. So close your eyes on the way in, or look at the floor."

I close my eyes and hold on to the door handle.

Strong, sturdy arms and small, fierce ones wrap around me. Collecting me up. Herding me back inside. There are footsteps. Milling wolves. Owl hoots to page the packmates up at Dorie's camp and the ones in the trees.

I stand where I've been put.

A furry nose nudges my hand, and a hot mug of tea gets held to my lips. "When is the last time you ate, woman?"

I blink my eyes open. Brown isn't usually the one doctoring patients.

He scowls. "Drink."

I don't argue. That would require words, energy, thought.

I drink and I wait.

KEL

Rio and Hayden give me regular shit for seeing too much of war in civilian life—but as I look at Shelley Martins, utterly exhausted and covered in splatters of paint, all I can think is that I'm looking at a soldier. One who just put everything on the line for her pack.

I know that's not what she just said. I heard her words, the ones about painting for herself, and if what she truly did in this room was let go of her unswerving adherence to loyalty and duty and family long enough for something else to breathe, she'll have my unswerving support.

I just don't think that's what she did. My gut doesn't believe it, and my heart doesn't believe it, and the veteran soldier who considers her a friend doesn't believe it at all.

I put a hand on Eliza's back as she teeters. The school is full of people trying to move gracefully around shelves and pillows and other hazardous objects with their eyes closed, and the last thing we need is an accidental game of shifter dominos. I keep my gaze at knee level and scan for pregnant mamas. Cori is in front of Eliza, but I've lost track of Fallon.

My wolf snorts. If Fallon goes down, the odds that

she'll land on anything other than her mate are approximately zero.

Fair enough. I steady Hoot as she bounces off of Reilly, which gets me an eye roll, and grab Adelina before she meets up with a glass wall. Definitely civilians. Soldiers never close their eyes. We're the wolves making our way to the far end of the room. Hopefully the people staying closer to the door are a little less discombobulated.

I make a mental note to add blindfolds to my next woodcraft lesson.

We eventually find something that resembles stillness, and we wait. The shuffling dies down, and the heartbeats of wolves who haven't been inside this building for eight days speed up.

Some kind of silent signal moves through the pack, and my eyes lift to the wall along with everyone else's. I scan the mural first. Gauging the territory. Looking for danger.

There's plenty—I just don't know why.

Neither does my wolf. He thinks he's looking at a sweet scene of pups and mountains and paw prints and trees, but that's not what everyone else sees. I have a good view of most of their faces. Shelley Martins just set off a bomb.

KENNEDY

I'm so confused. My wolf can feel the power of the wall, but she doesn't understand it. She doesn't know why Hoot is crying and Brandy is the color of death and Ben can't breathe.

It's the pups, though. Somehow. There are four of them painted on the wall, right in the center, and they're beautiful. I can tell their whole personalities just by looking at them. One is fierce and scrappy like Hoot, and there's one with sweet brown eyes and red fur who looks a little bit like Kelsey, and two more who maybe just played a trick on their alpha but he hasn't noticed yet.

Adorable pups—but they're not our pups.

Except that doesn't explain why Hoot is crying and Brandy is the color of death and Ben can't breathe.

Myrna walks forward, her legs stiff and her arms held out like a zombie. She freezes right before she gets to the wall. Her words sound like a chainsaw trying to whisper. "Can I touch?"

Shelley makes a noise that's probably *yes*.

Myrna's hand shakes as she touches the face of one of the pups who just played a trick. "That's exactly how he used to look. Full of fun and mischief. You got him exactly right, Shelley. You took the heart and soul of him and you put it on this wall."

There's an awful whimper from the far corner. Tara buries her face in Kenny's chest. Hoot grabs blindly for me.

Bailey turns to stone.

Brandy sucks in a ragged breath. "Dad?"

Myrna turns from the wall. Nodding, laughing,

crying. Swiping at her nose. "Yes. This is the four of us. Cleve and Aaron. Tara. Me. When we were pups. I've got a picture of us in my knitting basket."

Fallon's lips quirk. "It's not there at the moment. I borrowed it."

I can feel my pack desperately trying to clear enough water out of their ears to hear properly. Most of us aren't getting very far. I stare at the four pups again. At the one who looks so much like Kelsey. "That's Grandpa Aaron? He used to have red fur?"

Myrna manages a shaky smile. "Yes. It went gray right after Bailey was born, but when he was young, his fur was bright red like Grady's. He used to shine in the sun."

Hoot whimpers just like Tara did—but she keeps looking at the shiny red pup.

RIO

Everyone else is staring at a wall. I can't take my eyes off the woman who painted it. The one who is somehow finding the strength to stand and hold a cup of tea and watch her oldest friend. The one who painted the four origin pups of this pack on the wall inside our forever seed and put what a sentinel did up on a mountain to absolute shame. This took courage—and it took decades of loving and intimately knowing every wolf in this pack.

Brandy walks gingerly over to stand beside Myrna.

She touches the face of her father first. Stroking the wall. Murmuring. Then, ever so gently, she runs her fingertips over to the friendly red pup beside him. The one who would grow up to be alpha. The one who made Myrna shake. Her breath hitches. "I never would have guessed that Uncle Aaron belonged on this wall."

Neither did my sentinel. Aaron is the first wolf who died under Samuel's claws.

Brandy smiles. "Now that I see this, I can't imagine him not being here."

The shimmering column of nervousness surrounding Shelley eases a little.

Eyes sharpen all over the pack. Eyes that have finally stopped looking at a pack's soul in painted form and are suddenly looking at the woman who put it on a school-house wall.

Myrna finds her words first. "Shelley Martins, don't you dare think this is anything other than a masterpiece, or you and I are going to have words."

Shelley shrugs weakly. "I thought it might be too much. Too hurtful." Her eyes slide in the direction of Hayden's boots and scurry away again. "Or maybe it's not right for the pack that we are now."

All Hayden can manage is an indignant snarl.

Lissa pats his arm.

Myrna smirks.

My wolf snorts. The first person who tries to paint over a speck of that wall is going to find themselves face to face with a very irritated wolf and her frying pan.

My sentinel is far less at ease. An elder has taken her

stand, and that matters, but this is huge and raw and Shelley knows it. She took her own pain and darkness and grief and figured out how to use them. She didn't try to fix or transform or heal them—she accepted those parts of who she is and let them share hold of her paintbrush.

The result is a dreamy, ethereal mural. It isn't bright, and that took some effort, given the paints Muriel sent. It's a study in muted, translucent tones, even the four pups. A wall that tells its searing story gently. Origins and heartache. Innocence and loss. Pain and belonging. And layers upon layers of ghosts.

Most of the rest of our pack is still stumbling their way through the pieces, at least on the surface. I need to go deeper. I don't bother reaching into the earth, not while I stand here in knitted socks with floors and pipes under my feet. I reach for pack sense instead. For the instinctive knowing that's the birthright of every wolf and those who love us.

And marvel at what I see.

I will be needed—but not today. Underneath the puzzled eyes and careful touches and murmured words is a song of absolute clarity. These walls were built for pack and by pack and with pack, and now they hold the story of pack where it can be touched and felt and seen.

We built this place.

It is safe.

It is our seed.

Some will go soon and do the work that this wall demands in small pieces, because this is a seed with exit doors. Some will do it fast and fierce because that's the only way they know. Some will take a long time to get here at all.

It doesn't matter.

The hard truth of a garden or a meadow or a forest is that not all seeds grow.

This one already is.

SHELLEY

I had a bad fever once, one that lasted for days and days, and I kept waking up with odd moments of lucidity in the middle of spinning dreams.

Maybe I'm sick again.

My eyes struggle to find the faces of the packmates that my mural will have hit hardest. Hits that I painted, knowing they would land. Hits that I didn't have permission to deliver—I only had the wild spinning of my artist as she painted and dreamed.

Fingers wrap around my arm, strong and trembling. Tara clears her throat. "I can look at him like this. See him like this. Thank you."

My heart breaks for her, just as it has every day since Aaron died. "I remember his stories. He loved you, even back when you were pups. You took a little longer to come around."

She snorts. "I led him on the merry chase that he deserved."

That was the part of the story he always loved best. I lean

against her shoulder. "I didn't put in Anna Maria. Maybe I should have." There were five pups in the beginning, not four, but I never knew the fifth. She moved east before I came to Ghost Mountain, found a mate in Manitoba.

Tara points to one side of the mural. "She's right there in the paw prints that have left us." A long pause. "Maybe Aaron should have been a set of prints, too. But it does me good to see him here with me."

The wild spinning of my artist didn't give me a choice. "I wasn't sure if paw prints would be enough." There are prints on the other side of the pups, too. The ones of those who have joined us. Paw prints and foot-prints and raven claws and bear tracks, because some of the wolves of this pack have very strange feet.

Some have come. Some have gone. The seed remembers.

A wolf growls, and I turn, because he is a friend.

Kenny stares at the right side of the wall like it will gut him any minute. It might. I took special care with one of the sets of prints on that side. I had to work from memory, and Jason's paws grew so very quickly in his last years, but I did my best. From the look in Kenny's eyes, it was more than enough.

I go to him.

His arms wrap around me, fierce and tight and shaking like the last leaf in late fall winds. But his eyes don't leave the paw prints of his dead son, and he doesn't ask me to paint over them.

I let my head rest against his chest a moment. I'm so

very tired. "You can touch. When you're ready. I made it safe for pup hands."

His breath is a rasp in his throat. "Can't."

The seed knows that, too. "One day."

Another rasping breath. Two. He wraps his fingers around mine and squeezes hard. "Look."

I follow his gaze. Kelsey is standing in front of the wall, one hand on Fallon's belly as she chatters away at a small, red, painted pup. My heart chokes. "She's telling Grandpa Aaron about the baby."

It takes Kenny three tries to get the words out—but he tries. "Yeah. She is."

My wild, spinning artist closes her eyes.

The wall isn't hers, anymore. It is pack.

CLEVE

There's a single light shining on the painted wall. I don't look just yet. I try to close the door behind me, but my wolf won't allow it. He's already cranky about the scratchy, uncomfortable clothes.

I chuckle, a sound strange and rusty to my ears. He never much liked putting shoes on for the first time after the summer, either. But I won't walk naked into a school. It doesn't seem right. Neither did the baggy sweatpants and loose shirts that Myrna's been leaving for me in the kitchen.

Tonight there was a nice set of jeans, a flannel shirt with the tag still on it, a knit cap, and a note.

I swallow and look back at the open door. I could step out onto the porch. Just long enough to catch my breath. The rest are eating up at Dorie's camp. They won't be back for a bit.

My wolf scrunches his shoulders against the discomfort of a collar and sleeves and tells me to get it over and done with so that he can get back to his ledge and get some sleep.

I shake my head. I've been sleeping on that damn ledge all week. The one with blankets and hot tea and a lovely view of the den. He wouldn't let me leave.

I've been too afraid to ask him why.

I take the knit cap off, because that's what I was taught to do in school, but I don't know what to do with it. There's a basket by the door with a book and some rocks and a cooking whisk inside, but when I bend down, it's got a drawing of Lissa's pup on the front.

I trace the letters of his name. Robbie.

I set the basket up on a shelf next to some others. There's one for the nice young lady in the kitchen. Mikayla. Her basket smells of cinnamon. The next one is Moon Girl's. It's got bits of fur in it, and soft yarn. I move down the row. Sniffing. Touching.

I want to close my eyes when I get to my son's basket, but I can't. His sister captured Ben's gentle eyes with her pencils—and his strength.

He didn't get that from me.

My hands shake. I need to look at the wall, before I

can't. Before I am too afraid. Before I lose the little bit of curiosity that somehow came to life when I read Myrna's feisty, mysterious note.

She didn't mention the baskets, but I can come back to visit those again.

I will. They help me to remember.

26

SHELLEY

I stick my finger in the dirt up to my second knuckle and pull it back out again. "That far?"

Jade solemnly measures the hole with her special stick and nods. Then she carefully drops in a watermelon seed. She shines a tiny, bright flashlight down the hole to make sure it didn't accidentally end up somewhere else and brushes dirt over the seed.

I pick up my pencil. "What should we name this one?" I don't think Reilly expected his science experiment on planting depths to take this particular turn, but it has, and like a good research assistant, I'm taking notes.

Jade tilts her head and contemplates. "Ruby."

The artist inside me tilts. So far, this row has a Grady, a Milo, and a Rennie.

These are the seeds we're planting deepest.

Kel looks at us from the other side of the planter.

There's pain in his eyes—and reluctant amusement. "Are we naming the watermelons after packmates, too? Because that might cause some trouble when it's time to eat them."

Jade giggles. Silly beta.

I eye him and his fellow ninth-graders. "How's the soil testing going?"

Kennedy scowls at the sat phone in her hand. "I put the probe in the dirt just like Reilly said to do, but the app says it can't find any soil to test."

Molly, who is managing Kel's presence from a reasonable distance, smiles faintly.

Adelina snickers. "Maybe you need to stick the phone in the dirt."

Kennedy produces an enormous baby-alpha sigh. "Stinky tried that last week, remember?"

Oh, dear. Reilly is enamored with the high-tech gardening gadgets that mysteriously fell out of the supply cupboard along with my paintbrushes. His fellow students aren't quite so impressed. Which is probably why these ones have a beta keeping watch over their antics.

Antics from some of them, anyhow. Molly has been sitting quietly, barely breathing—but her eyes shone while Ghost did her talk about the minerals necessary to grow strong plants, and she keeps inching closer to the book on soil science that one of the cats sent over.

I'll have to get her baking in the kitchen with Cleve. There's plenty of science in a good recipe.

Kennedy looks longingly out the greenhouse

windows. "I'm making Reilly transfer me to third grade. They got to go out into the woods with Wrinkles to look for mushrooms."

I hide a smile. The sat phone has somehow ended up in Adelina's hands, and she's busy tapping and making adjustments to the probe. One very reluctant student, neatly herded by a thoughtful friend—and another one given a choice in case she needs to escape the presence of the adult male in the greenhouse.

A fine morning's work. I pat Jade's bottom. "Go tell Reilly that we've finished with our planting, sweet pea."

She scampers off because she's a sweet pup and because Reilly almost certainly has some of the new honey berry bars that Cleve made earlier. I heard him cursing. They're a bit stickier than muffins.

Kennedy elbows Adelina. "Are we done yet?"

"No." Hoot is standing in the doorway, breathless, her eyes wide. "I mean yes. I need everyone to come outside really slowly and not panic and keep your domi-nant stuff locked down. Maybe leave all the doors open, too—and I'm not sure what else."

Kel's arm is already around her. "Someone's coming."

It isn't a question. My wolf quivers.

Hoot sucks in a really shaky breath. "Yes. Just like Rio said they would, but he didn't say it would be this many and he didn't say it would be this soon and I don't know how to help them all get here."

We were just having that conversation at breakfast. I haven't even made up my special grocery list yet. I thought we had time.

Kel drops to his knees and looks up at Hoot, his hands on her shoulders. "You know what *you* need to do. Start there."

Hoot lets out a breath bigger than she is. "I have to go. Grady is trying to come and he's stuck and I have to go to him. The others will get here first, but my brother needs me."

Kel's smile is absolutely beautiful. "Go."

She hesitates.

He growls. "That's why your pack has betas. Go."

She spins around, already running.

Kel slips out the door after her, Ghost hot on his heels.

I stare. They didn't even ask who else was coming.

I use the planter to pull myself to my feet. We'll just need to get ready for anyone, then. "Adelina and Katrina, go get some of those berry bars and a pitcher of tea to leave on the table in the school. Molly and Reilly, pick up anything on the floor in there and open all the doors. Kennedy, crack a few of the windows in here, too."

Wolves are already moving.

I try to think. "Eliza, grab some soft clothes from our spare hamper and leave them on the porch. And maybe some of those small blankets we just finished."

Ebony sticks her head in the greenhouse door. "About fifteen minutes until we need to clear out of the way."

That's not enough time, but we'll make it enough. "Do we know who's coming in first?"

She shakes her head. "Not yet. Ghost is checking. Rio

vanished, but before he left, he said to tell you to find Kelsey and stick to her like glue."

My hands scrabble at thin air. "Where is she?"

"She's fine." Ebony smiles. "She's in the kitchen with her alpha, picking some flowers."

HAYDEN

I back my wolf up a millimeter. Two. That's pretty much all he's going to allow. He can't make any sense of the lines on the back of my eyelids, and he wants to have his teeth and claws close at hand.

I don't know much more than he does. Whatever's coming, it's urgent enough and important enough that nobody has bothered to keep a mere alpha in the loop. All I know is that we need to keep our distance from the school, dominants are supposed to be furry, and Kelsey picked every last flower from the small pots in the kitchen.

My wolf frets.

I try to think wolfy happy thoughts. If he scares someone away with his worrying, he'll feel awful.

His ears orient. Listening. They come.

I back him up another millimeter. We're near the main trail into the den, and he can be a very scary dude.

A shadow emerges from the trees.

My wolf quivers. He knows her, but Moon Girl isn't

walking like the diffident, shy packmate that he knows. She's walking like a leader.

A second shadow emerges from the trees.

Terrence. Furry Terrence, shaking so hard he can barely stay on his paws. His head is down so far that his nose is almost on the ground. The quiet, proud man who visits the den quite often—and whose wolf absolutely can't.

Mine walks forward, trusting instincts as old as time.

Moon Girl leans into Terrence, letting him shake. Asking him to stay.

I pause, close enough for him to feel my breath and see my paws. Then I back away and off to the side. The welcome of an alpha wolf to a trusted and respected packmate.

Terrence shakes a little less. His head comes up the barest fraction.

I stand where I am. I've done all that I can as his alpha. The rest are the fervent, heartfelt wishes of a pack-mate, and those aren't going to do a damn bit of good coming from me.

Reuben pads out of the forest, a wolf strolling over to greet a visiting friend. Glow joins him. Dorie. Some-where off in the distance, a wolf howls, a painful, defeated cry. A chorus howls in return. *We love you. Try again on a new day*.

My wolf watches the wolf in front of him—the one who must make the same choice. Forward or back. I swallow the indignant yowl trying to force its way out of my throat. Wolves would finish this one way. Wolves with humans inside of them need to finish it another.

Terrence huffs out a breath strong enough to make the dry leaves on the ground in front of him dance. Then he takes a single step forward. Another. Moon Girl and Reuben and Glow and Dorie match him like it's entirely normal to be moving through the forest at the speed of snails.

Terrence's head lifts a little more.

I watch his achingly slow procession toward the den, my heart beating high and fast in my chest. I hope he can't hear it. I hope he likes the new honey berry bars. I hope he makes it to where he wants to go.

Moon Girl turns her head as they pass the rock that serves as the official boundary line of the den. The one we give to the pups. The one they cannot pass without responsible supervision.

Terrence keeps walking.

I yearn, with everything in me, to follow him—but there's another shadow emerging from the trees. Human this time. Teesha. Leader of the baby pack who mostly can't tolerate their fur. She flashes some quick hand signals. She's got four with her, back by the mossy tree. They will wait.

I look around frantically for the bag I dragged out here with me. Wolves are hard to bribe without enough time to chase tasty bunny snacks, but I brought good human treats. Cookies. Crispy-rice squares. Chocolate.

She smiles and holds up a very similar bag.

I shake my head. The wolves of this pack are at our

very best when we descend into fifteen minutes of chaos. Shelley's brisk choreography in the kitchen was a thing of condensed, jumbled beauty.

Teesha's head turns toward the den. Her eyes are wistful.

I trot over to her side and nudge her hand. Offering an alpha's hope.

She scratches behind my ears. Then she crouches down and wraps her arms around my neck, her words warm by my ear. "I have two who won't make it in. They did well to make it this far. Tomorrow, they'll need to know that you're still proud of them."

I lean into her cheek. I will come.

She stands back up. One last look at the den and she heads off into the trees, running with the long, loping stride of a human who has grown wolf appendages from her soul.

I herd my wolf back over to his post. There are more coming.

He sniffs at the air, skeptical.

Silly wolf. He doesn't need his nose to know that there are far too many wildly protective den wolves who are still missing. There's no way that they're just hanging out in the woods for no good reason while the pups are so scattered and unprotected that his fur is standing on end.

He sobers. Watches. Paces a row of baskets in his mind—the ones with the drawings of every wolf in his pack.

I smile. He wasn't a big fan of the whiteboard's funny lines and squiggles, but it gave him the names of his pack and he guarded it as treasure. Right up until he saw the baskets. It nearly killed him that he couldn't go visit them for a whole week while Shelley was painting.

Especially the one with the drawing of a yellow-gold nose and a white one.

SHELLEY

"I need to be closer."

I look into convinced brown eyes. "We're already pretty close, sweetheart."

Kelsey scowls, which is about as typical for her as snow on a summer's day. It happens, but when it does, a smart wolf pays attention.

"We're trying to give them space to make choices, remember?" Even the ones that hurt very much, like when Terrence turned around two steps before the porch and walked away. "You got to give Teesha a flower. And Blaze."

She smiles. "Blaze will come back. She liked the paw prints."

I shake my head. Kelsey has been out here with me this whole time, but I don't doubt her one bit. "Good. I worked hard on those."

She sits back down beside me, her eyes on the scraggly trees where our visitors have been emerging. "Rio says you painted our soul."

My heart thumps. Myrna said something similar,

right after she handed me a good, strong cup of tea. "I painted what my heart needed to paint."

Kelsey's lips curve up a little as she keeps watching the trees.

My wolf twitches, uneasy. She wants her good nose, the one that can smell things, instead of this silly human one.

I tried that back when we started our wait, because it's chilly, and because if danger somehow came out of the trees instead of friends, Kelsey is far faster in her fur. I lost. Wolf paws can't hold flowers. "Maybe we should head over to the cook shack and see what needs doing." It's been more than an hour since our last visitor.

She shakes her head. "Grandpa Cleve is coming."

Her radar is fierce today. "To make some muffins?" We could surely use some, or our very late lunch is going to be a hodgepodge.

A quiet sound escapes Kelsey, something between a sigh and a whimper.

My wolf sits bolt upright, alarmed. "What's wrong?"

Her head shakes slowly, her eyes glued to the scraggly trees. "Don't be scared. Rio says not to be scared."

My bones gelatinize.

Kelsey pats my hand. "He says we should change into our fur and we'll know what to do and we shouldn't be scared."

That doesn't help me to breathe any better, but I stand up to unzip my jacket and shake off my rubber boots, because the small girl beside me is losing no time getting rid of hers. She folds up her sweater neatly and sets it on her jacket. It's special and purple and Lissa just finished knitting it.

She trembles as she reaches for the hem of her t-shirt.

Everything in me wants to snatch her up and run and not look back, but I have no idea what's coming. I only know that Rio loves Kelsey Dunn to the absolute bottom of her oceans-deep soul. If he says to shift and stay, I need to trust him.

The small, naked girl beside me looks up, her eyes full of messages I don't understand. Then she shifts, and a small red wolf with equally mysterious eyes stands in her place.

I join her as quickly as I can. My wolf yanks for my nose, but all she scents are the last ones who passed by. Teesha and Elijah and Blaze. I try to listen instead, but all I can hear is Kelsey's panting and my heart hammering in my ears.

Peace. Help steady their path.

My heart skips several beats. I've felt Rio before, but not like this. He's speaking from somewhere deep inside me. That place where my wolf would go on the very worst days, when she could do nothing more to keep me safe except hide so deep that Samuel could never find her.

The one who comes has such a place. A long pause. Great sadness. *Hers is much smaller.*

A ghost. Hoot left to find Grady. I step my paws around his small cousin, tucking her quivering body under mine. Knowing it's useless, even as I do it. I'm not one of the psychic Dunns. I have no idea how to help keep either of them safe.

That's my job. A smile. Glowing warmth. *Yours is to be her grandmother.*

I don't argue genealogy with him. Kelsey was mine the first moment Ben laid her in my arms. My paws nestle her in closer, trying to make her smaller. Grady was ripped apart by violence. Hoot says that it sometimes rips through him still.

Grady will not come today. A quick, shimmering image of two much younger pups playing in the forest. *He is with Hoot.*

My artist spins to life with dizzying speed, trying to remember the details. I will paint them. Not on a wall this time. On one of the special canvases that Muriel sent.

You will. Certainty. Conviction. *But there is one you will paint first.*

My throat closes. I touch my snout down to the head of the small, red pup who stands tall between my legs, her gaze never leaving the scraggly trees. If it's not Grady who comes, then there can be only one reason I'm standing here with Kelsey Dunn and orders to protect her heart.

Cleve walks out of the shadows first, a limping gray wolf.

The wolf who slinks out next, belly to the ground and eyes wide with fear, is one I haven't seen in over five years. Not since the awful day when I lost track of Eamon and took too long to find him.

Bile rises in my throat, a hot river of acid and guilt.

The small pup between my legs whimpers.

My heart hammers a staccato song of panic. I have no idea how to help. I try to ask, but Rio feels different. More distant. Busy.

The cowering wolf works her way a little further forward. She opens her mouth and snaps her teeth at thin air, a wolf sensing threat in the simple act of breathing.

My entire body wretches. Oh, Rennie. I am so sorry.

RIO

Fuck. My wolf jolts as yet another secret finds its way out of the deep-dark of this pack. I wasn't expecting Shelley's drowning guilt, but I can't let it touch Rennie or the small, brave pup who is curious and confused and trying to read currents she shouldn't even be able to see.

I don't have enough skill to block them all.

I spare a glance at Cleve, who is standing patiently, a wolf with all the time in the world. He places no demands on his youngest daughter—he isn't even really looking at her. That he can do that after the dozen hours it has taken them to come down from the high mountains is a moment of pure grace. I know how much of that journey she did on her belly.

He wasn't patient for all of the trip. He had his own demons. His own guilt.

My sentinel contracts in for a breath and then expands out again, doing the subtle, difficult alchemy required to keep three highly sensitive empaths from doing anything more than brushing against each other gently.

My wolf growls. No pup should be anywhere close to this.

I agree with him, fully and completely—but my sentinel understands enough of what lives in Kelsey Dunn to know that she could never be anywhere else.

He did what he could. He put her here with a guardian. Far too often, the wolves of this pack look at Shelley Martins and see what she wants us to see. Our brisk, wonderful cookie baker. We forget that underneath that exterior is a woman who chose to walk into hell because of her fiercely maternal love for her pack—and we forget that she is a Dunn.

Not the distant-cousin kind.

The bedrock kind.

The breath-of-her-family-and-her-pack kind.

The ancient, old-growth-tree kind.

Even as I watch, she finds the steadiness that is her most impressive superpower and wraps it around Kelsey like a cape.

The storming energies inside a small red pup ease.

I take every scrap of sentinel power that frees up and throw it at containing the disintegrating fear trying to eat Rennie Dunn. I don't know how long I fight that battle. I only know that it eases a little when she walks through the doors of the schoolhouse.

When they walk out again, fathomless time later, Rennie isn't on her belly and Cleve is no longer patient and steady. Their exit is ungainly and hasty, two wolves at the absolute ends of their ropes. Cleve throws a desperate look my way and disappears into the shadows. Rennie moves off into the trees at a skittering run, a wolf entirely bewildered by the finger of dream that has somehow reached into her nightmare.

She doesn't see the small red pup who shifts into a naked girl and blows her a kiss.

Shelley does.

27

SHELLEY

I'm not painting alone, this time. Jade and Mellie and Mikayla all have brushes and easels and canvases just like I do. Brown built the two small easels just last night.

We're tucked away in a corner of the school because it's too cold outside for paint to behave properly, and because there's a lovely beam of sunshine coming through the windows. Mellie keeps sliding her easel over to stay in the brightest light. We might make an artist out of her yet.

Mikayla sets down her brush and steps back to look at her work, laughing. "I have no idea how you do it, Shelley. I swear that I'm trying to paint a wolf, but this looks more like a sheep. Or maybe a bear."

Reilly giggles from the table behind her.

She turns and shoots him a look of mock disgust.

"Enough out of you, or I'll be putting old socks in your berry bars."

He grins. "I think Kenny ate those already."

The wiry beta wolf lying down in the middle of the room while Kelsey and Adelina brush his fur growls.

I chuckle. He was not happy to discover that his wolf has some of the softest fur in the pack. Just right for a raven baby's nest. I step back from my own painting and tilt my head. It's coming along nicely. I don't have Grady's tail quite right, and Hoot's ears need to be a stitch bigger, but I've got the gist of it.

I look over at the two sketches Brandy did for me so that I can overlay her memories with mine. Definitely bigger on Hoot's ears. She's grown into them some, but the pup of six years ago hadn't, quite yet.

A hand pats my leg. Kelsey smiles up at my work in progress. "I like Grady's eyes. Is this one for Mama, too?"

I look into eyes that look so much like the Rennie I remember. "Not this one, sweetie. It's for Hoot. I think your mama got just the right painting for her."

A small smile. "It was a really pretty flower."

I worked almost as hard on the flower as I did on the small girl holding it. Eliza made me a beautiful frame and Rio carried it up the mountain to Rennie's caves because her wolf will let him get close, now.

Kelsey leans her head against my leg, still looking at her cousins with the ears and tail that need to be fixed. "Grady got closer last night."

He did. A few of the teenagers had an impromptu pinecone war out where he could watch. Which seemed like maybe not the best way to make a very sensitive wolf feel welcome, but Rio just smiled a little and Kel snuck a whole bag of extra pinecones to the troops in the trees.

I ruffle hair that has more strings of beads in it than yesterday. "Did Martha come by to visit Fallon?" The ravens have two hatchlings due any moment, but she still makes the flight over at least a couple of times a week.

Kelsey shakes her head. "She can't leave because a storm is coming and babies usually hatch when it's not convenient."

She stumbles a little over the last word and makes me smile. Then she pats my leg again and moves off, headed toward her baskets. She's set two of them in a sunbeam, each of them holding a small pot with seeds. The one in her basket hasn't sprouted, yet. The one in Rennie's basket has a small, green stem poking out of the dirt.

I exhale quietly.

Mikayla leans against my shoulder. "Wanna trade?"

I grin at her wolf that really does look like a sheep. "It's good that you've got other talents."

She snorts. "Bailey, Shelley's picking on me. Make her stop."

The aggrieved sigh behind me makes all the students at the high table snicker. "You're not even one of my students today. I checked."

A cackle from Myrna. "You can fix that, can't you, Reilly?"

Rollicking bear-cub giggles.

I add a few brush strokes to Hoot's ears before my paint dries.

Life is never boring inside a seed.

HAYDEN

I glare at my sister. "You can't have her."

Jules tries to look innocent. "I didn't even ask, yet."

"You were going to." I lean back in my makeshift office, which I only have to myself because I promised not to let the muffins burn. "She can paint canvases for other dens. Big ones, if you send up more of the special ones that Muriel uses."

A wry look. "Ames is already loading them on the plane."

I don't ask if she included more paint. Jules Scott is the queen of logistics. "How many orders have you taken without asking her if she wants to be HomeWild's painter-in-residence?"

She grins. "Only a couple. From some bears who will trade paintings for anything on Phil's furniture list."

I make a face. Jules is also the queen of really excellent negotiating tactics and she knows it. "Don't let this get ridiculous. Please." I have some idea of what the bears might be willing to pay for work from the artist who kept their favorite bear cub safe.

My sister snickers. "I think it's fairly safe to say that you won't need to pay for any of your bunk beds."

Those won't be all that useful until we have somewhere to put them. Sleeping modules are not in this year's budget. "That works. Let her pile up credits for a while. I'll make sure Lissa hides that spreadsheet."

A mischievous grin. "I hear she's good at that."

I have no idea what the secret project is, but half my pack knows and so does Jules. Which isn't exactly reassuring. "Don't let that get ridiculous, either."

Her peeling laughter rings through the cook shack.

I'm obviously way too late with that request. "Whatever. What was it you needed to ask that required my personal attention?"

She makes a face that's oddly hard to read. "I did a thing. I need you to tell me if it's a mistake."

The hesitation in her voice has my wolf perking his ears.

She sighs. "I'm going to put a video up on the screen. Watch it all the way through and let me know what you think."

Her face disappears before I can nod, and music streams into the kitchen. It's a catchy tune, probably a Scotty original. It isn't the song that has my undivided attention, though. It's the visuals. Snippets of our live feed as we built the greenhouse school, but in true Jules fashion they've been assembled into something that doesn't seem like it could have possibly come from the parts.

Ghost bossing the unloading of three trucks. Pups carrying pipes through the forest. Reilly explaining how the wall will go up and Kennedy nearly getting her head stuck as the first corner snaps into place. Eliza pouring footings while three big guys make slightly burnt cheesy sandwiches. The women of the pack raising the roof and Kelsey carefully shining the greenhouse panels before they went up.

It's a marketing video. A very slick, professional one, and it will make every pack with a couple of a teenagers and a hammer crave a HomeWild building kit. But it's so much more than that. I wait for my sister's face to come back onto the screen.

She looks at me for a long time. "I won't use it unless they agree. All of them."

I smile a little. "I know that."

She sighs. "I'm doing the same thing for the build in the Arctic. I know this shouldn't feel any different, but it does. Sometimes business and life need to stay separate. I need you to tell me if this is one of those times."

The sister I love wouldn't have the foggiest clue how to separate HomeWild from her heart. I don't bother telling her that, though. As soon as the muffins are done, I'll carry my tablet over to the school and play the video again and let Jules watch their reactions on a live feed, and then she won't have any doubt at all.

Because my pack is going to see exactly the same thing as I do.

Right after they stop laughing about the cheesy sandwich I accidentally set on fire.

RIO

I didn't expect to find her here. I slide my boots under my basket and look over at Bailey. If I'm disturbing her, I can leave.

She smiles a little. "Cleve's jacket is hanging on his hook."

I make my way over to where she's sitting. The high table has two open laptops and what might be math homework, done in crayon. The low table is completely covered in various drying art projects.

The students have all gone for a recess run with their alpha. I'm curious about why their teacher stayed behind.

She picks up the crayon math, looks at it, and sighs. "So many of them are so far behind, and they know it."

I'm not entirely sure we're talking about students. "Six years is a lot to work through. We have time."

She makes a face. "It doesn't feel that way, some days."

She's carried such a huge load for so long. I sit quietly. Perhaps today is a day where she would like some of that to be seen.

She sets down the math homework and picks it back up again. "Ruby is doing better. She's sleeping most days."

She's also dumping volatile energy into seven dominant wolves on a really regular basis. Which gives me some idea of just what Bailey Dunn was handling on her own for the last six years. I keep a sharp hold on my wolf —he hasn't quite calmed down about that yet. "That's good."

The look she shoots at me has daggers lurking in the

background. "Ben says Brandy is handling it, and I trust him. Ebony and Dorie could both be lying through their teeth and I wouldn't know it, and I don't see the others regularly enough to have a good read."

That's because she still insists that she lives out in the far orbits. My sentinel says it isn't time to have that particular wrestling match, so I smile and answer her question, instead. "Several of you are good enough to lie to me, too."

She snarls quietly. "Brandy is taking the most. You could stop her."

Setting down huge loads can be the hardest job of all. "Her anxiety doesn't get in the way of being this kind of strong, and every bit she takes is helping to protect Rennie from more harm. She's more than handling it. She's proud."

The storm in Bailey's eyes eases.

I pick up a crayon and fill in an answer on the math homework. "I can help Adelina with her algebra. She's got a good head for it."

A reluctant smile. "Yeah, she does."

I draw a flower on another page that started out as instructions for a science experiment and is about halfway to becoming a paper airplane.

A long sigh. "Do you think Shelley knew what she was doing?"

I look up to find Bailey staring at the mural. "Which part?"

Something less certain than a storm swirls in her eyes. "When she put my dad up on that darn wall and now my wolf drags my ass in here three times a day so I can chat with him?"

I take the ragged gift that she just expelled and hold it as gently as I can. "Tara had an argument with him this morning. Something about a blue mug and a bad haircut."

Her lips quirk. "I don't think I know about that one."

I finish folding the paper airplane. "It wasn't going all that well for him."

She chuckles. "He never won an argument with her. He never needed to. She just needed someone to love her, sharp edges and all. Once he did that, she mostly talked herself around."

I toss the airplane in the general direction of a cheeky gray pup. "Sounds like a smart guy."

Another long sigh as a head lays itself gently on my shoulder. "I loved him so much. I miss him every day."

I tip my head against hers, and together, we contemplate a wall.

The one where Shelley Martins knew exactly what she was doing.

Next up: Ronan is coming. He's a big bear—an enormous bear—and arriving in Ghost Mountain is going to change the shape of who he is forever. Get Bear, book six in the Ghost Mountain Wolf Shifters series!

Printed in France by Amazon
Brétigny-sur-Orge, FR